Three Times as Deadly

by Erin Wade
Edited by Susan Hughes

Three Times as Deadly
by Erin Wade
Edited by Susan Hughes
© 2017 Erin Wade

ISBN-13: 978-1976466472
ISBN-10: 1976466474

www.erinwade.us

DEDICATION:
To the one that has always supported me in everything,
I have ever undertaken. You have encouraged me and
have always been my biggest fan. Life is sweeter with
you. Erin

* * * * * * *

Erin Wade

THREE TIMES AS DEADLY

Contents

Chapter 1...7
Chapter 2..10
Chapter 3..16
Chapter 4..20
Chapter 5..24
Chapter 6..30
Chapter 7..39
Chapter 8..47
Chapter 9..52
Chapter 10...55
Chapter 11...62
Chapter 12...70
Chapter 13...78
Chapter 14...84
Chapter 15...90
Chapter 16...96
Chapter 17..105
Chapter 18..109
Chapter 19..119
Chapter 20..123
Chapter 21..135
Chapter 22..141
Chapter 23..146
Chapter 24..152
Chapter 25..158
Chapter 26..162
Chapter 27..170
Chapter 29..185
Chapter 30..189
Chapter 31..195
Chapter 32..201

Chapter 33...211
Chapter 34...216
Chapter 35...222
Chapter 36...228
Chapter 37...238
Chapter 38...243
Chapter 39...251
Chapter 40...265
Chapter 41...272
Chapter 42...274
Chapter 1...286
Chapter 2...291
Chapter 3...302

Chapter 1

Rhinos are dangerous, I thought as I pulled my long blonde hair into a high ponytail and slid it through the opening in the back of my cap. I had shipped all my belongings to the States last week. I did a quick check of my room one more time before pulling my camera bag over my shoulder and heading out for my last attempt to capture the beast.

I curled the bullwhip that had saved my life on several occasions and attached it to my belt. Indiana Jones has nothing on me when it comes to using the whip for self-defense. I can break a man's arm or his neck from five feet away.

My cameraman, Ross Taylor, and I have been in the tiny province of Sdratsab—the *S* is silent—on the coast of South Africa for over a year. It is finally time to go home. We will shoot a couple of hours of film to intersperse throughout our documentary, drive ten hours, and then catch the red-eye flight from Johannesburg to Heathrow in London and finally to the States—Dallas, to be exact. The total travel time is twenty-five hours, and I plan to sleep most of the way. I intend to be well rested for my homecoming.

For the hundredth time, I read the last text from home. "I miss you, baby. I can't wait to hold you in my arms. I have a very special homecoming planned for you."

Every night in this godforsaken country, I had dreamed of being in the arms of my—

"Sloan, get your butt out here," Ross bellowed as the jeep skidded to a stop amid a cloud of dust. "I'm not missing that plane for you or anyone else. My woman is waiting for me."

I slid into the driver's seat, and Ross manned the high-powered video camera we had mounted in the back of the vehicle. We are after rhinos today. For a year, we have lived among a crash—or herd—of rhinoceros for a documentary we are doing for the Natural Habitat Network. Save the Rhino Consortium funded the documentary.

While we do care about the magnificent animals, Ross and I have a more secretive reason for accepting the challenge of running with rhinos for a year.

"Over there." Ross pointed to a mother and baby partially hidden by brush. "Try to get beside her so I can film her running with her baby."

I circled the mother and calf to approach her from behind. Sometimes it's difficult to flush a cow with a calf from the brush. The mother seems to know it's safer in the bushes than to run into the open.

"What the hell?" A bullet zinged by my head and nicked the hood of the jeep.

"Someone is shooting at us," Ross yelled as he ducked behind my seat. "Get us out of here, Sloan."

A quick glance in my rearview mirror brought into focus two armored Hummers bearing down on us.

THREE TIMES AS DEADLY

"Who are they?" I stomped the accelerator to the floorboard and bent low as a volley of bullets peppered our vehicle.

Angered by the noise, the mama rhino decided to join the *Kill Sloan and Ross Club* and rammed the side of our jeep.

"Son of a bitch!" Ross screamed. "She will turn this thing over."

I pressed the gas pedal but nothing happened. The rhino had lifted the driver's side of the jeep off the ground and was pushing the vehicle toward a cliff. Ross and I had two choices: stay in the jeep and hope the drop wasn't steep, or bail out of the vehicle and take our chances with the enraged rhino and the killers in the Hummers. I gripped the steering wheel and prayed. Ross grabbed the brake lever between the seats and held on for dear life.

##

Chapter 2

"Hello, Sleeping Beauty." A tall, stout nurse smiled at me. I squinted to shut out the bright light she was trying to shine into my eyes.

I slowly realized I was in a hospital bed, hooked up to all types of machines, and my head was killing me.

"What happened?" I asked

"We have no idea." The nurse smiled as she wrapped the blood pressure cuff around my upper arm and pumped it tight enough to cut off all circulation to my hand. "Someone dumped you at the emergency entrance of the hospital. You've been in a coma for about ten days.

"You looked like a pride of lions played keep-away with you." She grinned at her own humor. "You have a concussion, couple of broken ribs, and various and sundry other cuts and bruises, but you'll live.

"I am glad to see you awake." She ripped the cuff from my bicep. My hand tingled as the feeling returned to my numb fingers. She ran a temperature wand across my forehead. "I need to get some information from you."

I nodded, and my head kicked me hard. The pain was unbearable. I closed my eyes and opened them to find a name tag with *Sadie* engraved on it blocking my view. "Can you give me something for my headache?"

"I will as soon as I complete my paperwork." Sadie wrinkled her nose and logged into the computer on the stand beside my bed.

"Date of birth?" Her attitude was efficient and direct.

"I don't know." I said.

"We'll just skip the hard stuff and start with the easy questions," she said with a smirk. "What is your name? I need the middle initial too."

I stared at her in disbelief. *This is a joke, right?*

"Your name, sweetie," she insisted.

"I . . . I don't know," I whispered.

Loud arguing in the hallway outside my room sent Sadie charging toward the door. Before she could reach it, two different, but equally stunning women burst into my room.

Sadie took a stance between the women and me. I raised my head and tried to look around my nurse.

"You two do realize you are in a hospital, don't you?" Sadie scolded the women. "Keep your voices low, or I'll have you escorted from the premises."

The women looked contrite and edged around Sadie, but my protector wasn't letting them get close to me.

"Who are you?" Sadie glared at them.

They answered in unison. "I'm Sloan Cartwright's wife."

"Well, I'll be damn." Sadie laughed as she turned to me. "Is that what happened to you? You got caught between these two."

"No!" I blurted out. "I mean, I don't know them."

Both women glared at me as if I had defamed God."

"Honey, I'm glad I'm not in your shoes right now," Sadie said, chuckling. "Sloan Cartwright, is that your name?"

I struggled to sit up so I could get a better look at the two visitors. Obviously, I had good taste in women.

"Why don't you introduce yourselves." Sadie grinned, enjoying my predicament too much.

The beautiful blonde stepped forward. She was tall and slender, like a runner. She wore black slacks that hugged her perfect hips. A short-sleeved lavender blouse was tucked into her waistband. Toned arms and a flat stomach testified to her workout regimen. She wore a gold watch and pendant. Her green eyes seemed to change color as the light reflected from them.

"Sloan, honey, it's me. Leigh." Distress filled her eyes as she moved toward me. "Leigh Redding-Cartwright, your wife. We make our home in the United States. I'm here to take you home." She blushed and added, "You call me LeeRee."

"No! No!" Sadie intercepted her. "We still need to hear from this black beauty."

She was a beauty indeed. Her features were fine and chiseled. Her ebony hair was stylishly cut. She reminded me of the actress Halle Berry. When she spoke, her French accent mingled with a touch of high English. I loved her accent. *How do I know who Halle Berry is?*

I looked from one woman to the other. Apparently I am an equal opportunity lover.

THREE TIMES AS DEADLY

The black beauty smiled. "I am Amarosia Cartwright." She bowed her head slightly. "You call me Amy. We live together here in Africa."

Both women were earthshaking beauties.

As I gazed at them, mouth agape, the door to my room flew open, banging against the wall a couple of times as if doing a drum roll to announce the arrival of the gorgeous brunette who burst into my room. "Where is Sloan?" If the woman was also my wife, my taste in women had just shot off the Richter scale.

I realized I was holding my breath when the cardiac monitor attached to me went crazy. I didn't know if the brunette or my predicament caused the increase in my heart rate.

"Tachycardia," I muttered, one hand to my chest. I didn't want the other two women to know how the brunette was affecting me. If one of them was my wife, I didn't want to hurt her.

"Bullshit." Sadie laughed gleefully. "You have your butt in a crack and can't get it out. No wonder you have amnesia."

"What is going on here?" The brunette demanded, glaring at the other women. "Sloan, what have they done to you, baby? I begged you not to come to this heathen hellhole."

"Who are you?" Sadie demanded.

If looks could kill, Sadie would be pushing up daisies any minute. The brunette narrowed her icy blue eyes and moved to stand toe to toe with the nurse.

"I am Alexander Roland Cartwright." She tilted her head, tossed back her long, dark hair, and stared down Sadie who stepped back to allow her access to me.

13

THREE TIMES AS DEADLY

My heart jumped to triple time as Alexander Roland Cartwright moved closer to me. "What do I call you?" I gulped.

"The love of my life," she said with a mischievous smile. "When you aren't acting grandiose, you call me Alex."

"What's going on, Sloan?" She lightly stroked my cheek. "Ross managed to sneak a call to me before he disappeared. He said you're in trouble and to trust no one."

"I . . . I honestly don't know," I whimpered. Something about Alex's soft touch brought out the baby in me.

"I flew all the way from New York to take Sloan home with me," Leigh declared.

"Our home is here," Amy said. "We have always lived here. Sloan is going home with me."

Alex possessively pulled my hand into hers. "I am not letting Sloan out of my sight."

I leaned forward to stare at the three women, and my front opening hospital gown took the opportunity to expose my ample breasts. I must admit, I am nicely endowed. Determined to resolve the uncomfortable situation, I pointed out the obvious. "You all seem to be missing something, ladies. I am a woman. I doubt that I am married to any of you."

I didn't miss the way each of them licked their lips as they ogled me. I pulled the treasonous gown tight around my chest. I felt like the most succulent lobster at the lobster fest.

I tried to bring some sanity to my situation. "Look, I've been in an accident and had a loss of memory. I don't even know my name, much less to whom I'm married."

The women looked at each other and then began talking all at once,

"You can take turns sitting with her," Sadie instructed, but all of you can't stay here all the time. You can sit in eight-hour shifts. You work it out among yourselves."

Sadie pushed the women out the door and shoved it closed behind them. I was glad I wasn't involved in the arguing taking place in the hallway outside my door.

##

Chapter 3

"Sadie, where are my clothes?" I asked after she herded the women from my room.

"Sweetie, your clothes were shredded rags when we admitted you to the emergency room."

"Surely I had some form of identification," I insisted. I looked at my left hand. A white band around my wrist was evidence that I usually wore a watch. A matching strip of pale skin encircled the ring finger on my left hand.

"There were only the rags on your back," Sadie said with a sad smile, as if she suddenly had some compassion for me.

I gratefully swallowed the pills she held out to me. My headache had returned with a vengeance. "Why does my head hurt so badly?"

"Concussion, remember? That's why you don't know which of those smoking-hot women is your wife." She chuckled as if she found my predicament funny.

Sadie narrowed her eyes and studied me intently. "Or maybe you *are* married to all of them, and this is the first time they've met. You're gorgeous, definitely a chick magnet. I bet you have a girl in every port."

"Oh, God, Sadie, don't even say such a thing out loud." I chewed my bottom lip. Part of me thought she could be right, but another part of me was certain I was the type that mated for life, like a wolf. What I wasn't sure about was which one of the women—if any—I had chosen.

##

"I get the first shift." Amy said, a broad smile on her face as she entered the room. "Miss Redding will relieve me at four and sit with you until midnight. Miss Roland will sit with you from midnight to eight in the morning."

I noticed how she insisted on referring to the other two women as *Miss* and dropping my last name from theirs.

"I brought the book you were reading before the accident," Amy said. "I thought you might want to finish it."

I looked at the book by D. J. Jouett. It was *The Destiny Factor*, a lesbian murder mystery. A book marker indicated I had read a third of the book. Nothing about the book looked familiar to me. *I'll have to read it from the beginning.*

"Thank you." I watched Amy as she pulled a chair closer to my bed. She was beautiful, fashionably dressed and perfectly manicured. If she was my wife, we obviously had money. She wore no wedding band.

"My love, can I do anything for you?" Amy fidgeted. She was skittish and appeared to be ready to bolt and run at the slightest disturbance.

"I am sorry, Amy. It is very disconcerting. I know nothing about my life—our life. Perhaps you can enlighten me."

"Oh, yes, my love." She smiled, placed the book on the bedside table, and pulled her chair even closer.

"Your name is Sloan Cartwright. You are married to me, and we live in a lovely home that is safe and secure. We've been married five years."

"How did we meet?" I asked.

"You are with the US Embassy," Amy said with a shrug. "I met you at a formal dinner, and we became friends. One thing led to another, and we became lovers then married."

"What is your job?" I inquired.

"My job is to take care of you and make certain our home is a sanctuary for you. I strive to please you in every way." Amy's eyes darted around the room as if our conversation was embarrassing her.

"I'm sure you do. How did I end up in the hospital?"

She laughed. "Sloan, you know how you love speed. I told you jeeps couldn't take sharp corners at high speeds."

I grinned at the merriment in her eyes. "You aren't angry with me for wrecking the jeep?"

"I never get angry with you, my love," she said earnestly. "I only worry about you."

"What is my job at the embassy?"

"You are the chief of security," she said with pride. "You are someone extremely important."

"What happened to my identification and jewelry?"

Amy's big brown eyes opened wide as she stared at me. "I don't know. We live in an extremely poor province. I am sure bystanders were on you like a pack of hyenas. You are lucky your clothes were shredded, or they would have stolen the shirt off your back, leaving you naked in the dirt."

"How did you find out I was in the hospital?"

She chuckled. "This is a small town. Everyone rushed to our home to inform me of your accident and that you were here."

"Where is 'here' exactly?"

"Hospital Central de Maputo." She furrowed her lovely brow. "In Maputo, Mozambique."

"You are from here?" I watched her dark eyes as she relaxed.

"Yes. I was born here but educated in France and England." She lifted her chin proudly.

"I can tell you're well educated." I grinned at her. The smile on her face told me she was pleased with my observation. "I love your accent."

"I think that is what attracted you to me," she said, almost giggling.

I surveyed her voluptuous body and smiled. "Yes, I am sure it was your accent that caught my attention."

Her light-brown complexion darkened in what could only be described as a blush. She bowed her head as if my comment had embarrassed her then slowly looked up at me through long black lashes.

"Sloan, the doctors say you must stay here for several days." There was obvious distress in her big brown eyes. "I know I can nurse you back to health in our house. Make them release you so I can take you home and take care of you."

I closed my eyes and pretended to be asleep. I didn't want to go home with anyone until I knew who I was and what they wanted from me.

##

Chapter 4

I kept my eyes closed as Leigh Redding exchanged words with Amy.

"Why are you doing this?" Leigh was around five seven and towered over Amy. "We both know Sloan isn't married to you."

"Who are you?" Amy said with a haughty toss of her head. "What are you doing in our town?"

"I *am* Mrs. Sloan Cartwright," Leigh hissed.

Suddenly, Sadie bumped open the door with her hip. "Ladies, which one of you is on your way out?"

"She is." Leigh smirked as she jerked her head in Amy's direction.

"We will see you in the morning, Amarosia," Sadie informed the dark beauty.

"Sloan," Leigh touched my arm.

I opened my eyes, pretending to be half asleep. Sadie was checking my vital signs as Leigh struggled to stay close to my bedside but out of Sadie's way.

"It must be four," I smiled at Leigh. "Changing of the guards."

Leigh wrinkled her nose and waited for Sadie to leave the room.

"I'll be on duty tonight," Sadie announced. "If you need anything, just push the button."

"Thank you, Sadie," Leigh said.

THREE TIMES AS DEADLY

"I'm not talking to you," Sadie said with a smirk. "I am talking to my patient." She leaned down to me and whispered, "We're taking bets on whether you survive spending alone time with all three of your wives. I'm betting on you, so don't piss them off." She laughed out loud as she left my room.

"You survived Amarosia," Leigh said.

"Yeah," I murmured. "One down and two to go."

"You're safe with me, Sloan." Leigh pulled the chair beside my bed. "I have never hurt you."

"I don't want to be insensitive," I told her, "but I don't know who you are. I don't know how we met or how long we've been married."

Leigh looked down at her hands in her lap. She wore a plain gold wedding band. She raised her eyes and started talking.

"We've been married seven wonderful years. We met while you were in New York on a publicity tour for your newest book. You are a highly successful author."

"And your profession is . . . ?" I asked.

"I am the news liaison for the New York governor's office," she said. "When you made your first tour through our town, I was assigned to escort you to the various news interviews. The governor likes to make celebrities feel at home in the Big Apple. He tries to encourage the wealthy to move to New York to increase his tax base."

"So, we live in New York?"

"Yes, dear." She took my hand. "I'm here to take you home."

"I think they're going to keep me for a few days," I informed her.

"I'll wait for you," she said, smiling mischievously. "Believe me, you are worth the wait."

"What am I doing in Mozambique?"

"You're doing research for your next book." She shifted in the chair and leaned forward, giving me a clear view of her breasts. I tried to look away.

Leigh placed her hand on my cheek and pulled my eyes back to her. "It's okay, Sloan," she whispered. "You're allowed to look. I am your wife. You may even touch if you'd like."

"I shouldn't," I croaked. My voice failed me as I stared at Leigh. It took everything in me to pull away from her.

"How did you know I was in the hospital here?"

"Celebrity news travels fast," she said. "It came across the news wire that a woman resembling Sloan Cartwright had been admitted to the Maputo Central Hospital in Mozambique.

"I tried for hours to call you then finally flew here. I knew you were in this area working on your book, so I concluded it was you. It never occurred to me that you wouldn't know me."

"I'm so sorry," I mumbled.

She nodded then pulled my hand to her soft lips and kissed my knuckles. "It's okay, sweetie."

I studied Leigh for a long time. She didn't seem to mind my scrutiny. She was beautiful in a girl-next-door sort of way. Long blonde hair curled around her lovely face and her figure was perfect.

"You look more like one of those gorgeous anchor women the news stations like to hire," I finally commented.

THREE TIMES AS DEADLY

She laughed. "I was. The governor's office pays better and will still be there when my looks are gone."

"I think you'll always be beautiful," I said honestly.

"I know you'll always think so," she said. "I think you love me for my mind even more than my body."

I let my head fall back on the pillow and I closed my eyes. I was learning the best thing I could do in an uncomfortable situation was to feign sleep.

##

Chapter 5

Alex entered my room without making a sound. I watched her through half-closed eyelids. She had changed clothes. Her hair hung loosely around her shoulders, and her mesmerizing blue eyes reflected the night-light over my bed, giving her a feral look. The expensive pair of designer jeans looked as if they were custom-made for her. They hugged her perfect body and were a shade darker than the blue silk blouse tucked into them. Soft leather knee boots caressed her calves. A single blue sapphire hung from a gold chain and rested between the tops of her ample breasts. She wore a gold and diamond wedding band.

Unwittingly, I licked my lips as a fire spread through my body. My cheeks burned, and I knew I was blushing. Hmmm. If lust is any indicator, I am definitely a lesbian.

A smile played at the corners of Alex's full red lips. "I always affect you that way," she informed me.

"What way?" I pretended grogginess.

"The heat wave that just consumed you." She grinned, pressing her lips together to keep from laughing at me. "I could just slip into the hospital bed with you," she said. "It's been a long time, and I've missed you desperately."

"I don't think that's a good idea," I mumbled. Actually, I thought it was a wonderful idea but refrained from acting on my desire to kiss her full, soft lips.

She nodded and stood at the end of my bed. "I brought you some magazines." She lifted a stack of publications so I could see them. "Would you like me to read to you?"

"No, I would like you to tell me about us." I pushed the control and raised the head of my bed to a sitting position. I was thankful my headache had diminished.

Alex placed the magazines on the table next to my bed and pulled a chair close to my side. I couldn't take my eyes off her. She was one of those women who exuded sexuality. There was something about her that warned you not to touch for fear of being consumed by the heat.

"Why don't you ask me questions and I will answer them?" she suggested.

I asked her the question that had been burning in my mind since the first time I laid eyes on her. "How did someone like me get a woman like you?"

"Are you serious?" She laughed. "Do you even know what you look like?"

I suddenly realized I had no idea about my appearance. I hadn't bothered to look at myself in a mirror. "No," I whispered. "But you, you're a goddess."

"Um . . ."—she nodded—"so are you, darling. But to answer your question, I belong to you because you are honorable, brave, idealistic, strong, trustworthy, beautiful, *and* an incredible lover."

The heat surged through my body again, and I clenched my thighs as I allowed myself to envision making love to the beauty sitting beside me.

I licked my lips, trying to find a spot of moisture in my heat-scorched mouth.

Alex took pity on me and held a straw to my parched lips so I could drink water. "We have several homes. My business requires me to travel more than I like," she continued, "and you always accompany me whenever your job isn't sending you in some other direction. I also travel with you when I can.

"We live in Texas, own a loft in New York, a villa in Italy, and an apartment in Paris. My work demands that I spend several weeks each year in those locations."

"What is your work? Wait, don't tell me." I grinned. "You're a model."

She nodded. "Cosmetics."

"Ahh! That explains the perfection." I admired her flawless complexion. I couldn't keep from staring at her lips.

I vocalized my thoughts. "I suspect we're different. You are caviar and champagne, and I am pizza and beer."

She laughed. "You underestimate yourself, darling. You fit in anywhere, and you hate beer. You do consume an inordinate amount of pizza for one so slender."

"How did you know I was here?"

"Ross, your cameraman, called me. He said you'd had an accident and were in the Maputo Central Hospital." She tilted her head slightly, and a frown furrowed her beautiful brow. "He said you were in trouble and I had to get you out of Africa."

"Where is this Ross?" I queried.

"Hiding," she said with a grimace. "The agency pulled him in after the attack on you."

"Agency? Attack?" I dragged my hand down my face. "Alex, I have no idea who I am or what I'm doing here. Please tell me all you know about me. Maybe something you say will trigger my memory."

She lightly raked her nails from my shoulder to my wrist, sending unbelievable tremors throughout my body. "I think I know something that will make you remember me." She had a devilish twinkle in her eye.

I suddenly realized I was holding my breath. I am surprised I didn't pass out. The sensations she aroused in me were breathtaking.

"I . . . I—"

"I know, darling. You're not certain I'm your wife. I told you, you are honorable."

She settled back into the chair and crossed her long legs at the knees. "You are Sloan Cartwright. I call you my soldier of fortune. The truth is, you are a video journalist. You cover hard news and make documentaries.

"You are passionate about everything you do," she said. "I mean *everything*." And with that, she paused for a split second and winked at me. "You are highly regarded in your field. Your recognitions include an Oscar for Best Documentary Feature for your film titled *Ivory Traders in Africa*.

You won a Pulitzer Prize for your investigative reporting on the human sex trade in the United States.

A report that sent many politicians—men and women—to prison, by the way."

"Why am I in Africa?"

"You just completed a year's work on a documentary about the slaughter of rhinos. Poachers murder the magnificent beast for their horns. It's disgraceful."

The vision of a female rhino running with a baby at her side thundered through my mind. It disappeared as quickly as it had materialized.

"You were supposed to arrive at the Dallas/Fort Worth Airport two weeks ago. When you didn't show up, I started trying to contact you. I was frantic.

"I contacted the state department and threatened to go to the newspapers to report you missing. Within an hour, Ross called to tell me where I could find you. He said the two of you had evidence that would crack the rhino horn trade wide open and bring down governments. He said you have the evidence."

Alex leaned forward and took my hand. "Why don't you tell me where you hid the evidence and I will turn it over to the agency?"

"Agency?" I raised my brows. "I thought you said I was a video journalist."

"You are." Alex's smile was condescending. "That is your cover. You are also a secret service agent for the US Treasury Department."

"And I have something someone is willing to kill me to get." I closed my eyes and tried to will something from my blank mind that would confirm Alex's story.

I suddenly realized the reason I have three gorgeous women claiming to be my wife. Are any of the women my wife, or are all of them after whatever mysterious evidence I possess?

I kept my eyes closed, pretending to sleep. Is Alex my loving wife or my own personal Mata Hari?

##

Soft lips on mine pulled me from a deep sleep. "Alex," I whispered without opening my eyes.

"Um,"—she nipped my bottom lip—"how did you know it was me?"

"I just knew you would kiss like that," I said truthfully. The suffocating band around my chest tightened.

##

Chapter 6

"Where is she, Amy?" A man's voice bellowed outside my door. Alex instantly jumped to her feet and positioned herself between me and whoever was entering my room.

An impressive black man filled my doorway. He was over six feet tall, muscular and distinguished looking. His tailored black suit, white shirt, and red tie added to his air of authority.

"Father, don't upset her," Amy said, her tone much more timid than her words. "She has severe injuries."

The man scoffed. "Knowing Sloan, she is probably faking amnesia to get out of your marriage."

My headache rebounded. The pain almost blinded me. I squinted against the daylight that filled my room when the man yanked open the blinds.

He turned to glare at Alex. Something akin to pride swelled in my chest as she stood her ground, not backing up an inch. "Sadie," she said firmly, "close the blinds, please."

Sadie sidled past the man and returned my room to the subdued lighting I craved. I opened my eyes in time to see the man reach for Alex.

"Touch her and, so help me, I will kill you," I growled as I sat up. Everything seemed to stand still as everyone turned to glare at me. Alex flashed me a brilliant smile. I knew she was pleased. Strangely, that made me happy. I was surprised I had experienced such visceral emotions when I thought someone meant Alex harm. As pain shot throughout my body, I wondered why I thought I could protect her. I couldn't even stand. I fell back on my pillow, groaning in pain.

Sadie quickly moved to my side and punched the button that fed me morphine. Standing on the other side of me, Alex caught my hand and gently squeezed it. "It's okay, baby," she said.

"Look here,"—the man harrumphed at Alex— "who are you?"

"Sloan's real wife." Alex lifted her chin.

"I am Governor Makin," the man said with a scowl. "My daughter is her wife."

Thankfully, I slipped into a drug induced sleep.

##

Hours later, Sadie lifted my free hand and checked my pulse. I slowly opened my eyes, wondering who would be with me.

"It's just you and me," Sadie said, chuckling. "None of your wives are here right now, although Amarosia is roaming the hospital."

I groaned and pushed the control to raise the head of my bed.

"Sadie, have you found out any more about me?"

"You mean other than the fact that you're a philanderer and appeal to all types of women?"

I moaned. "I think I'm in real trouble, but I don't know why or from whom."

31

THREE TIMES AS DEADLY

"I'd say that three wives are three times as deadly as one," Sadie said. She continued to tease me, but I sensed something ominous in her words.

"Which one of them do you think is my wife?"

"I'd gladly go home with any of them." She giggled. "Just pick one."

"I wish it were that easy," I mumbled. "I think I'm in danger, and I am in no shape to fight."

Sadie studied me intently. "Stay here as long as possible," she advised. "Give yourself a chance to heal, in case you have to fight your way out of Africa."

"What do you mean?"

"My love, you are awake." Amy smiled as she pushed open the door.

"Are you hungry?" Sadie asked.

I nodded.

By the time, Amy had pulled her chair close beside me, Sadie had grabbed a meal from the cart outside my room. She pulled the lap table across my bed, forcing Amy to back away from me.

"Call me when you finish eating." Sadie wrinkled her nose. "The respiratory therapist has to give you a breathing treatment. I can't have you getting pneumonia on my watch."

"I can breathe just fine," I argued.

Sadie gave me a wicked look. "Breathe deeply!"

I inhaled loudly just to show Sadie. *Oh, damn, damn, that hurt.* I thought I would pass out. I tried to pretend it didn't hurt, but Sadie growled, "Exhale."

Excruciating pain. "Damn, Sadie is a good name for you. You are a sadist." I gasped.

"Call me." Sadie pointed toward the remote button and left the room.

Slow, shallow breaths. I tried to breathe as little as possible as the searing pain eased in my chest.

Amy sat observing my struggle to breathe without pain. "Should I get a doctor?" she asked.

"No, no, I'm fine."

She stood and lifted the cover from my plate. "Oh, this looks good, my love." She unwrapped a knife and fork and cut up the meat on my plate.

"Taste it," I said. "Is it good?"

She obeyed and nibbled the food. "It's delicious."

"Now the potatoes and carrots."

She did as I instructed. "All delicious." She held out a fork full of food, and I opened my mouth.

She was right; it was delicious. Since she hadn't dropped dead, I assumed it wasn't poisoned. What kind of person uses her wife as a poisoned food taster?

Amy settled another mouthful of food on the fork and held it to me. I must admit it was pretty good being fed by a gorgeous woman. I pulled myself from my indulgent stupor and gently took the fork from her hand.

"I can feed myself."

"I don't mind, Sloan. I have always enjoyed taking care of you. If we were home, I would cook your favorite meal. You love my home cooking."

"What's my favorite meal?" I watched her eyes as she answered my question. She tilted her head a bit and cast her eyes to the right as if thinking.

"You love beef dishes," she said, "and potatoes and bread. You love ice cream."

I wondered how I knew she was lying just from the way she'd shifted her eyes before answering my question. "Uh-huh." I nodded as if agreeing with her.

"I must apologize for my father's behavior this morning." She bowed her head. I was pretty sure the look of embarrassment she shot me was fake.

"He was rude to you and Miss Roland."

"Why was he here?" I tried to direct the conversation away from my overreaction to her father's movement toward Alex.

"He wanted to check on you, to make certain everything is being done to make you comfortable. He is fond of you."

"Yes, I could tell he's crazy about me." I refrained from rolling my eyes.

"At first he had trouble accepting that I was hopelessly in love with you." Amy blushed. "It was difficult for him to comprehend that two women could care for each other as we do. My family is of the Muslim faith. My feelings for you go against everything he believes."

"And what do you believe?" Now I was curious.

"I don't believe," Amy whispered. "I know I love you. I can't help it."

Before I could respond, a perky tech pushed his rolling treatment center into my room. "Time to suck and blow," he said before addressing Amy. "Do you mind stepping out for a few minutes, ma'am?"

"No," I said, "I want her to stay with me."

Amy's face brightened, and she moved to the head of my bed. "I'll stay out of your way," she said to the tech.

The breathing treatment was sheer torture.

"Suck the ball to the top," the tech instructed as I gasped from the pain caused by my inflating lungs.

THREE TIMES AS DEADLY

The treatment exhausted me. Amy was talking about her father when I fell asleep.

##

A nurse gently shook me awake. "Dinner time, Miss Cartwright."

I cautiously opened my eyes, not certain which of my wives would be present. To my surprise, Leigh was sitting in a chair next to my bed.

She stood, raised the head of my bed, and fluffed the pillows behind me. "How do you feel today?"

"Better." I moaned as I struggled to sit up straighter. "Still sore."

The truth was, my ribs and head hurt like a son-of-a-gun. I was happy to see Sadie enter my room. "Drugs?" I couldn't hide the hopeful sound in my voice.

"Eat your dinner," Sadie instructed as she checked my vital signs. "Then I'll give you some pain medication."

She shook my water pitcher and held it toward Leigh. "Please take this to the nurses' counter and ask them to fill it with fresh ice and water."

Leigh looked a little perturbed but did as she was told.

Sadie leaned close to my ear. "Listen, Sloan, there are two extremely nasty-looking men asking to visit you. I told them you were too critical to have visitors. I'm trying to keep a close watch on you, but they may attempt to sneak into your room, so stay alert."

"I . . . I can't defend myself, Sadie."

To my surprise, Sadie slipped a pistol under the hospital blanket. "Do I even know how to use a gun?"

"It's already racked," she whispered. "I don't think you're strong enough to rack it yourself."

I stared in disbelief. "What is racking?" I croaked, as I slipped my hand around the gun handle. It felt good.

"Don't be fingering it," Sadie said, her brow furrowed. "Glocks have no safety. When you pull the trigger, it will fire."

"Who are you?" I wanted to inhale deeply to catch my breath but knew it would hurt like hell.

"Your best chance of survival," Sadie whispered.

"Swallow these, my little Casanova." She winked as she shoved a tiny paper cup of Advil into my hand and then keyed in more morphine for me.

Leigh entered the room and poured fresh water into my glass. Her fingertips fluttered across my cheek. "I love you," she whispered.

"Call me if you need anything," Sadie said over her shoulder as she left the room.

Leigh leaned down to brush her lips against mine. I turned my face away from her. The hurt in her eyes was heartbreaking.

"Am I still a stranger to you?" She wrinkled her lovely brow.

I slowly exhaled. "In my mind, I just met you yesterday."

"How long are you going to hide behind the memory loss story?" Leigh glared at me. "I accepted your womanizing years ago. I'm okay with it. I'm not surprised to find you have three wives."

"I . . . I'm not hiding," I mumbled.

She looked down for several seconds. When she raised her eyes to meet mine, they glistened with unshed tears.

"I'm sorry," she said. "You've always been the strong one, the one who takes care of everything. I'm having trouble reconciling the woman I've shared my life with for the past seven years with a woman who doesn't even know my name."

I caught her hand and smiled. "We will work this out. I promise you everything will be okay."

Leigh's phone rang. She answered and listened intently to the caller. "Yes, I'll be right there."

"Sloan, I have to leave for a little while," she said. "Someone has broken into my hotel room and rifled through all my belongings. I'll be back as quickly as possible."

"Please be careful," I said. "Leigh, there is something wrong going on, and I have no idea what it is."

She studied me for several long seconds. "You truly don't know, do you?"

Before I could answer, she was out the door.

My first two visitors had given me plenty to think about as I lay flat on my back. I was a little appalled that I'd been willing to use Amy as a food taster. I was even more distressed that Leigh had called me a womanizer. That destroyed my *lone wolf* image of myself.

Maybe I am a total scoundrel and not a very nice person. I hope Alex gets here soon.

##

THREE TIMES AS DEADLY

Movement in the shadows jerked me awake. I tried to see without opening my eyes too wide. I could tell there was someone just outside the circle of light cast by my nightlight. Then I heard whispers.

"She's asleep," someone whispered. "Now's the time."

Someone crept beside my bed and grasped my IV. They inserted a needle into the tube and pushed the plunger, sending a liquid into my drug conduit. Under the cover, I crimped the line, hoping I could keep the liquid from entering my bloodstream.

"What the hell?" Sadie stormed into the room as two men shoved past her and ran into the hallway. Sadie immediately rushed to me.

"IV," I said, gasping as she turned on the overhead lights, temporarily blinding me. "They put something in my IV."

Sadie yanked the needle from the back of my hand and clamped the tube shut. Without a word, she took the IV line and bag out of my room.

I could hear a lot of activity outside my door as Sadie called security and the search started for the culprits. Her back filled my doorway as she barked instructions to others.

"Let me know as soon as you have information," she said before returning to my bedside.

"Where is Miss Redding?" Sadie glared at me as if I had injected myself.

"Her hotel room was broken into," I said, yawning. "She had to go check on what was stolen."

Sadie snorted. "Humph. I'm glad you had enough presence of mind to crimp that line. You just missed death by lethal injection."

THREE TIMES AS DEADLY

For the first time, I realized that my life was still in danger.

##

Chapter 7

The room was dark except for the light over the head of my bed. I opened my eyes slowly, peering out from between my lashes as I tried to determine if I was alone. I was.

I raised the bed to a sitting position and considered calling Sadie, but then I saw the stack of magazines Alex had brought me. I carefully reached for the top one and was pleasantly surprised to find I could move my arm without the killer pain I had experienced the past two days. *Probably the lingering effects of the morphine.*

The cover of the magazine was mouthwatering. The cover copy screamed "Cosmetic Tycoon Weds Soldier of Fortune."

The photo was of Alex and a gorgeous blonde woman who obviously adored her. I fumbled through the magazine to find the lead story. My vision blurred, and I struggled to read the type as it kept going in and out of focus. The photos told the story. My heart stopped beating. Alex was married, but not to me.

I stared at the photos. The tall woman Alex was draped all over was slim and shapely. Long blonde hair fell around her shoulders in a golden cloud. Her beauty rivaled Alex's. Her pink lips reminded me of

Cupid's bow. Her emerald-green eyes danced with happiness. *She* was Alex's wife, not me.

##

"Good, you are among the living." The bubbly respiratory therapist had pushed open my door and was filling my room with his traveling torture chamber.

"I'm going to skip this treatment," I informed him, eager to return to the magazine article.

He laughed as if I'd told a joke. "You act as if you have a choice," he said with a look of amusement on his face. "You don't!"

He pulled the magazine from my hands and glanced at the cover. "Wow!" He pointed to Alex's photo. "She is something."

"Yeah," I huffed as he shoved the ball-sucking apparatus into my hands.

"Fifteen minutes then I will let you rest." He flipped through the magazine and moaned his approval as he read the article about Alex's wedding.

I wanted to throw up. Of the three women who claimed to be my wife, she was the one I'd wanted. At least I've narrowed my wives down to two. I decided to keep my new knowledge to myself and see what kind of game Alex was playing.

Sadie brought in my dinner as the sadistic therapist wrapped up the breathing treatment. "How is she doing?" Sadie asked the man.

"Great." He grinned. "Miss Cartwright can pull the ball all the way to the top and hold it. That is not an easy thing to do in her condition."

THREE TIMES AS DEADLY

I waited until the therapist left my room before querying Sadie. "Are the two characters still hanging around?"

"I've been watching for them but haven't seen them," she said. "Do you still have the gun?"

"Yes."

She advised me to keep it hidden as she placed clean towels and a wash cloth on my bed.

"I need to give you a sponge bath," she said, a mischievous twinkle in her eye.

"I would kill for a shower," I pleaded pathetically.

"You can't get into the shower alone," Sadie said, "and I have no one to help you."

"I'll help her." The sultry voice floated from the doorway.

I couldn't keep my heart from kicking into double time as Alex walked into my room. "A sponge bath is fine," I mumbled.

"Nonsense." Alex grinned. "I need to wash your hair. You still have dried blood in it.

"Sadie, if you'll disconnect her IV, I will take it from here."

"You do need to get out of bed and move around," Sadie informed me. "A shower will be good for you."

Sadie disconnected the IV tube and wrapped plastic around my hand and the remaining IV needle. "That will keep it dry. I am going to unwrap your ribs, but be careful. You've only been healing about three weeks."

She helped me stand, removed the ace bandage around my ribs, and then moved away so Alex could take my elbow and steer me toward the shower.

"Are you okay?" Alex said. I could tell the concerned look on her face was sincere. "Let me know if anything hurts you."

I nodded and stood outside the shower as Alex set the water temperature. I caught a glimpse of myself in the bathroom mirror. I looked like a street urchin. My hair was greasy and matted. My face was pale and gaunt. My eyes were so recessed into dark sockets their color was indiscernible. I looked nothing like the woman married to Alexandra Roland Cartwright. I gasped as she pulled the tie on my hospital gown and let it drop to the floor.

"I . . . I'm naked," I whined.

"Yes, baby, you are." Alex smiled. "I didn't think you wanted to shower in your gown. Let me look at you."

"Umm, nasty bruises around your torso. Looks like a few stitches on your back and hip, but otherwise you look good enough to eat."

She opened the shower door and held my arm as I settled on the tile bench inside.

"I need to wash your hair." She bit her bottom lip. Her action made me catch my breath.

"You want me, don't you?" she said, her voice a husky whisper.

I didn't answer. I knew I couldn't lie to her.

Before I realized what she was doing, Alex undressed and stepped into the shower with me. No words can describe her beauty. Every glorious inch of her was perfect. I couldn't stop staring at her. I realized that she was surveying my body with the same carnal admiration.

THREE TIMES AS DEADLY

Without a word, Alex soaked my hair with the shower wand then placed it back on the showerhead. She poured shampoo into the palm of her hand and gently massaged it into my scalp. I inhaled deeply. Alex's closeness overshadowed the pain. I wanted to wrap my arms around her waist and bury my face between her perfect breasts. Of the three women claiming to be my wife, Alex was the one I wanted.

She seemed to know my desires. She slid her knee between my legs so she could press her body against mine. She gently tilted my chin upward and pulled my face between her soft breasts. I stopped breathing.

She continued to massage my scalp as she held me close. Everything in my world disappeared. The only thing I was aware of was Alex. Her softness assaulted my senses like nothing I had ever experienced. Smooth, soft skin gently rubbed against mine. The water from the hot sprayer filled the shower with steam. The scent of Alex filled my nostrils as I fought to catch my breath. I closed my eyes and gave in to the feel of her hands as they slowly moved down my neck to my shoulders.

She lathered her hands and gently soaped my skin. She touched every inch of me, lathering down my sides, skimming over my ribs and across my stomach. Her hands were gentle as she covered my thighs with soap and washed between my legs.

"Sloan." Her voice was husky with desire. "I need you, baby."

I slid my arms around her and cupped her firm, round hips. Everything about this woman felt right. I didn't care if she was married to someone else. She slid to her knees and looked up at me. Her lips captured mine as I caressed her back and shoulders, pulling her closer. Her lips were even softer than in my dreams. Her firm, full, lower lip moved relentlessly against my mouth, reminding me of what it felt like to kiss a woman. I groaned half in passion and half in pain as my ribs reminded me I was injured. The passion quickly overshadowed the pain.

I tentatively caressed her lip with my tongue. Her tongue touched mine, enticing it into her mouth. I moaned as our lips communicated our need for one another and our tongues stoked the fire.

She threw back her head, allowing me to explore her neck with my lips. I traced my tongue from the soft spot in her throat to her nipple and gently pulled it into my mouth. I cupped her perfect breast as I circled her nipple with my tongue and then sucked harder, slowly drawing my tongue across her nipple at the same time. Alex moaned and crushed me to her.

I couldn't silence the scream of pain that ripped from my throat as Alex tightened her grip on me. "I can't do this," I said, panting. "God, that hurts."

Alex instantly jerked away from me. "Oh, baby, I'm sorry. I didn't mean to . . ."

I doubled over in pain, trying not to faint. I rested my forehead on Alex's shoulder.

"What the hell is going on in here?" Sadie bellowed as she threw open the shower door. "I knew this would happen." She glared at Alex who was still on her knees. "Rinse her off and get her out of there."

The alarm in Alex's eyes told me that she hadn't intended to let things get out of control. "I am sorry, baby," she murmured as she used the shower wand to rinse the shampoo from my hair and body. "I didn't mean to hurt you."

"I was a willing participant." I tried not to gasp.

She dried me and helped me slip into a fresh hospital gown. I sat on the commode lid while she dried and redressed. Her hair was as wet as mine.

She gave me a sheepish look before leaning down to kiss me. It was the sweetest kiss possible, filled with tenderness, apology, and—did I dare hope? —love.

I kissed her back. "I wish you *were* my wife," I whispered against her lips.

"I am, darling." She pulled back and gazed into my eyes. "You should sit on the bed while I dry your hair." She took my arm and led me to the bed, where Sadie stood with her arms crossed over her chest.

"Is it safe to leave the two of you alone?" Sadie gave us an angry look.

"You!" Sadie shook her finger in my face. "I am not surprised at you. You're a scoundrel." She whirled to face Alex. "But you! I expected you to take care of her."

"I was," Alex said in self-defense. She pressed her lips together trying to suppress an impish grin.

The three of us exchanged glances then burst into laughter. Jesus, it hurt to laugh.

"Behave yourselves." Sadie glared at us as she left the room.

"Alex, I'm sorry. I shouldn't have—"

Alex shook her head. "No. It's not your fault." She turned on the hairdryer, ending any further conversation.

I sat on the side of my bed and watched as she dried and brushed her thick, dark hair. The light danced off it as she turned her head. "You truly are beautiful," I commented when she turned off the dryer.

"So are you, darling," she said. "While I rather enjoy it, I thought you might like something other than that revealing gown. I brought you a pair of lounging pajamas."

"I think I love you," I said as she pulled the pajamas from a bag.

"Don't tease me." She tossed her shiny black hair back from her face. "Here, let me help you get dressed."

The soft, warm pajamas were a welcome change from the scratchy, airy hospital gown.

Alex picked up the book Amarosia had brought me and started to read. Her voice was low and sultry. It made me think of fine Scotch poured over ice cream—sweet but with a hint of fire.

The entire ordeal of showering and almost making love to Alex had exhausted me. I slipped into a deep sleep filled with dreams of Alex.

##

Chapter 8

I was sitting in the hospital recliner when Amy entered my room.

"You are just in time to join me for breakfast," I said as I held out a fork loaded with scrambled eggs.

She frowned then took the egg from the fork. I held out toast and bacon which she also ate. My juice bottle was sealed, so I didn't worry about it containing poison.

Amy sat on the side of my hospital bed. "You look wonderful," she said. "Your hair is glorious. How did you manage a shower?"

I mumbled around the food in my mouth so she wouldn't understand me. I swallowed and then did the Texas sidestep, avoiding her question. "I was hoping your father would accompany you this morning. I wanted to apologize to him for my behavior yesterday."

"He's on a short business trip." Amy cocked her head, still studying me. "Where did you get the new pajamas?"

"Alex brought them last night. I'm surprised you didn't bring me pajamas from home."

She laughed out loud. "What you wear to bed at home is not something they will allow in this hospital."

THREE TIMES AS DEADLY

I was afraid to ask, but curiosity overcame my better judgment. "What do I wear?"

"Normally, nothing," she said with a suggestive twinkle in her eyes. "Or an old T-shirt and no bottoms. One can't expect Alex to know that. Obviously, she doesn't know you very well."

I nodded as I contemplated her dig at Alex. I recalled how Alex had gently brushed my hair and helped me apply a little makeup earlier that morning. Lord, I missed her.

My musing came to an abrupt halt when Sadie trotted in with her iPad and proceeded to check all my vitals. "You need to be walking," she said. "I brought you a pair of nonskid socks for the trek."

I donned my socks, took Amy's arm, and headed out for a stroll. The more I walked around the hospital floor, the stronger I felt. Amy tried to lead me back to the room, but I insisted on walking. I didn't want to answer her questions about the night before.

We were in the hallway when Leigh stepped off the elevator. Her eyes sparkled when she spotted me. She hurried toward me with outstretched arms. I stopped her before she could embrace me. "My ribs are still too sore," I explained.

I was relieved to see the cafeteria cart roll off the elevator behind her. "Dinner time, Miss Cartwright," the attendant said.

"I'll take over now," Leigh said to Amy. "There's no need for you to walk Sloan back to her room."

Amy opened her mouth to reply but changed her mind. She tiptoed to kiss me on the cheek. "I'll see you in the morning, my love."

THREE TIMES AS DEADLY

I nodded and watched her walk away. She had a beautiful derrière. I suddenly realized that Leigh was watching me stare at Amy's swaying hips.

I shrugged at her with a sheepish look on my face. *Now would be a good time for a nap*, I thought as we headed back to my room.

"Tell me about the break-in at your apartment yesterday," I said as I slipped back into bed and waited for the attendant to serve my dinner.

"It was nothing serious," Leigh replied. "Someone ransacked my room, but nothing was taken."

"What were they looking for in your room?"

"I have no idea." Leigh wrinkled her beautiful forehead.

"They probably thought I gave you the evidence I collected." I took a shot in the dark that Leigh was here for the same reason as Alex.

Leigh got up and closed the door. She moved back to my bed, her eyes never leaving mine. I began stuffing my mouth with food. I could tell I was about to be interrogated.

Leigh waited as I shoveled the last of my dinner into my mouth. I looked around for anything that would distract her or provide me a reason to avoid answering the questions I knew she was going to ask.

Oh, thank God for Sadie! My savior bounced through the door with her iPad and a broad smile. "Looks like the walking was good for you," she noted.

"Yes, but I'm exhausted." I yawned and laid my head back on my pillow as Sadie checked my pulse.

"You should sleep, sweetheart," Leigh said, though the look in her eyes told me she had no intention of letting me do so.

I closed my eyes and slowed my breathing, feigning sleep. I listened as Sadie spoke with Leigh.

"She's improving every day," Sadie whispered. "But she's not out of the woods yet."

I heard the door click shut as Sadie left the room.

Soft lips brushed mine then increased the pressure. No mortal could sleep through that kiss. I pretended to jerk awake. "What are you doing?"

"Something I should have done the moment I entered this room." Leigh sat on the side of my bed and traced my face with her fingertips until they rested on my lips. "I have missed you so much."

Wow! One mention of the evidence and I became irresistible. I wondered who Leigh really was and what she expected from me.

I swallowed hard and nodded.

"Sloan, where is the evidence you and Ross collected?"

I told her the truth. "I have no idea. I have no clue who I am or who you are or why I'm in Africa."

It suddenly occurred to me that I might be in grave danger. All three of my so-called wives were after secrets that I supposedly knew.

Sadie had provided me a gun, because she knew I was in danger. I was the only clueless one here.

Leigh stared at me in disbelief. "You're lying."

"No, I'm not," I declared. "Honest, Leigh—or whoever you are—I have no idea what is going on here."

She caught me by my pajama lapels and pulled me forward for a torrid kiss. "I'm your wife, you jackass."

"My ribs!" I whined as I pulled my lips from hers. "You're killing my ribs."

51

She let go of my pajamas and plopped into the chair beside my bed.

"Seriously, Sloan, I need to get you out of Africa. If you stay here, they'll kill you. The only reason you're still alive is that they know you always mail your reports and videos home ahead of you."

"Why are you involved in this? Why are you here?"

"How many times must I tell you, Sloan Cartwright? I'm your fricking wife. I am trying to keep you alive."

I had to admit I loved her fire. I could see being married to her.

"I can't leave until the hospital releases me," I mumbled.

Leigh sighed in obvious exasperation. "You certainly are not the woman I've lived with for the past seven years. The Sloan Cartwright I know wouldn't let anyone tell her whether she can stay or go."

Hopefully, I wouldn't let anyone badger me into doing something I didn't feel good about, either. I closed my eyes and pretended to sleep.

##

Chapter 9

"If anything happens to her, so help me I will hunt you down and kill you." Alex was in Leigh's face, whispering a bit louder than she realized as I pretended to sleep. "I have cooperated with you people, but that is about to come to a screeching stop."

"You need to go back to the States and leave this to the pros," Leigh growled back

"You mean, leave her at your mercy? I think not. You so-called pros are the reason she's in this mess."

Alex's anger was palpable, though both women turned on the charm when Sadie burst into the room with fresh linens in hand.

"Time for you to leave, wife number two," Sadie said to Leigh.

Leigh glared at the nurse, grabbed her purse, and stomped out without even a goodbye kiss.

Alex stood for a long time with her back to me. She was probably collecting her thoughts. Alex struck me as a woman who always had a plan.

She turned to face me, her eyes were filled with love and tenderness. "I brought you some real clothes."

I realized I was holding my breath as I watched her walk toward me. "Thank you."

I wondered how she knew my size. From a bag, she pulled a pair of jeans, a red-and-black plaid shirt, and a short-waisted denim jacket. The outfit looked perfect for a plane ride home or a jeep dash through the bush. Alex was good.

She eyed the fresh linens at the foot of my bed. "Are you up to another shower?" She grinned wickedly.

I laughed. It hurt, and I nodded. "You know those movies where the hero gets shot, run over by a bus, and dropped from a ten-story building?"

Alex's grin widened. "Yes."

"Then the beautiful woman drags what is left of him from the street into her bedroom, where she washes him and attends to his wounds."

Alex nodded.

"Then he flips her over on the bed and makes mad, passionate love to her."

Alex giggled.

"I'm not that guy, Alex."

She laughed out loud. "I promise not to do anything that will hurt you." She moved to my side and leaned down, her breath warming my face. "But sooner or later, you will make mad, passionate love to me."

I inhaled deeply, causing a little pain, but the thought of making love to Alex vanquished the discomfort.

"Shall I call Sadie to remove the bandage around your ribs?" She leaned closer and brushed my lips with hers.

"I think I can handle that." I said.

THREE TIMES AS DEADLY

True to her word, Alex helped me shower without trying to arouse me. Not that I needed a stimulus. Just feeling her soft hands on my body shot my heart rate and blood pressure up. The look in her blue eyes told me she knew how she was affecting me.

"I have walked all over this hospital today," I informed her as she finished brushing my hair. "I'm getting stronger each day."

"That's good, Sloan, because we may have to make a run for it."

"What do you mean?"

"I tried to make airline reservations for us to leave next week. The reservationist assured me that there were two seats in first class, and everything went fine until I gave them your name. The agent put me on hold and returned to tell me she had made a mistake; no seats were available for that day.

"I told her we would take any day. She said all the first-class seats were sold out for the foreseeable future. I said we would take any seats anywhere on any plane. She informed me all seats were sold out indefinitely."

If Alex was telling me the truth, not only was I in danger, but so was she. I didn't like the idea of anything happening to her.

##

Chapter 10

Today was my tenth coherent day in the hospital. I was beginning to get cabin fever. I'd walked every hall in the facility and felt like I could now sprint through them. Between the exercise and the sadist with the breathing treatments, I'd grown stronger every day.

I knew I was in a desperate situation. I had no money, no identification, and no idea how to get out of Africa. I knew my life was in danger. I was no closer to knowing which of my wives to trust than I was the first day I awoke to find them in my hospital room.

I daily fought my increasing attraction to Alex. I suffered through Amy and Leigh just to spend the rest of the night with Alex. She consumed my thoughts and my dreams. I knew it was just a matter of time until I succumbed to her advances.

Amy showed up every morning and fixed my hair for the day. I still couldn't lift my arms high enough to brush my hair. I didn't bother looking into the mirror. I knew I still looked like something the cat dragged in.

I searched through the drawers of my bedside table for the paperback Amy had brought me. I settled into the recliner to read.

"Don't you want to talk?" Leigh craned her neck to read the title of my book.

"I think I know everything you're willing to tell me," I said without looking up at her. "When you decide to be honest with me, we can talk."

"Sloan, I—"

Sadie pushed the door open with her hip and set my dinner on the lap tray. "Wife number three just got off the elevator." She tipped her head in Leigh's direction. "Time for you to leave."

Leigh walked over to me and lightly kissed the cheek I turned to her. "When I get you home, I'm going to kill you," she whispered before heading out the door.

I hoped she was teasing.

"You should call them by their names," I chided Sadie, "not wife number one, two, and three."

"Or I could call them all Mrs. Cartwright."

"You are enjoying my misery, aren't you?" I liked the nurse who had been my constant companion. "Do you ever sleep?"

"My job is to see that you leave this hospital alive," Sadie said with a sudden seriousness. "I intend to do that."

I narrowed my eyes and surveyed the powerfully built Ethiopian. Sadie was tall—probably six feet—slender, and the color of light caramel. Her English was perfect with a slight French accent that I loved. Sometimes I engaged her in conversation just to hear her delightful voice.

"I know you're from Ethiopia," I commented. What region?"

"Tigray," she said. "You are trying to figure out why my features and coloring are more white than Negroid, aren't you?"

"No, you're just different from other Africans I've encountered."

"According to Ethiopian traditions, I am descended from Tigrayan nobility. We trace our ancestry to King Menelik I, the illegitimate son of Makeda, the son of the Queen of Sheba and your revered King Solomon. I am of the Christian faith."

"You seem to know more about me than I do," I noted. "Who *do* you work for, Sadie?"

"Darling! I have a new outfit for you." Alex said as she burst into the room. And just like that, my chat with Sadie was over.

Alex hurried over to me and leaned down for a serious kiss. For some reason, I couldn't turn my cheek to her, so the kiss landed solidly on my lips.

"You look wonderful." She scanned me from head to toe. "I knew that outfit would look awesome on you. It is so you."

"Sloan has already showered today," Sadie said, her nostrils flaring. "You don't have to bother with that tonight."

"It's no bother," Alex said, waggling her brows at me. "I enjoy it."

I do too, I wanted to say, but I kept my mouth shut.

After all the nurses and therapists had traipsed through my room and left us alone, I turned to Alex.

"How did we meet?" I watched as her sparkling blue eyes moved to the left before she answered, the sign for recall. I wondered how I knew that.

"We met in college," Alex said, settling onto my empty bed. "Both of us were in the UT system. You were a local celebrity, state tennis champion, and Olympic swimmer."

"Don't tell me . . . you were the head cheerleader. I was a jock, and you were my girl, right?"

She gave me a dirty look.

"I was studying marine biology in Houston, and you were completing your journalism degree in Austin."

"UT Austin?" I raised a quizzical brow, trying to find a way to distract her from my shallow statement about her being a cheerleader.

"The University of Texas in Austin, Texas. In the United States." Alex frowned at my inability to recall.

"We were in our senior year," Alex continued. "I had to take courses that UT Houston didn't offer, so I was attending in Austin. We were roommates."

I couldn't hide my delight as I thought of sharing a room with Alex. I nodded for her to continue.

"Well, one thing led to another. We became lovers and have been together ever since."

"So, you've always been my only lover?"

"Hardly." Alex snorted. "You *were* a jock. You did have a thing going on with the head cheerleader. When I met you, you were going steady with her. The girls crawled all over you—the straights and the lesbians. I, however, have only been with you."

"A looker like you?" I glared at her. "I find that difficult to believe."

Alex shrugged. "Believe what you want. I can honestly say that since we've been together, you have always been faithful.

"You could have been a professional tennis player, but chose to pursue hard-news reporting. I went into research and hold several patents on skin creams that truly work. You and I have built the cosmetics company into a multi-billion-dollar operation."

I looked down at my hands, wishing that Alex was telling me the truth, but I knew better.

"Do I have parents?"

"Yes, they live in Dallas," Alex said with a sigh. "I speak with them daily to keep them informed on your recovery."

"You and I are married?"

She nodded.

"You *are* a cosmetic mogul," I said, ready to take the plunge. "And yes, you *are* married . . . but not to me."

"What are you talking about?" she said. I saw her wince. "Of course, I'm married to you."

I stood from the recliner, walked to the bedside table, and pulled out the magazine with Alex and her gorgeous wife on the front cover. I tossed it onto her lap.

She stared at the cover for a long time and then looked at me with a confused expression. Finally, she stood.

I backed away from her as she moved toward me. My back hit the wall, and she pushed her body against mine.

"Tell me what you're thinking," she demanded as she pinned me against the wall.

"That you are the most desirable woman I have ever met and that you scare the hell out of me," I mumbled.

She slid her hand to the back of my head and grabbed a fistful of my hair.

THREE TIMES AS DEADLY

"Ouch!" I squealed as she dragged me to the dresser and stood me in front of the mirror.

"Look," she commanded. "Who do you see?"

My eyes were instantly drawn to Alex's face; then I zeroed in on the gorgeous blonde next to her. I moved my hand to touch my face, and the reflection in the mirror emulated me. I touched my cheek, my nose, and my forehead. All my movements mocked me from the mirror.

"You are my wife, Sloan." Alex's eyes pleaded with me to believe her. "The woman on the cover of the magazine, the woman I am married to, is you."

"I'm . . . you're my—"

Soft, demanding lips cut of my foolish babbling as Alex claimed what belonged to her.

She moaned as I pulled from her arms. "Hold that thought." I grinned as I wedged the back of a chair under the door handle so no one could open the door.

"Now, that's the woman I married," Alex said, her voice thick with desire as I backed her onto the hospital bed.

##

"Good God!" Alex said as she struggled to catch her breath. "You'd better let her in before she hacks down the door with that ax in the fire alarm box."

I gave my wife one last, wonderful kiss and then slipped from the bed. I waited until she grabbed her clothes and ran into the bathroom. I slipped on my shirt and opened the door.

"Please tell me you haven't done what I think you've done." Sadie growled as she looked around my room.

"And that would be . . . ?" I asked in my most innocent-sounding voice.

"That you crawled into bed with wife number three," Sadie said, glaring at me.

"I can honestly say I did not *crawl* into bed with wife number three."

I *jumped* into bed with her as fast as I could. I tried to hide the satisfied grin that was spreading across my face.

"Why wouldn't the door open?" Sadie eyed the chair sitting nearby.

I shrugged.

With that, Alex strolled from the bathroom, looking like a million dollars. "Oh, hello, Sadie," she said, feigning surprise. "I didn't realize anyone was in here."

Sadie harrumphed and almost pawed the ground. For a second I thought she was going to attack Alex. Her dark eyes flashed from Alex to me, and then she whirled on her heel and stormed from the room.

Alex looked at her wristwatch. "At least they left us alone for three hours," she said. "Thank God for small favors."

"Uh-huh." I sighed as I moved toward her.

"We must be careful, darling." Alex placed her hands flat against my chest, holding me back, but it didn't last long. She collapsed against me as I pulled her into my arms. "Sloan," she whimpered as our lips met.

#

Chapter 11

At midnight Leigh stood and gathered her things. "I want to leave before Alex arrives," she said. "I don't think she likes me."

I chuckled at her understatement of the year.

"Thank you for the hamburger," I said. "That's the best thing I've eaten in three weeks."

"Hospital food isn't very tasty." She looked pleased that I was happy with her offering. She leaned down to kiss me on the cheek then left the room.

I threw on the jeans, shirt, and jacket Alex had brought for me. *Alex knows my size. Alex knows everything about me.*

I pulled on the soft leather knee boots and fastened them securely. I pulled the Glock from under my mattress and slipped it into my waistband behind my back. I was careful not to touch the trigger. I wasn't certain I would know how to use the gun.

Sadie had checked on me ten minutes before. It was after midnight, and the lights on the floor were dim. I checked the nurses' station; there was no sign of anyone. I slipped into the stairwell and hurried to the garage level. I was glad to learn that I could move fast without pain.

I crept into the dark garage and looked around, my eyes adjusting to the dim lighting.

"Sloan!" Alex hissed. "Over here, baby."

I followed the sound of her voice and located the tan-colored jeep she had rented. Alex was in the passenger's seat.

"You drive, baby," she whispered as she kissed my cheek. "I have a map and will be the navigator."

I nodded. "Sexiest shotgun ever."

She squeezed my bicep as I shifted the gears and put the vehicle into motion. The cool breeze that greeted us as we left the garage was heaven-sent. Leaving the hospital was almost as good as escaping a prison.

"I found this in the hospital," Alex said as she pulled a leather bullwhip from the floorboard. "I knew it was yours. It has your initials on it."

"Umm, that looks promising," I said, my face lighting up as my imagination kicked into gear.

"You use it for self-defense, Sloan, not for fun."

"Seriously, am I supposed to know how to use that thing? I scowled as I fingered the soft leather. "Are you sure we don't . . . ."

Alex slapped my arm and laughed. "I am positive."

"I got a bush plane," Alex said as she reached into the console. "This is the map showing where it's hidden." She cast the bright light of a small LED flashlight onto the map. "It's hidden in some brush halfway between here and Johannesburg. It's a three-hour drive. We should arrive before daybreak."

I nodded and drove carefully until we were outside Maputo. Then I drove the jeep as fast as the road would allow.

"Why didn't we pick up the plane from the rental agency?" I asked.

Alex wrinkled her forehead in disbelief. "You really are out of it. No one would rent me a plane."

"How did you get one?"

"I bought it," she said. "Even that was difficult. I had to get cash from our home office and pay the manufacturer. There's a travel advisory out on you. The authorities will arrest us if we're caught trying to leave the country. They'll imprison the manufacturer who sold me the plane if anyone finds out he helped us."

"What the hell?" I gasped. "You're in danger too, Alex. You should have gone back to the States without me."

"Haven't we shared the same hospital bed the last three nights?" she said. "You must know by now that I'd rather die with you than live without you."

I squeezed her hand and kept my eyes on the road.

"We should be able to get onto the EN4 Toll Road at the next turn," she said.

"Good. We can pick up some speed," I said, trying to sound enthusiastic.

At one time, the EN4 had been a nice blacktop highway. Now it was full of potholes and suffering from chronic neglect. I was forced to keep the jeep in four-wheel drive.

Somewhere along the way, a vehicle pulled in behind us. I watched it in my rearview mirror. It kept its distance, and I decided it was a tourist foolish enough to drive at night in this dangerous country.

THREE TIMES AS DEADLY

We had traveled about ninety miles when our headlights fell on a group of men gathered in the middle of the road. "Who are they?" Alex asked.

"I'm not sure."

As we drew closer, I realized a ragtag gang of bandits were blocking the road. They were on foot and waving guns at us.

"Keep your head down," I yelled at Alex.

There was no way I would stop. I shoved the accelerator to the floorboard and held my hand on the horn to let them know we were crashing through their human barricade. They scattered like bowling pins as we sailed past them.

They must have been too surprised to shoot at us, and I maintained my speed until continuous potholes forced me to slow down for fear of blowing out a tire. A glance in my rearview mirror told me the vehicle that had been following us had fallen prey to the bandits. Poor bastards.

We were within forty miles of our rendezvous spot when we encountered a highway checkpoint. I slowed as we approached the lone officer manning the station.

Alex pulled our fake identification papers from the front pocket of her backpack. The guard looked at the photos of us and then flashed his bright light into our faces. His evil grin made my skin crawl as he surveyed Alex's face.

My heart stopped. The guard had a gun, as did I— and I wouldn't hesitate to use it. He walked to Alex's side of the jeep and scrutinized her closer.

"Come with me," he commanded in heavily accented English.

"No," I said as I prepared to spring from the vehicle.

"It's okay." Alex touched my arm as she opened the jeep's low-slung door and stepped out.

The guard pushed her to the other side of the guard shack, out of my sight. I put the jeep in park and reached for the bullwhip. I had no idea what to do with it. Maybe beat him to death with the stock.

I stepped around the side of the building just as the guard slammed Alex's back against the shack's wall. As if possessed, I unfurled the whip and snapped it around the guard's neck, the tip just missing Alex's face as she ducked.

I yanked hard and held the tension on the whip until the guard stopped struggling and collapsed on the ground. I pulled tighter until his eyes bugged out and his tongue lolled out of his mouth.

"He's dead," Alex declared.

"Yeah," I whispered. I felt neither regret nor guilt, only joy that Alex was okay. I wondered how far Alex would have gone to guarantee our safe passage. "Let's go."

An hour later we were circling the spot indicated on the map. "I don't see a plane anywhere," I grumbled.

"It looks like a zebra," Alex informed me.

"A BushCat! You bought us a BushCat." I wondered how I knew what the hell a BushCat was.

Alex nodded.

"Over there, through those trees."

I looked in the direction she was pointing and got a glimpse of something black and white.

I drove under the low-hanging tree limbs and exhaled completely for the first time since leaving the hospital.

I grabbed the bullwhip—my new best friend—and ran behind Alex to the plane. We hoisted ourselves up, and Alex tossed her backpack behind my seat.

"Where's the pilot?" I looked around. The BushCat was small. There was no room to hide anyone in the cockpit.

"It's a two-seater," Alex declared. "You have to fly it, darling."

"Me?" I choked on my one-syllable word and swallowed hard. "I know nothing about flying a plane."

"You've been flying our planes for years," Alex informed me. "You can fly this in your sleep."

My heart dropped to my stomach. "Alex, I can't fly this plane."

"Just like you can't use a bullwhip?" She gestured to the fine leather attached to my belt.

"I didn't have to use it two thousand feet off the ground." I sucked air.

"You better do something quick," she yelled as she pointed toward a half-dozen government jeeps fanned out and headed our way.

"Buckle up!" I shouted as I searched for a way to start the engine.

I pushed all the red buttons to the *on* position. That just seemed like the right thing to do. Thank God there was a key in the ignition and a compass.

I pushed a button that turned the propeller and frantically searched for a throttle. To my surprise, the throttle was in the armrest that was folded up beside the seat. I pulled the armrest down and pushed the throttle forward, causing the plane to taxi out of our hiding place. I prayed the small bush plane would stand up to a quick takeoff.

I opened the throttle and shot in front of the government vehicles. After running full-throttle for about 250 feet, I pulled back on the control stick and prayed I had gained enough speed to leave the ground. The plane's nose lifted a bit, dipped back down, and rose again. Then, much to my surprise, we were airborne.

"I knew you could do it, Sloan." Alex leaned over and kissed my cheek. I motioned for her to put on her headset so we could talk without screaming over the sound of the engine.

"I'm not sure how far we can fly on a tank of gas," I informed her. "If we land in any of the African countries, we are dead in the water. I'm sure that by now I'm wanted for murdering that guard."

I looked over the lightweight plane we were flying. "This thing is made of aluminum and cloth," I pointed out. "We are basically in a motorized hang glider. Look around and see if you can find any information that came with it, like an instruction manual. I need to know if it uses regular gasoline— which I doubt—or jet fuel."

Alex found a large envelope containing instruction manuals, warranties, and part replacement information.

"Sloan, I'm sorry," she said into the headset. "I thought a plane would get us out of Africa."

"It would, honey, if we weren't at the furthest tip of Africa, almost five thousand miles from the nearest non-African country. Madagascar is no help."

THREE TIMES AS DEADLY

How did I know that? Things kept coming to me in bits and pieces. I was surprised memories of Alex weren't flooding my mind. I squeezed her hand to let her know everything would be okay. *Now, how do I deliver on that promise?*

"It says this plane runs on ordinary automobile gasoline," Alex said as she flipped through one of the manuals.

"Only the government and major cities in Africa have gasoline," I said, my concern increasing by the second. "If we land close to any of those, we'll be arrested."

##

Chapter 12

We had been airborne about three hours when the sound of soft, steady breathing in my headset told me Alex was sleeping. *God, she's beautiful.* I overcame the urge to reach out and touch her. I knew she was exhausted and needed to sleep.

I climbed as high as the plane could withstand and killed the engine. I would use it as a hang glider. I alternated between catching updrafts and using the plane's engine. I knew I could extend the distance we could go on a tank of gas.

Without warning, Camp Elephant popped into my thoughts. *What the hell is Camp Elephant?* I tried to clear my head, hoping additional epiphanies would jump into my mind. Erindi. *Erindi whatty?* I struggled to pull additional information from my contrary brain. I failed.

I had been flying for hours, and everything still looked the same. There was nothing but sand and the occasional oasis. Alex stirred as I looked at her lovely face. Her long eyelashes fluttered open like delicate butterflies. I wanted to lean over and kiss her.

"Oh, Sloan, honey, I didn't mean to go to sleep and leave you alone." A contrite look clouded her beautiful face.

71

THREE TIMES AS DEADLY

"You didn't miss anything. Alex, does the name Erindi mean anything to you?"

She furrowed her brow in thought. "No."

"What about Camp Elephant?"

"Camp Elephant?" She searched her memory for a minute, and then her eyes lit up. "Yes, right after we married you did a documentary on ivory traders. I went with you. We stayed a month at a place called Camp Elephant in the Erindi Private Game Reserve in Namibia." Excitement filled her voice as she found answers to my questions.

"Tell me about it," I said.

She shook her head as if trying to shake loose memories. "There were twelve or more camp shacks—they called them chalets—that meant they had running water for a shower. We loved it. The camp management knocked on our door the third day to make certain we were okay."

"Were we?" I frowned.

"We were wonderful," Alex said, a warm blush spreading across her cheeks. "We just didn't want to leave our chalet and interact with the rest of the world. The wildest animal I encountered during our stay was the one in my bedroom."

I grinned from ear to ear, quite pleased with myself—though I couldn't recall a single moment of our time there.

"Would you recognize the chalets if we fly over them?"

"I think so," she said. "It was an unforgettable month."

"I think I am flying over the reserve now," I said, distraught that I couldn't recall the memories I'd made with Alex.

We flew in silence as we watched for any sign of a campsite or buildings.

"It was near a large watering hole," Alex said. Thirty seconds later, she grabbed my arm and nearly bounced from her seat as she pointed to a semicircle of shacks about a hundred yards from a watering hole below us. "There, Sloan! There it is."

The BushCat coughed and sputtered. "Not a minute too soon." I exhaled, unaware that I'd been holding my breath.

I caught a wind draft and glided into the open desert behind the campsite.

"What do you hope to find here?" Alex asked as we deplaned. She carried her backpack, and I carried my bullwhip. We were a pair.

"Gasoline—or even better, a jeep." I caught her hand as we walked toward the campsite. "Do you have any cash?"

She patted the backpack. "That's all I have in here."

"Awesome." I leaned down and brushed my lips across hers.

To my dismay, no one was at the campsite. It was off-season. "Looks like a ghost town," I muttered.

"Maybe we can take a shower," Alex said, her face beaming, as if a shower would solve our problems.

"Have I told you how much I love you?" I laughed.

"Let's take a shower, and you can show me," she said as she tugged me toward the nearest chalet.

THREE TIMES AS DEADLY

For a moment, I forgot the dire situation we were in and thought only about showering with my wife. It was easy to jimmy the lock on the chalet door. White sheets covered everything. Alex ran to the shower and turned on the water. Nothing happened.

"I'll check outside. I bet there's a cutoff valve," I said, eager to wipe the look of disappointment from her face.

Just as I'd hoped, I found the valve behind the building and turned it on to allow water to run into the shower.

We took a cold shower then fell into the bed, content to forget about the outside world for a little while.

I lay beside Alex, trying to catch my breath. She snuggled into me. You're so soft and yet so strong," she murmured as she kissed the top of my breast.

"I still don't know how I got so lucky." I hugged her tighter.

"I'm the lucky one," she murmured as she drifted into sleep.

The sun was going down when we awoke. I hadn't planned to sleep the entire day. I was even more exhausted than I thought. I tried to slip out of bed without waking Alex, but soft fingers curled around my wrist and pulled me down beside her.

"I'm starving," she whispered.

"I'll check the main lodge to see if anyone is there." I pulled on my jeans and shirt.

THREE TIMES AS DEADLY

"I'll go with you," she said. "I don't like being away from you."

The absence of light in the lodge told me there was no one at the compound. I tried the massive door and found it locked.

We walked around the lodge, looking for an unlocked window or loosely fitting door. I finally jimmied a lock and gained entrance.

Alex practically flew to the kitchen and had her head stuck in a massive commercial refrigerator by the time I entered the room.

"Bacon and eggs!" she said, squealing with delight as she pulled the items from the fridge. Then she opened the freezer. "And bread for toast."

The hum of the refrigerator indicated the generator for the lodge had been left running to provide electricity. I found a toaster and coffee while Alex fried bacon.

I walked through the common area of the lodge and was pleased to find a map of Africa. It showed all the game reserves on the continent. I figured it might come in handy, so I slipped it in my pocket.

After we ate and cleaned up our dishes, we walked toward the barn or farmstall, as the natives called it. I don't know how I knew that, but I did. I hoped there would be gasoline stored in the barn for use in the generators and industrial-size tractor I'd noticed behind the lodge.

Alex gasped as she spotted a jeep through the pipe fencing around the barn. "The gods are smiling on us."

"We'll make better time and get further in the BushCat," I noted. "We won't have to deal with checkpoints."

"Hmm. And that means fewer bodies in our wake," Alex said. "Travel by air, it is."

I climbed the pipe fence and sprinted into the barn in search of gasoline cans. Alex was right—the gods were smiling on us. Ten 5-gallon cans of gas were lined up along the back wall behind the jeep.

We loaded the cans into the back of the vehicle.

"We have no key for the jeep," Alex said. "You'll have to jump-start it."

"I'm glad you have so much confidence in me."

I had no idea how to jump-start a vehicle. I sauntered toward the jeep, hoping Alex wouldn't sense my general lack of knowledge.

I raised one side of the jeep's hood. The battery cables were disconnected. I connected the cables and somehow knew the small wire to the cable led to the starter. In less than five minutes, I had cranked the jeep and motioned for Alex to get into the driver's side.

"Let's stop by the lodge and stock up on food and water," Alex suggested. "No telling when or where we'll land next time."

We gathered chips, bread, cheese, candy bars and water from the lodge. Alex left two hundred dollars on the counter to cover the gas and supplies then we headed back to the plane.

"We'll fill the BushCat with gas and carry the extra five cans in the cargo bay," I said. "That will give us sixteen hours of flying time."

I didn't add that we would still be in Africa when we ran out of gas again. Taking advantage of the wind drafts and gliding every chance we had, we could eke out about eight hundred miles on a tank of gas. The BushCat's tank held a little over twenty-four gallons.

THREE TIMES AS DEADLY

The gas we had would get us to Gabon, a tiny country on the African coast.

We still had to fly from Gabon to the Algerian border and then to Morocco. The final leg of our trip would take us from Morocco, across the Strait of Gibraltar into Spain.

Once we reached Spain we could get to the States. Of course, we might be unable to find gas en route, be shot down, or simply wear out the little BushCat's engine. The plane wasn't designed for the effort I would require of it.

"We'll have to fly during daylight hours," I informed Alex. "I don't know enough about the mountain ranges in Africa. I'm flying strictly by sight. The plane's navigation system is an iPad which is worthless out here."

She nodded and gave me a thumbs-up. Somehow, I knew Alex had always been a trooper. I wasn't worried about her.

I filled the plane's tank—saving enough to prime the engine—while Alex loaded the extra five-gallon gas cans into the cargo bay.

We returned to the chalet for a good night's sleep. I was sore and needed rest. My ribs were killing me, and a dull ache haunted the back of my neck and head. It had been a grueling day.

"I'm not sleepy," Alex whispered as she wrapped her arms and legs around me and cupped my breasts. Her warm breath on my ear suddenly rejuvenated me. More than anything in the world, I wanted her. I pushed her onto her back and began to kiss my way down her body. "Maybe, I am that guy!" I murmured.

We awoke just before sunrise and drove the jeep to the plane.

I poured a little gas into the plane's fuel pump to prime it and closed the cowling. Alex was already buckled into the passenger seat. I climbed into the plane, buckled my seatbelt, and kissed Alex soundly for good luck. The engine sputtered for a second, but that was it. I pulled out the choke, adjusted the air mixture, and said a quick prayer before attempting to start it again.

This time, the engine jumped to life and purred like a kitten. I was beginning to have feelings for the tough little plane.

Alex squeezed my arm. "I love you, Sloan."

"I love you too, honey." I winked at her as I pushed the throttle forward and the BushCat picked up speed. A few seconds later, we were airborne.

##

Chapter 13

Alex studied the map we had found in the lodge. "It looks like another reserve is about four hundred miles from here. We should reach it just before sundown.

"Sloan, it looks like we might be able to jump from reserve to reserve and get the hell out of Africa."

"Good, because that's our only chance." I grinned at her. Even though we were facing certain death, I couldn't suppress the happiness I felt being with Alex.

As we flew, Alex read me every piece of literature we had on the BushCat. I felt like an authority on the light bush plane. It was originally designed for game reserves to use in their pursuit of poachers.

Africa is plagued by thugs willing to kill rhinos and elephants for their horns and tusks. The regal, nearly extinct animals are being killed by poachers faster than they can reproduce.

"I could fly for a while," Alex said. "You need to rest. I'm afraid I didn't let you sleep much last night." She nibbled on her bottom lip and cocked a brow at me.

I laughed. "I'm not complaining. Can you fly this thing?"

"Uh-huh. I didn't want to be the one getting it off the ground, but after reading all this, I'm fairly certain I can keep it in the air."

"We both have throttles on our armrests," I pointed out. "Why don't you take over, and I'll stay awake and observe?"

"That's a better idea," she said. "I'd be more comfortable knowing you can take over in an emergency."

"Put your hand on the rudder controller." I winked at her as I covered her hand with mine. "This is your steering wheel.

"Move it right, left, up or down and the plane will respond to your directions." She nudged the controller, and the plane swayed to the left. "Feel it?"

"I wish we could act on what I'm feeling right now," she said, blushing.

I moistened my lips and nodded. "There's not much room in this cockpit."

"I'm sure you'll think of something once we are on the ground, darling." She shot me a lust-filled look. "You've always been incredibly inventive."

I exhaled slowly, trying to dissipate some of the heat my body was producing.

"You are deliciously evil," I said, wishing we were somewhere—anywhere—other than the tiny cockpit.

##

"Sloan, wake up, baby." Alex stroked my cheek. "We're entering a game reserve."

I looked around as I wiped the sleep from my eyes. "How long have I been asleep?"

"About three hours," she replied as she watched the landscape below us. "Why don't you take over, and I'll try to find the campsites on the map?"

I took control of the throttle and the controller then leaned over to kiss her.

"Um, unless you've come up with some innovative ideas, don't start anything you can't finish."

I pulled back from her. Making love in the cockpit of a BushCat would be harder than making out in a Smart car.

I must admit I'd been eyeing the cramped space behind the seats.

"We should be close to an encampment." Alex furrowed her brow as she concentrated on the ground below us.

"I see water," I said with enthusiasm, pointing toward my left.

I know, my mother taught me not to point, but sometimes I get excited and can't stop myself. This was one of those times. We had eaten all our food and were down to our last few sips of water. We were hungry, hot, dirty, and thirsty.

I lowered the plane and trimmed the speed back to forty-five miles per hour so we could see better.

"Over there." Alex whispered, as if it would disappear.

Multiple campsites encircled a huge compound enclosed by a high stucco wall. I killed the engine and glided the plane toward a dense copse of scraggly trees about a mile from the compound. I wanted to check out everything on foot.

"Did you see anyone?" Alex said as the plane came to a stop.

"No."

"Neither did I. I think we're in Kainji Lake National Park in Nigeria."

"Those are two good things in our favor." Grabbing my whip, I crawled from the BushCat and stretched my legs and back. I was certain rigor mortis had settled in my knees.

"Let's approach the main buildings on foot," I suggested.

"It will feel good to walk," Alex said, though I saw a glint of concern in her eyes as she surveyed the thick jungle between us and the compound.

To my dismay, I had not only landed a good distance from the park compound, but I had also landed on the other side of the river from it.

"Where the hell did that come from?" Alex blurted.

I shrugged. "I didn't see it."

"Of course, we didn't see it," Alex said. "It's enshrouded in trees. A swim will feel good." She tried to lighten the mood.

"Not in this river." I pointed out two pairs of beady eyes floating lazily in the water. "Hippos."

Further scrutiny revealed a bask of crocodiles sunning on the river bank. A waterfowl landed midstream, and the crocs slid into the river without a sound. A few seconds later, the bird was yanked underwater.

"I'm not certain where we fall on the food chain out here," I mumbled to Alex. "I think our best bet is to fly the plane to the other side of the river."

She nodded and turned back toward the plane. I slammed into her back when she stopped dead in her tracks. "Sloan!" she whispered.

For just a second—as her back pressed against me—a wave of desire swept my body. Then I saw the lioness and her two half-grown cubs romping between us and the plane. *Damn! Damn! Damn!*

"Don't move," I whispered, slowly kneeling in the grass. "Maybe they won't see us. We're downwind from them."

It was almost dark when the lioness and her cubs strolled toward the jungle. We waited until they disappeared and ran for the plane.

I helped Alex into her side of the plane and climbed in on the other side.

"Honey, I can't take off in the dark," I said, frowning at her. "I'm not certain I can clear the jungle without visibility."

Alex leaned in for a sweet, soothing kiss. I fought to keep from taking it deeper, because I knew we would only end up frustrated and aching.

Sometime around midnight, the sound of Alex whimpering awoke me. "Cold," she murmured. She was curled into a tight ball, trying to stay warm.

We had taken the doors off the BushCat to lighten the load when we put the gas cans in the baggage compartment.

Most of our trip had been in sweltering heat. Africa is the hottest continent on earth and the dirtiest. Tonight, frigid air had settled over the area where we waited for the sunrise.

I reached behind me and pushed Alex's backpack against the side wall then climbed into the narrow space behind the seats. My movements aroused her. I pushed my body as far back as I could to make room for her. She immediately snuggled into my arms. We used the backpack as a pillow.

"I knew you'd think of something," she mumbled as she spooned against me, wiggling her perfect butt into my lower abdomen.

"I just want to keep you warm," I whispered. "Go back to sleep."

"In the morning," she murmured as she slipped back into oblivion.

##

Chapter 14

"Sloan, stop licking me!" Alex giggled.

"Not me, babe," I whispered as I opened my eyes to find myself eyeball to eyeball with the lioness. "Lay still. Don't breathe."

The big cat and her cubs had made themselves at home in the seats of the BushCat. I didn't know if she was washing Alex's face like one of her cubs or tasting her before eating her. I was so wedged into the tiny space I couldn't move without riling the lioness. Our safest plan was to play dead.

The big cat dragged her tongue across Alex's face and onto the side of mine. She gave me the sloppiest wet willy I've ever experienced. My ear would never be the same.

My lips were right against Alex's ear. "Be still," I whispered as the cubs began to wrestle in the front seats.

The two reared up on their hind legs and batted at one another with their front paws. Suddenly, one of them fell backward out of the BushCat. The other one jumped on him, which resulted in a lot of snarling and growling.

The lioness turned her attention to her cubs and jumped from the plane to administer jungle justice. Two blows of her powerful paw sent the cubs rolling in the dirt. They jumped to their feet and ran from their mother. Fortunately, she ran after them.

"Oh God! Oh God!" Alex squealed as she rubbed her face with her hands then scrambled into the front seat.

I realized I wasn't breathing and exhaled with an audible sigh of relief. "Let's get out of here before she returns."

I had learned just the right amount of air and fuel mixture favored by the BushCat. The little plane's engine kicked off with the first start. I pushed the throttle forward, picking up speed as quickly as possible. I breathed normally once we were airborne.

"Oh my God!" Alex was still shuddering with disgust. "That was the scariest thing I have ever lived through."

I kept the plane as low as possible to avoid being seen above the trees. About five miles from the encampment, Alex spotted a break in the jungle, and we flew through it. Once we crossed the river, I turned back toward the compound.

Alex released the death grip she had on my arm and began to laugh. "When you asked me to marry you, you promised me three things, Sloan."

I shot her a quizzical look.

"You promised always to be faithful and to love only me. You promised to protect and respect me, and you promised that life with you would never get boring.

"I can honestly say, Sloan Cartwright, that you have always kept those promises."

We were still trying to laugh at our predicament when I spotted the perfect place to conceal the

BushCat. I landed and taxied into a U-shaped copse of trees.

After I killed the engine we pushed the plane around so it was positioned for a quick takeoff. Alex grabbed her backpack, and I fastened on my whip.

I fingered the soft leather. It felt good, almost sensuous. "Are you certain you've never let me . . . ?"

"Never." She laughed. "Never. It's not going to happen, Sloan."

"Feel this leather." I held out the tips of the bullwhip to her.

She played with the fine, soft leather, her eyes glued to mine.

"I wouldn't be opposed to"—I caught my breath—"using it on you," she said.

"Oh!" I grunted. "You do know I was teasing, right?"

Her smirk told me she had her doubts.

Outside the wall, sturdy huts circled the compound.

We lay on our stomachs and observed the activity as people left the huts and walked inside the wall. A noisy group of camera-toting tourists climbed into a safari bus.

We waited until the bus disappeared then ran to the closest hut. The door was unlocked.

"A shower!" Alex shrieked as she shed her clothes, turned on the shower and stepped under the stream of water. I quickly stripped and joined her.

I can't remember a shower feeling so good, unless it was the one Alex gave me in the hospital. My body snapped to attention as she slipped her arms around my waist and pulled my nipple into her mouth.

"This won't take long," she said as she took away my breath.

Dear God, I love this woman.

We traded our clothes for the clean ones belonging to the tourists staying in the hut. To my surprise, they fit.

"Clean clothes," Alex said with a loud sigh. "Sloan, I'll never be particular about clothes again, as long as they are clean."

I eyed her. The jeans she fastened fit her like they were made for her. My jeans were not as flattering.

"The jeans are loose in the stride." I pulled on the excess material.

"You have men's jeans, darling." Her eyes danced. "They're like that to keep from binding their junk."

"Okay," I said with a slow nod, thankful I had no "junk."

"Let's see if we can bluff our way through the general store," I said as I zipped my borrowed jeans.

We took some bands from our unknowing hosts and pulled our hair back into high ponytails.

One elderly black woman was behind the cash register when we entered the store.

"I can't believe we missed the bus," I huffed as we walked into the store.

"Don't worry, Miss," the woman said with a toothless grin. "There will be another one in the morning."

"What time will they return?" Alex treated the woman with respect.

"Around sundown, Miss."

THREE TIMES AS DEADLY

"We have to leave this evening," Alex said, her forehead furrowed in feigned distress. "I so wanted to be on that tour. Is there any way we can rent a jeep and catch up with them?" Alex blushed as she slid a hundred-dollar bill across the counter to the old woman.

The woman slipped the bill into her pocket with one hand and selected a key from a keyboard behind her.

"Number 5," she said as she handed Alex the key. "They're in the barn. The number is on the hood. I'm supposed to walk up there and get it for you, but I can't leave the store unattended."

"I'm sure we can handle it." Alex's grin lit up the entire room. "Thank you so much, ma'am. We'll just purchase some snacks and be on our way."

"Are those sausages fresh?" I eyed six beautiful kielbasas slowly turning on a rolling rotisserie.

"I just put 'em on," the old woman said.

We took the kielbasas, anything that looked halfway nutritional, and a dozen bottles of water. Alex paid for the food and water with a twenty and gave the old woman another hundred. "For you," she said as she gently folded the woman's hand around the bill. "Don't let anyone know you have large bills. They'll take them away from you."

The woman nodded and wished us well as we headed out the door.

I'm not certain how I ever convinced this gorgeous creature to marry me, but thank God she did. She is incredible. She owns my heart.

THREE TIMES AS DEADLY

We ran to the barn. As in other barns we had raided, this one had cans of gasoline. We scrambled to get the jeep loaded and headed for the BushCat.

As soon as we were airborne, Alex unwrapped the sausages and handed me one. We ate in silence, grateful for anything that would quiet our growling stomachs.

We moved away from the coast of Africa as we flew toward Algeria.

##

Chapter 15

The last leg of our trip would be the most difficult. The Sahara Desert and the Atlas Mountains stand between us and Morocco.

Soft breathing told me Alex was sleeping. I glanced at her. Her beauty made my heart hurt. I was concerned that she had never seemed worried that two other women were trying to get their claws into me. From the bits of conversation I overheard between her and Leigh, I was certain they knew one another. I had hoped Alex would be more forthcoming with her knowledge of my situation.

I would have interrogated her, but I didn't even have enough knowledge to question her. Maybe I could fake it—something I'd never done with Alex before.

She shifted in the seat and yawned, stretching her arms above her head, her blouse pulling tight across her breasts. She smiled when she caught me staring and then kissed me on the cheek.

"How many more days of this?" She swept her hand to encompass the desert we were flying over.

"Two, maybe three," I said. "We still have a desert and a mountain range to get over. Then we need to get from Morocco to Spain."

She pulled water from the back and opened a bottle for us to share.

She searched my eyes as I turned to accept the water bottle. "You seem troubled. What's bothering you?"

"I've just been thinking. You said before that I'm a US Treasury agent. Tell me what you know about my government job."

"Not much." She shrugged. "I know it's dangerous, and you are extremely secretive about it. You said the less I know, the better off I'd be."

"But you know Leigh Redding? You knew her before she showed up at the hospital?"

"Yes." Alex closed her eyes as if trying to avoid the discussion.

"And?"

"She's your partner," Alex mumbled. "You, Leigh, and Ross make up an elite investigative team. You take down crooked government officials who trade in exotic animals and endangered species. Instead of protecting the rhinos and elephants, many African governments are the culprits behind the illegal exportation of the horns and tusks."

"Jesus, Alex, I wish I could remember this stuff," I said. "It sounds like I may have gotten you into a dangerous situation."

"You're usually allowed free rein in the African countries, because your documentaries result in huge donations from all over the world. People want to save the magnificent beasts you fight to protect.

"I don't think they know how cunning you are. People don't know you dig deeper than poachers. You look for the money men."

"Do you know how the three of us work together?" I asked.

"You and Ross do the investigative work, and Leigh handles the prosecution of the criminals. Ross is an award-winning videographer, and you are an award-winning reporter. Your cover is perfect.

"Leigh is frantic because you shipped your tapes and documented proof to a safe place unknown to her."

"Do I always do that?"

"Yes," Alex said. "If you feel the information you've accumulated is dangerous or would endanger your team, you always ship it to a location in the US. You never try to carry it through customs. You pretend to, but you don't. You have had your videos confiscated on several occasions. They always return them to you, erased. So you always have a backup."

"Do you know where I ship them?" I asked.

"No, you never tell me. You're afraid I would be in danger if anyone thought I had the information. You ship it to a mailing address unknown to me."

"Who knows that this is my normal procedure when handling dangerous information?"

"Ross, Leigh, and me. You tell me everything— except the things that might get me killed." She chuckled but I saw sadness in her eyes. "I thank you for that."

"If the four of us are the only ones who know I have damning information," I thought out loud, "why are people after me?"

Alex shrugged. "Obviously someone informed the bad guys. You are the world authority on the illegal animal trade. You have information that could bring down governments. We have to get that information into the hands of the US government."

"How do you know that?"

"What do you mean?" Her clenched jaw and pursed lips told me told me she didn't like the direction my questions were headed.

"How do you know I have that kind of evidence? Who provided you that information?" I watched her eyes as they darkened from Caribbean blue to deep-ocean black.

"You did," she said, all but growling at me.

Like a dog with a poisonous snake, I couldn't let it go. "When? I don't think I'm a stupid woman. I don't think I would tell you that during a phone call."

"Seriously? You suspect me?" Her voice was a mixture of disbelief and anguish.

She rubbed her temple with her fingertips. "Look at me, Sloan! Do you honestly think I would do anything to hurt you?"

I knew right then it didn't matter. Like Samson and Delilah, I knew I would let her lead me to my destruction before I'd walk away from her.

I didn't answer her. I couldn't talk because of the lump in my throat.

"Sloan, look!" The anxiety in Alex's face told me something was wrong before I spotted the dark cloud that had materialized ahead of us.

A loud boom sounded as a sudden gust of wind caught the BushCat and threw us upward. I fought to keep the plane upright. Flying a BushCat in a thunderstorm was like flying a kite in a hurricane. The plane's wings were merely aluminum frames covered in cloth, like the sails on a sailboat.

THREE TIMES AS DEADLY

"Hold on!" I screamed as another gust of wind sent us higher. I'd been coasting on the wind currents, but now I desperately needed to get out of them. They were taking us higher and higher. At some point, we would lose oxygen and consciousness.

I cranked the plane's motor and opened it full-throttle to fight my way below the storm. It took all my strength to keep its nose pointed downward. It seemed like every time I descended two feet, the wind tossed us up five more. The rudder shook, fighting my efforts to keep the plane's nose aimed down.

Soft hands wrapped around mine as Alex grabbed the controller and helped me steady it. We were pushing with all our might to keep the plane in a downward dive. The little BushCat vibrated from its tail wings to its propeller. I knew that we would have to pull it up as quickly as possible when we escaped the high winds. Otherwise, we would crash.

The winds lessened as we dove below the storm. We pulled back on the controller to stop the plane's death spiral. It continued to plunge toward the ground. I grabbed the flap handle and pulled with all my strength, hoping the flaps would slow our descent.

The plane shuttered and groaned. I waited for it to fall apart. Alex kept a death grip on the controller, as I let all my weight hang from the flap handle. After what seemed like hours, the little BushCat leveled off and stopped shuddering.

Thank you, God! We're going to live!

"We need to land," I yelled over the downpour that had suddenly engulfed us. "I can't see to fly."

Water seemed to be hammering us from all directions. We were drenched, and it was freezing.

THREE TIMES AS DEADLY

On a rudder and a prayer, we glided to the sands of the Sahara Desert. What I wouldn't give for the plane's doors we had discarded.

I immediately killed the engine, afraid to taxi. I had no idea what was around us. The BushCat wedged between two sand dunes.

Without a word, I climbed behind the seats. They offered the most protection from the forces of nature that seemed to be at war all around us. Alex didn't hesitate to settle into my arms.

I moved so that Alex was between my body and the back of the plane. It was the most protection against the storm I could provide for her.

We clung to each other as the storm raged. Exhausted, we fell asleep holding on to the only things that matter in our lives—each other.

##

"Sloan," Alex whispered as she wiggled against me. "Wake up, baby."

I tightened my arms around her and lightly kissed her lips. "Are you okay?"

"I am now."

I shifted my weight to give her more room.

"Don't go," she said, moaning as she pressed closer to me. "I need you."

"I'm not sure I can—"

"Just do it, Sloan." Her voice was thick and husky.

I slipped my knee between her legs so she could ride my thigh. She pulled up her shirt and unhooked her front-clasp bra. "Suck me, baby," she whispered.

I was certain that making love in a BushCat would be impossible, but I must admit it was one of the most pleasurable experiences I'd had in a long time. Of course, I'd discovered that everything with Alex was gratifying and possible.

Chapter 16

I poured the last of the gasoline into the plane and dug the sand from around its wheels. The deluge we had experienced the night before had soaked into the parched earth, and only dry sand remained. Within a couple of hours, our clothes had dried on our bodies.

I was thankful Alex had purchased a BushCat with a nosewheel configuration. It made the plane easier to maneuver. I checked the wheels to make certain there was no damage. BushCats don't have a landing gear. Their wheels don't retract like those on most planes. They constantly stay in a triangular formation.

Alex slid from the top of a dune. "Nothing but sand for as far as I can see," she informed me.

"We need to pull this baby to a place that will give us room to take off." I secured the cowl of the plane and pulled all the empty gas cans from the cargo hold.

"What are you doing?" Alex said as she watched me scurrying about.

"Making our load as light as possible," I explained. "We should be able to make it to Spain on this last tank of gas."

Alex drew in a deep breath and let it out slowly. "I'm afraid to hope."

"We have a radio. I haven't turned it on for fear of being located by our signal. Once we fly over the Strait of Gibraltar, we can begin radioing for help and a landing strip."

"Let's get this plane airborne." She grinned as she grabbed hold of the plane and helped me push it out of the dunes.

##

"Is there any way we can land in Spain and make a run for it?" Alex asked.

"What do you mean?"

"I mean we still don't know where we stand with the authorities. It would be best if we could land the plane and lose ourselves in a city. Maybe rent a vehicle or take the train into Seville and then fly from there to New York.

"Sloan, I don't trust turning you over to any authorities until we're in the States. Whatever you've uncovered, it is serious. They pulled out all the stops when they sent in Amarosia. The African authorities want you badly."

"We can try," I said, but I didn't feel too confident about our chances. "I agree with you; I would rather remain incognito until we're back in the States."

I kept an eye on the fuel gauge. Flying over the Atlas mountain range that divided Morocco and Algeria had required constant use of the engine. At 12,000 feet, the altimeter told me I was pushing the limit of the plane's capabilities. The map showed the Atlas Mountains reached over 14,000 feet in some areas.##

Alex's eyes widened as the BushCat shuddered and sputtered. I looked at the fuel gauge. "Looks like we'll have to add a boat trip to our travel plans," I said as I glided the little plane to a landing inside Morocco.

Alex laced her fingers through mine as we looked around us. "I don't think we're even close to civilization," she said.

"You may be right," I was thankful to be on the right side of the mountain range. At least we wouldn't have to spend days hiking over the Atlas Mountains.

I handed her the backpack and fastened my whip to my belt. We had four bottles of water and two Snickers bars. For the first time, I slid the Glock into the back of my jeans.

Each of us put a hundred dollars in small bills into our pants pockets. If we needed to buy our way into or out of something, we knew it wasn't a good idea to let anyone know how much money Alex was carrying in the backpack.

I pried the compass from the dash of the BushCat. I had no idea where we were, but I knew a due-north course would lead us to the ocean sooner or later.

As the sun slipped toward the horizon, we searched for a haven for the night. There were facts in my head that just seemed to reside there. How in the world did I know about the deadly nocturnal Egyptian cobra that was prevalent in the hot, desert-like regions of Morocco?

We located a cave-like space protected by boulders. With only one way in, it seemed like the best place to spend the night. The desert temperatures dropped quickly after sundown.

We sat in silence as we shared one of the Snickers bars and drank a few sips of the water. I could tell Alex was still miffed at me because of the way I'd questioned her.

"You lean against the rock," I instructed her as I settled between her legs, my back against her chest. I knew she would be warmer between the rock and me. She seemed to realize my motives and wrapped her arms and legs around me.

"Are you warm enough?" she whispered into my ear. Her hot breath felt good on my cheek.

"Very." I lied. "Are you okay?"

She rested her chin on my shoulder. "Yes."

I was dozing off when she whispered, "Damn it, I love you, Sloan Cartwright."

##

The sound of a baby crying invaded my sleep. I moved, and Alex's arms tightened around me. "Shush," she whispered before I could make a noise.

We sat motionless, waiting for the sound to come again. The cry seemed to emanate from the rocks surrounding us. I scooched toward the opening in our sanctuary.

Sheep! The crying was the bleating of sheep. I motioned for Alex to crawl up to the opening and see the herd of sheep spread out over the valley. One lone shepherd seemed to oversee them.

"Maybe he can tell us where we are," Alex whispered. "He's just a young boy. Do you think it's safe to reveal ourselves to him?"

"We don't have much choice," I said. "Wait here. I have no idea if he has a village or tribe close by."

THREE TIMES AS DEADLY

I knew I could overpower a boy, but I didn't want to take on an entire tribe.

I slipped out of the rocks and walked toward the boy. I watched the emotions play across his face as I approached: shock, interest, and then fear. He was probably sixteen or seventeen years old—almost a man.

He held up his hands when I moved closer. "Please, no trouble," he said, wide-eyed.

I was shocked that I could understand him and could easily converse with him in his native language, bastardized French.

"Friend," I said, bowing slightly to him to pay my respects. "I am trying to reach the closest town." I held out a twenty-dollar bill to him.

He reached for the money. "I will help you. Come. My sister is going to town. She will take you."

His eyes lit up as he craned his neck to look around me. "Ahh." He sighed as he scrutinized Alex. "Your friend?"

"My wife," I said stoically.

"I trade you camel for her." He flashed me a toothy grin.

I laughed out loud. "No, she is my favorite."

He looked shocked. "You have many?"

"Two more than I want." I tried not to laugh at his excitement.

"Then I take one of them." He leaned around me as he watched for more women to emerge from the rocks.

"Get me to the closest town, and I will give you enough money to impress all the women you want," I told him.

"The closest town is Tata," he explained. "It is an oasis about ten miles from here."

"What is he saying?" Alex wrapped her hand around my arm and took my breath away.

"He wants to trade me a camel for you," I explained with a devilish grin.

"I take you to Tata," the man spoke to Alex in his native language. "Tata."

"He wants to see my breasts?" Alex gasped as the man repeated the name of the town again. "Sloan, I don't think—"

"You don't expect him to trade me a perfectly good camel without seeing what he's getting, do you?" I couldn't suppress my laughter as I teased her.

I yanked myself from thoughts of Alex's glorious breasts and explained the situation. "Tata is the closest town. He can get us there."

"Oh, thank God," Alex whispered, releasing the breath she'd apparently been holding.

"Come, come." The boy motioned for us to follow him. He took one last look to make certain his sheep were safe and then led us to the top of a hill.

In the valley below was a house built of pink clay. It blended with the surrounding terrain. A small herd of camels milled in a corral.

Alex looked at me, perplexed. "You're not trading me, are you?"

"No, I promised him enough money to get all the women he wanted, but he can't have mine."

The boy led us to the house and pushed open the front door. "Malika, we have strangers," he yelled.

A beautiful, dark-haired woman entered the room. I was surprised to see that she was wearing none of the traditional Muslim apparel. She had on a simple skirt and blouse. She was tall and stately. Apprehension filled her dark eyes.

"Wasim, what is the meaning of this?" she demanded.

"Malika, they need to get to Tata," Wasim answered. "They have money. They can pay."

She contemplated both of us. "You have names?" I was surprised she spoke English.

"This is my wife, Alex Roland, and my name is Sloan." I intentionally left off Cartwright, just in case the authorities were after us.

"Your wife? You are married to her?" She seemed more interested in the fact that we were married than the fact that we had emerged from nowhere in the middle of the desert.

"Homosexuality is a criminal offense in this country," she said, narrowing her eyes.

"Will you help us?" I spoke to her in French.

"Yes," she said.

##

"You will be less conspicuous wearing these." Malika placed a pile of neatly folded clothes on the dresser in a bedroom. I was pleased to see we would wear black cotton shirts and pants under a hijab. I could hide my bullwhip and Glock beneath the clothing.

"I have drawn you a bath," she said to me. "You will need one if you are to travel with me."

I nodded. I was sure neither Alex nor I smelled like roses after our ordeal. I stepped aside so Alex could bathe first. I was certain there would be only one tub of water for us both to use.

"You are American," Malika said once Alex was out of earshot. "How did you get here?"

"The less you know, the safer you will be."

"Have you visited Morocco before?" she asked.

"I think so," I said. It was an honest answer.

"You think so?" She raised a perfectly arched brow.

"I don't remember," I said. "But you have been educated in America."

She nodded. "Texas A&M University. I did my doctoral research in animal science there."

"Why A&M?" I queried. "Other universities are higher ranked."

"Your Texas most closely compares to our climate and some of the challenges we face."

"You must let me show you Texas," I said, laughing. "It is truly nothing like Africa."

"You are correct. Texas is nothing like Morocco, but you must admit that your Texas badlands are quite barren."

I had to agree. "What will you do with an animal science degree?"

"The Rhino Conservation Project in Mozambique just hired me as their new director," Malika informed me.

I cringed as I thought of the extreme danger she would be facing. I innately knew it was dangerous.

I looked up as Alex entered the room. She looked gorgeous. She wore no makeup. Her hair tumbled loosely around her face and caressed her shoulders—

something I longed to do. I couldn't stop the blush that crept up my chest to my face.

Alex nibbled her bottom lip as she approached me. "I always have that effect on you," she whispered.

Then she turned her charm on Malika. "Thank you so much for your hospitality." She all but purred at the woman, who soon was blushing too. Apparently, Alex has that effect on everyone.

##

Chapter 17

"A camel?" Alex shrieked. "It's not even a real camel. It only has one hump. How can anyone perch on top of that?"

Malika rolled her eyes at Alex's antics. "We have saddles," she patiently explained. *I have a feeling she thinks my wife is as cute as I do.*

Wasim lifted heavy blankets and pads onto the largest camel, followed by a two-seated camel saddle. I ducked under the neck of the beast and started cinching the saddle in place.

Wasim moved to another camel and placed a single-seat saddle on it.

Alex frowned as she gauged the distance between the ground and the camel's back. "Where are the stirrups?"

"Unlike Western equine saddles," Malika explained, "camel saddles have no stirrups."

Alex turned to me with a what-the-hell? expression on her face. "They lay down so you can mount them," I said.

"Oh, of course they do," Alex rolled her eyes. The look of disbelief on her face was priceless.

Malika made a soft *kooshing* sound, and both camels quickly bowed and then lowered to their knees and stomach.

I gave Alex a told-you-so grin and reached out to help her into the saddle.

"You drive," she whispered. "I want to sit behind you so I can squeeze you."

The thought sent a tremor through my body, and I hoisted myself into the front saddle.

"Have you ridden a camel before?" Alex murmured into my ear.

"I think so," I mumbled.

Malika led the way as we tried to find our balance on the rocking animal. A camel's gait doesn't compare to a horse's pace. The long-legged beasts rock from side to side as they lumber along, because both legs on the same side move in unison.

Alex was clinging to me for dear life, and both of us were flopping around like rag dolls on a mechanical bull. I gripped the saddle's pommel and let my body relax as I tried to find the rhythm of the animal.

Malika slowed her camel so we could ride abreast one another. "Tata is only ten miles away," she said. "We will arrive there in an hour."

Camels don't run; they just shuffle faster. But I was pleased to find that we were moving about ten miles per hour.

Alex laid her cheek between my shoulder blades. It was a feeling I liked.

"Are you aware of the dangers in Mozambique?" I asked Malika.

Her soulful eyes fixed me with a long, cold stare. "Yes, that is why I accepted the job. There is tremendous corruption in the entire game reserve system. I intend to make a difference."

"You do know that ninety of the rhinos slaughtered on their game reserves so far this year died as a result of the reserve police working with the poachers?" I said it with confidence but wondered how I knew this.

"Yes."

"They will kill you too, if you get in their way," I added.

She stared at me for a long time as our "ships of the desert" lumbered toward Tata."

Suddenly, Malika caught her breath. "I know you. You spoke to our class on the preservation of elephants and rhinos. You're Sloan Cartwright."

Alex squeezed me tighter and pushed her soft breasts into my back. *God, give me strength!* I knew it was her way of saying, "What are you going to do now, Bwana?"

"I'm not. Really." I shook my head. It was a lame response.

She studied me closely. "Yes, you are. I could never forget your eyes. They are exceptionally green. I think they would glow in the dark."

Alex lifted off me momentarily and turned her head so she was facing Malika. Alex can be possessive. I hoped she wasn't making the Muslim woman uncomfortable.

"I purchased your documentary, *Ivory Traders in Africa,*" Malika declared. "It made me cry. I watched it over and over, determined to help stop the carnage."

She paused for a minute and waited for me to respond. When I said nothing, she continued.

"You're in trouble, aren't you?"

"Yes, we're in trouble," Alex huffed. "Sloan is hiding from the very people who just hired you."

"How can I help you?" Malika asked. "Do you need help getting out of Africa?"

"Yes!" Alex shouted when I didn't reply fast enough to suit her. "We need to get the hell out of Africa."

God, I love her. I leaned back into Alex, seeking more contact with her. She squeezed the breath from my body. I wondered if she has always been able to read my mind.

"I can help," Malika said as she urged her mount to move faster—something I deemed completely unnecessary.

##

Chapter 18

Tata is a city of great discrepancies. For the few wealthy enough to afford it, there were modern conveniences and luxuries. For the natives who were unfortunate enough to be born in Tata, there was poverty and hopelessness.

It was a city of contrasts—the ancient versus the ultra-modern. We rode through centuries-old ruins, remains of civilizations long past.

I had the strongest feeling I'd been there before.

Malika led us to a stable outside of town where we left the camels. A dollar tip to the old man watching the animals and a promise of the same amount upon our return guaranteed our rides would still be there.

Alex perked up as we walked past a delectable French restaurant. "Can we plan over dinner?" she asked.

"Yes," Malika said, "but not in there. That is an expensive place. We would draw unwelcome attention."

We followed her down streets which were no more than alleyways to a narrow storefront with a single-entry door. A snake charmer was entertaining a crowd on the other side of the alley.

Alex's shoulders slumped. I could tell her hopes for a savory meal had taken flight. Malika pushed the door open, and we followed her into the aromatic restaurant.

"Oh Sloan! What is that heavenly smell?" my wife exclaimed, suddenly relishing the taste of good food.

Malika led us to a cozy table in the corner and greeted the woman emerging from the kitchen.

"May I order for you?" Malika asked Alex.

"Of course," Alex said. "That would be lovely." Malika momentarily rested her hand on Alex's arm.

Was she flirting with my wife? She was indeed! I was quite certain of it. A sudden pain akin to being stabbed in the heart roared through my body. Malika excused herself and went to the kitchen to speak with the woman.

"What?" Alex shrugged as I glared at her. "Now you know how it feels when other women touch your woman."

"I don't like it," I growled.

Alex flashed that cute little smile I've become accustomed to when she is pleased with herself. "It won't happen again, dear."

I leaned over to whisper in her ear. "I want you so badly it hurts."

"Yes,"—that smile again—"I know."

Malika returned with ice tea—a rarity in Tata—and the woman bearing bread and fruit. I thought I was in heaven.

"We are ninety-five miles from Al Massira Airport," Malika informed us as we gorged ourselves on the fresh food. "It is an international airport, so you should fit in with the tourists nicely."

"Ninety-five miles on that camel?" Alex's painful expression made us laugh.

THREE TIMES AS DEADLY

"I have a friend who will drive you to Al Massira," Malika said, her voice syrupy-sweet as she spoke to Alex. "I will ride with you to guarantee your safety.

"When we are through eating, I will take you to my uncle who owns a travel agency and is the government passport agent for the Tata Province. He will issue you passports with photos of you in your hijab. That will completely change your appearance. Instead of looking like gorgeous models, you will look like peeled onions."

Alex laughed at Malika's description of us and touched her arm

I snorted, a little jealous that Alex was touching and laughing with Malika. I'd had Alex's undivided attention for the past few weeks, and I found it difficult to share her now.

She looked at me and placed her hand on my knee under the table.

"Signs of affection between women are greatly frowned upon here," Malika whispered.

Alex removed her hand, and a coldness settled on my leg where her hand had rested.

After a savory lunch, we followed Malika back into the alley. The snake charmer had attracted a group of tourists and a few local men who appeared to be his friends. The crowd watched in silence as the charmer played a flute-like instrument and an Egyptian cobra swayed back and forth in front of the face of a little girl. It was obvious the child was terrified.

THREE TIMES AS DEADLY

Alex inched toward the child. Before I realized what she was doing, she snatched the girl out of harm's way.

As Alex found the child a safe place to sit, a roar went up from the local men. Two of them grabbed Alex and forced her to her knees in the spot the child had occupied. The tourists gasped and backed away from the scene unfolding in front of them.

The local men laughed and babbled among themselves about how the snake might bite the beautiful woman. Alex remained motionless as the charmer continued to play his flute.

One of the locals poked the snake with a stick. The serpent drew back, flicking its forked tongue in and out of its mouth. It was clearly getting agitated. It fixated on the stick that was now between Alex's face and the snake.

Malika gasped. "She is in danger. They are trying to make an example of her by making the snake bite her."

It all happened in the blink of an eye. There was no thought on my part. I pulled the whip from my clothing and snapped off the viper's head. The man with the stick shook it at me. Another snap of the whip broke his wrist. I recoiled my whip.

The snake charmer screamed at me. "You kill my snake! He is harmless. No fangs. No fangs!"

Many charmers defang their snakes and replace the missing teeth with fake ones.

I picked up the snake's head and squeezed the jaws, forcing the mouth open. There were real fangs— deadly fangs.

"They are fake," the charmer yelled.

Alex caught my coiled whip, and I pulled her into a standing position as I sank the snake's fangs into the arm of the snake charmer. His eyes widened as he began to scream, "Poison! I will die!"

While the locals attended to the snake charmer and his buddy with the broken arm, Malika pulled us back into the restaurant. "Out the back door," she commanded as she pushed us into the kitchen.

Following Malika, we quickly lost ourselves in the marketplace. After walking in silence for at least a mile, Malika led us to an official-looking building in an upscale part of town.

"Wait here," she instructed as she went inside.

"I want to hold your hand," Alex said to me.

"As much as I would like that, we better not." I nodded toward two Moroccan soldiers strolling along the street.

"You were amazing back there," Alex said. She caught her bottom lip between her teeth, her eyes sparkling as she crinkled her nose at me.

"You are so sexy when you do that," I whispered, mesmerized.

"I know," she said. Then she winked at me.

Malika opened the door and motioned for us to follow her inside. The office was decorated with ornately framed prints of works done by the Old Masters. The furniture was sparse but of good quality.

Malika stopped in front of a door bearing a sign that said Government Passports. Inside, a portly man dressed in a black suit stood to greet us.

"My Uncle Benjamin," Malika said, introducing us. "I have explained your situation. He will help you."

"I will require a thousand dollars for my services and a thousand dollars for your airline tickets to Spain." His head wobbled on his shoulders as he shot us a lopsided grin—a human bobblehead. "In American money, of course."

"Of course." I nodded back at him.

"I'm sorry, but I am in dire need of the lady's room before we go any further," Alex said, fluttering her eyelashes at Malika.

"Of course." Malika caught her hand and pulled her from the room.

As the door closed behind them, the man got down to business. "So, you are Sloan Cartwright?" Uncle Benjamin walked around me.

Somehow I was certain I was not nearly as impressive in a hijab as I am in my usual attire.

"That's what I've been told," I said.

"My niece is enamored of you."

You mean enamored of my wife.

His smile had been replaced with a stoic expression. "Malika admires the work you have done to save the African rhinos and elephants."

"I'm afraid it's too little, too late," I informed him. "It's difficult to save a country's species when its own government is butchering them for a dollar."

Uncle Benjamin's eyes filled with dispair most Americans could never imagine. "Still, Malika and I appreciate your efforts to inform the world of the travesty that is happening in Africa."

Alex returned with Malika, and Uncle Benjamin motioned for us to follow him. In less than an hour, we had two airline tickets, passports, and US driver's licenses issued to Rita Smith and Melba Johnson.

THREE TIMES AS DEADLY

Alex produced twenty 100-dollar bills from her pocket, and we thanked Uncle Benjamin profusely. Malika led us out the back way, and her friend met us with an honest-to-God air-conditioned car.

In a couple of hours, we would be in a hotel where we would spend the night before flying to Spain the next morning.

I dozed during the trip while Malika flirted with my wife. What part of "she's married to me" did Malika not understand?

We checked into the hotel and headed directly to the lady's apparel shop on the first floor. We purchased suitcases and several outfits. I couldn't wait to get out of the hijab and back into real clothes.

"I'm exhausted," Alex mumbled as she fell onto the bed.

"Probably worn out from all that flirting." I was teasing . . . sort of.

I helped Alex remove her hijab and pulled off mine. I carefully folded the clothes, because we must wear them to board the plane in the morning.

"I'm going to take a shower," I informed Alex.

I expected her to join me, but she didn't. When I finished showering, I found her sound asleep. I slipped into bed, careful not to disturb her.

The sound of the shower disrupted my restless sleep. The clock on the bedside table showed five a.m. We had a ten o'clock flight. I got out of bed to search for coffee.

Alex and I hadn't talked much since meeting Malika. We needed to develop a game plan before we joined her for breakfast.

Our hotel was as nice as any I'd stayed in, complete with a Keurig coffeemaker and a wide selection of pods containing different coffee flavors. I selected a mocha cappuccino, slipped it into the holder, and pressed down the top.

I suddenly realized that things were coming back to me in bits and pieces—like details about other hotels where I've stayed and what kind of coffee I liked. The Keurig isn't easy to use the first time, but I did it like it was an old habit. Things were coming back, but still few memories of Alex.

"I'm sorry I fell asleep last night," Alex said as she slipped her arms around me and pressed her warm body against my back. "Did you make me a cup of coffee?"

"I . . . I don't know what you drink. "I can't remember."

"It's okay, baby." She kissed me between my shoulder blades as she released me. "It will all come back to you in time."

I pulled out the chair and sat down at the table in our room. Alex turned to me.

"What's wrong, Sloan?" Her eyes bored into mine, as if searching for answers to her question. "Are you still upset because I was flirting with Malika?"

"Maybe." I pretended to pout. I couldn't resist her sensual movements. She stopped making coffee and straddled my lap.

"You know I was just giving you a hard time." She nibbled at my lower lip. "I can make it up to you."

THREE TIMES AS DEADLY

I lowered my eyes "How?" My voice squeaked.

"I'll let you see my tatas." She giggled.

"Well, since I couldn't trade you for a camel . . . ."

In one smooth motion, she pulled her T-shirt over her head. She wore no bra.

"God, Alex." My breath caught in my throat as I stared at her. She kissed me softly, her full lower lip moved against mine. She sucked the soul from me as she deepened our kiss, teasing my tongue.

"I'll even let you touch my tatas," she whispered in her sexy way that left me breathless.

I trailed my fingers along her torso, tracing every curve as I made my way to her breast. I cupped the soft, firm flesh as my other hand held her tight against me.

She nibbled her way up my neck and breathed into my ear. "If you'll take me to bed, I'll let you suck my tatas."

A moan rose from the pit of my stomach and escaped my lips as I stood, still holding her. She wrapped her legs around me and began to grind into me. I could feel the warm moistness of her, and I wanted her more than I had ever wanted anything in my life.

For the first time, I realized we could take our time exploring each other. No one was hammering on the hospital door or hot on our trail, or likely to return to their campsite and catch us.

Making love to Alex was indescribable. She was warm and silky, soft and yet firm. Her scent was mouthwatering. Her mouth was everywhere—on my breasts, sucking my throat, nibbling my lips. Her teeth grated against mine as she pulled me down hard on her.

"You know what I need," she hissed.

And I did! I knew what Alex needed and what she liked. I knew just where to touch her and kiss her and suck her.

She clutched my hair in her fists and threw her head back, arching to meet me. *I know the next sound she makes will be a loud moan. Then she'll scream my name over and over as she gives me everything she has and we ride the waves of passion together. I know this because I remember. God, I remember!*

I moved to cover her screams with my shoulder. "Malika is in the room next to us," I cautioned her. "She'll hear you."

"Sloan, I can't . . . I can't stop."

"Bite me," I hissed, and she did.

She buried her teeth into my collarbone and ground against me. Her fingernails cut paths down my back. Pain and pleasure shot throughout my entire body. To muffle my own cries, I buried my face in her dark tresses and rode her to the most exquisite feeling I have ever known. We went over the top together and came down slowly, gasping for air, still clutching each other.

"Oh, Sloan," she whimpered, "I thought you had forgotten what I like."

"It came back to me," I whispered as I tangled my legs with hers and pulled her as tightly against me as possible.

##

Chapter 19

"Do you remember everything?" Alex kissed me gently after she fixed my hijab.

"Not everything," I said, "but I do remember the most important things."

"Umm, you certainly do, darling." She gave me a look that made me gaze at the bed hoping for a replay.

She laughed at me.

"You are evil." I kissed her.

"Malika is waiting for us in the coffee shop." Alex grabbed the pull bar on her suitcase, and I did the same with mine. "Do we look like Rita and Melba, Tourist?" She laughed.

I moved to the opposite side of the elevator, trying to keep my hands off her. "Why did you get a sexy name like Rita and I got Melba?"

"Because I *am* the sexy one."

I had to admit it; even a hijab didn't diminish her beauty.

Malika waved at us when we entered the coffee shop. She had ordered coffee for all of us and a fluffy French pastry.

"Do you have everything?" Malika asked. "We only get one chance at this. We can't afford for anything to go wrong."

I nodded. "We have a package for you. Don't open it until you get home."

"What is it?"

"Money and a gun," I whispered.

A look of concern clouded Malika's face. "I don't—"

"Please don't argue with us." Alex placed her hand on Malika's, and this time I found no room for jealousy in my heart. There was only love for my wife and deep appreciation for the woman who was risking so much to help us.

"We can't carry the gun or money through security. The authorities will confiscate both," I explained, "and we want you to have the money to use as you see fit." I leaned down and kissed her gently on the cheek. "If you ever need me, call me."

She hugged us goodbye and waved until we lost sight of her.

Uncle Benjamin didn't let us down. We breezed through security and customs. I feigned religious indignation to keep authorities from searching under my hijab. My bullwhip was secured around my waist and showed up on the x-ray machine as a leather belt.

##

Alex snuggled into my side as I studied our airline tickets. "Our destination is Florence." I tilted my head and looked at her.

"Yes." She hugged my arm. "To our villa there. Do you remember Florence?"

I leaned my head back and closed my eyes. Visions of a younger Alex flashed through my mind: Alex riding a bicycle on stone-paved streets; Alex eating ice cream from the cone I held out to her; Alex lying on white sheets, inviting me to join her; Alex wearing a white dress and veil as she stood next to me.

"We were married in Tuscany," I murmured. "That's where we vowed to spend our life together."

"See, darling? All the important things are coming back to you."

We had a layover in Spain and didn't reach Florence until early the next day. We were exhausted. At the Florence airport, we went into the ladies' room as two Muslim women and walked out as Alex and Sloan Cartwright. I ran my fingers through my hair, letting it fall across my shoulders.

"Even the air smells different here," I said as we waited in line for a rental car.

Alex leaned against me. "Wait until we reach our villa. It always smells like spring there."

Without warning, visions of a beautiful chateau filled my mind. I knew it was our home in Italy. "Do I even want to know how we became so wealthy?" I said as I placed our luggage in the back of the rental car.

"We did it together," Alex said. "I landed a research job out of college. During our senior year, you worked on an exposé of the university's football program, bringing to light how many rapes had been pushed under the carpet because star football players committed them.

"With your beauty and talent, every news station in the nation courted you. We both had high-paying jobs. We saved our money, were awarded several grants in our respective fields, and then we opened our own lab where I finalized my research on skin rejuvenation products.

"The scientific community lauded my research as a tremendous success, and A&S Cosmetics was born."

Alex and Sloan?"

She nodded.

As we drove, more memories seeped into my mind: the ocean, the vineyards, and the gorgeous woman sitting beside me.

##

We had been at our villa a week when a man on a bicycle delivered a telegram.

"What is it?" I asked as Alex opened it.

"It's from Leigh Redding." Alex handed the paper to me. "She isn't certain we're here. She sent the same message to all of our residences."

I read the telegram out loud. "Sloan, this is urgent. Do not ignore this. Must speak to you immediately."

"She wants the evidence I have."

"Where is it, darling?"

"I don't know. My memory is returning gradually. I seem to be able to recall things from my early life but not the past couple of years."

"You recalled the most important thing." She caught my hand and led me into our bedroom. "You have no doubt that I'm your wife."

"Yes." I sighed as she pulled me down beside her on the bed and began to unbutton my blouse. "That truly is all that matters."

##

Chapter 20

Alex snuggled into me and kissed between my breasts. "Thank you," she murmured.

We both laughed when I responded with the age-old phrase, "The pleasure was all mine."

"I can assure you that's not true." She kissed my lips. "Today let's ride our bicycles into the village."

"Sounds like fun."

##

The bicycle ride brought back additional memories. "Is that little café we loved still here?" I asked.

"It was last year," she said.

Try as I might, I could not recall the previous year. I was sure it would come to me sooner or later.

We parked our bikes and took a seat on the café's patio. A young woman greeted us like old friends. She hugged Alex and held out her arms to me. I hugged her. She took our order and hustled into the café.

"She seemed hesitant to hug me," I noted.

"She has had a crush on you since she was ten," Alex said, laughing. "I told you, you're a chick magnet."

A look of concern crossed Alex's face. "You look perplexed."

"Leigh, Amy, and even my nurse Sadie indicated that I'm a philanderer."

"No you're not, Sloan," Alex assured me. "They were trying to influence you to be unfaithful to me. They know that's the only reason I would leave you."

"With every fiber of my being, I know that too," I said. "I would never take a chance on losing you. My mama didn't raise a fool." I chuckled, but it was halfhearted.

"Honestly, I can't believe I could stay away from you for an entire year." I raked my eyes over her beautiful body and licked my lips.

"You didn't. We met once a month for four days. Sometimes here or in Paris. I often flew into Spain, and you would meet me there. We aren't able to stay away from one another for very long."

"I'm glad." I caught her left hand in mine and kissed her knuckles. The sun sparkled off the diamond in her wedding band.

"Did I have a matching one?" I asked as I touched the stone.

"Yes." Alex's eyes sparkled brighter than that diamond. "The artisan who designed them for us lives here. Oh Sloan, let's have a new one made for you."

We spent the rest of the day locating the jeweler who had crafted our wedding rings. He had retired but agreed to make a new ring for me.

"One week." He scribbled a phone number on a note pad and handed it to Alex. "I will have it ready in one week."

THREE TIMES AS DEADLY

We wandered through the plaza and shared a gelato. I held it as Alex took a bite. "I love you so much," I whispered, unable to find my voice.

"Let's go home, Sloan." The way the words fell from her lips was so sensual that I couldn't suppress the moan that escaped mine.

The week passed quickly, as time always did when I was with Alex—at least what I could remember of our time together. We rode our bikes all over the countryside. Sometimes we took a picnic basket. Other times we searched for out-of-the-way cafés and spent hours just talking and touching.

We purchased burner phones so we could call each other if we were separated. When Alex called the jeweler, he assured her my ring was ready.

##

I was giddy as a bride as I waited for the old gentleman to show us my ring. I had butterflies in my stomach.

He gave it an extra shine then handed it to Alex. She inspected the ring and raised her eyes to my face. She dropped to one knee and said, "Sloan Cartwright, would you honor me by marrying me?"

"Oh yes!" I gasped. "Always."

She slipped the ring on my finger. I pulled her to her feet and kissed her.

We walked hand in hand to the café where we'd left our bicycles.

"This is our tenth year of marriage," Alex said, leaning against me as we strolled along. "We should reaffirm our vows."

"I'd like that." I hugged her closer. "Do we need to go through all the legalese or simply have a magistrate marry us?"

"Let's make it official," she said, "binding, like our first marriage."

I nodded. I was happy to do anything that would bind Alex to me forever.

We stopped by the local magistrate's office and filled out the required papers. "You must post your intention to marry in the square," the clerk informed us as she stamped and signed the necessary documents and slid them across the counter to us.

"This is so romantic," the woman said, hugging herself. "Come back next Monday, and the magistrate will perform the ceremony."

"I can't believe you're marrying me twice." I skipped beside Alex, as excited as if we were marrying for the first time.

"It's the least I can do." She laughed at my antics. "After all, you did fall in love with me twice."

I stopped in the middle of the street. "I did, didn't I? I had no idea who you were when you burst into my hospital room. I just knew my heart went crazy, and I couldn't catch my breath."

She laughed even louder. "Yes, I do remember how your machines went crazy. I thought Leigh and Amarosia were going to attack me."

I held her at arm's length and looked at her. "Do you have any idea how gorgeous you are?"

"Why, yes, I do."

I knew her answer was an honest one. She knew how drop-dead beautiful she was, and she still chose to marry me.

THREE TIMES AS DEADLY

We walked the rest of the way in silence. I remained in awe of her, humbled by the fact that this woman, who was everything a woman should be and more, was my wife.

##

"You are beautiful," I said as Alex joined me downstairs for our trip to the magistrate's. "Is that the same wedding dress you wore the first time?"

"Yes, darling." She tiptoed to kiss me. "Are you ready to make an honest woman out of me?"

I thought of all the nights we'd spent together since my accident. "It may be too late for that," I teased.

"Just as long as the world knows I'm your woman," she said. "That's all that matters to me."

"I'll shout it from the rooftops," I promised

##

Several people in the magistrate's office volunteered to serve as our witnesses, and two signed the documents. Alex requested a dozen official copies of the marriage license.

"Last time we had to file these with everyone and their dogs in the US," she said as she slipped them into her purse.

"I'll file the necessary papers for Italy." The magistrate smiled as he kissed Alex on the cheek.

A crowd followed us down the street, singing and laughing. "I can't wait to get home and have you get me out of this dress." Alex raised her eyebrows.

It was all I could do to keep from running to our car.

##

I was in my office making notes on our escape from Africa when Alex brought me a glass of ice tea. "What are you doing?" she asked as she leaned down for a kiss.

"Making notes on our adventure," I said. "If I'd had a video camera, our trip across Africa would have made a hell of a documentary. Certainly a testimony for the BushCat. I have a new admiration for that little plane."

"Why don't you write a book about it?" Alex suggested as she eased between my chair and the desk and straddled my lap.

Her kiss was unhurried and exploring, filling my body with heat and need.

"I'd have to leave out the best parts." I kissed the pulse point in her neck. "Otherwise I would be labeled an erotica writer instead of an adventure writer."

She squeezed her legs tighter around mine and pushed hard into me. "Umm . . . that wouldn't be all bad."

"Why don't we move this conversation to the sofa," I suggested as I stood, holding her against me. She wrapped her long legs around my waist and kissed me breathless.

Later, Alex lay on top of me, our chests heaving as we both fought to catch our breaths. "I love how strong you are," she whispered.

"I love the way you let me do anything I want." My voice was deep with emotion. "You satiate all my desires."

"Sloan," she whispered, "don't you know that your desires fulfill all my fantasies?"

"The bullwhip . . . ?"

"Never! Not in your wildest dreams." Her laughter warmed my heart "But you can keep trying."

I didn't tell her that I had no idea what I would do if she said yes. I was certain she already knew that.

"I've finished the rough draft of our African adventure," I informed Alex as I placed the manuscript on the table in front of her. She sipped her coffee and looked at the dedication: *To Alex, my love, my life, my reason for living. You are the only woman I have ever loved. Sloan.*

She fanned her face. "Just your dedication got me all hot and bothered," she said, laughing.

"Good." I leaned in for a kiss and then refilled our coffee cups.

"Did you write a smoking-hot love scene in here?" Her curiosity was obvious as she turned the pages.

"I did. I wrote about that morning in our hotel room in Morocco."

She thumbed through the manuscript until she located the scene. I watched as she read it. She began to breathe faster, gulping in air. Her chest and face flushed a dark pink, and she ran her tongue between her lips, rolling her lips together to moisten them. Watching her excited me.

She closed the manuscript and slowly raised desire-laden eyes to meet mine. "I want you," she said in a smoky, lust-filled voice.

"And I you." I sighed as I led her to our bedroom.

Afterward, we lay motionless beside each other, our hands laced together over her stomach. She turned to face me, and I gently kissed her lips. Her tongue explored my bottom lip, and she sucked it. "I love the taste of me on your lips," she whispered.

"Mmmm, So do I."

She snuggled into me and giggled. "That scene you wrote turned me on. When did you write it?"

"Yesterday afternoon," I murmured.

"Was that when you found me on the patio and made love to me—after you finished that scene?"

"Yes," I admitted, a little embarrassed.

She chuckled. "What would you do if you didn't have me to satiate you?"

"Masturbate." It was the truth. "That's why I don't write romance." I kissed her. "You aren't always around when I'm working on a book."

She raised up on her elbow and tilted her head to one side, studying me. "Do you think romance authors masturbate with their heroines in mind after writing a torrid love scene?"

"I would bet money on it. I know I would if I didn't have you."

It is mentally and physically exhausting to write love scenes.

"Do you realize that we've been here three months and haven't turned on the TV or the internet?" Alex said as we walked back to the villa."

"I've been reluctant to let the outside world into our little piece of heaven." I squeezed her hand.

"Still, we probably should find out what's going on in the rest of the world."

I shrugged. "I suppose we have to return to it sooner or later."

I must admit that I was disappointed when we heard no mention of us on the evening news.

"By now, we're yesterday's news," Alex said. "That's good."

A late-night newswoman popped onto our screen. "And now for a report on our continuing news coverage," she said. "The small plane believed to be used by cosmetic mogul Alexandra Cartwright and investigative news reporter Sloan Cartwright has been found in the Sahara Desert at the foot of the Atlas Mountains."

A beautiful photo of Alex and me walking hand in hand from a New York musical theater appeared on the screen.

"The two have been missing for more than 100 days and are believed to have perished in the desert.

"Alexandra was the founder and CEO of A&S Cosmetics, the worldwide distributor of Youth Serum. She and Sloan Cartwright hold several patents and all licensing rights to products that women all over the planet have come to depend on for a youthful appearance.

"Most of you have seen the riveting documentaries produced by award-winning journalist and author Sloan Cartwright. The world mourns the loss of these two outstanding women. The couple had been married ten years when—"

Alex clicked off the TV.

We sat in stunned silence.

"Everyone thinks we're dead," Alex said, fighting back tears.

I nodded, trying to comprehend the ramifications of the newswoman's report.

"At least they won't be trying to kill us," I said.

"We must let your parents know you're alive," Alex said. "Your mother must be devastated."

"This may be a trick to get us to make contact," I surmised. "I'm going to call my parents' next-door neighbor. They won't tap her phone."

I dug through my desk and pulled out a black book. "All my important numbers are in here. We need to notify your parents too."

The sorrow in Alex's eyes hurt my heart. "They won't care," she said. "They disowned me when I married you."

"Oh." I had no words for the sadness that settled in me at Alex's announcement. How could anyone disown the wonderful woman standing before me?

"I'm so sorry," I murmured as I pulled her into my arms.

"It's okay." A pleased look crossed Alex's face. "Your parents love me more than my parents ever did."

I called my parents' neighbor and asked if they would get my mother to the phone. I put the call on speakerphone so Alex could hear too. The wait seemed like forever, and then a familiar voice spoke.

"Hello?"

"Mom, it's me. Sloan."

"Oh thank God!" she yelled. "Daddy, it's Sloan."

I could hear my mother sobbing. "It's Sloan."

"Hello?" My dad's strong baritone voice came across the phone line. "Is that you, baby girl?" The emotion in his voice was heartrending.

I couldn't stop the tears that rolled down my cheeks as I realized the pain I had caused them. "It's me, Dad. Alex and I are okay."

"I knew she would get you out of that heathen country," my father declared. "Are you sure you're okay?"

"Yes, we're fine, but we need to remain missing for now." I took a deep breath. "It will take too long to explain everything on the phone, but someone is trying to kill us."

A long silence followed my declaration. "How can we help you?" Dad asked.

"Let me discuss some things with Alex, and then we'll call you back. Dad, can you get a burner phone so I can call you direct?"

"As soon as we hang up," my father said.

"Go on your Facebook page and place the first three numbers using the time matrix. Then do the same thing with the last four digits on mom's page. I know your area code, so I just need the last seven digits," I said.

"I'll do that tonight. I love you, baby girl."

"I love you too, Dad."

"Your mother wants to talk to you before you hang up," he said.

"Sloan, I just wanted to say I love you. I never believed you were dead, not for a second." She hesitated. "And I'm so happy you and Alex are back together. Tell Alex we love her."

"I love you, Mom. I'll call tomorrow night at eight." I disconnected the call.

"That was emotional," Alex said, wiping the tears from her face.

THREE TIMES AS DEADLY

"For all of us," I agreed, swallowing the lump that still lingered in my throat.

"What are we going to do, Sloan?" Alex laced her fingers through mine and led me to the sofa.

"We need to get back to the States. I must figure out what I have that is so incriminating that people are willing to kill me to silence me." I needed to think. So many questions swirled in my head.

"Do we have a photo of Ross?" I couldn't recall the image of my partner.

Alex nodded. "Yes. There's one in your desk."

##

Chapter 21

Using our remaining cash and the identification Malika had secured for us, we donned our hijabs and headed to my parents' home in Texas. We had a short layover in New York before flying into DFW Airport in Dallas.

Dad and I kept in constant contact through our burner phones. We didn't dare use our credit cards or withdraw funds from our bank accounts. When Dad picked us up at the airport in a pickup truck, I had to fight the tears of joy and relief that threatened to spill from my eyes.

Alex and I slid into the back seat of the vehicle and breathed for the first time since leaving Italy.

"I have rented you an apartment in the Marquis at Turtle Creek," Dad informed us. "I know how you like fast cars, Sloan, but I got you a pickup. You'll be less noticeable driving it."

"Thanks, Dad . . . I think," I mumbled as Alex snuggled into my side.

"I can't tell you how great it is to see the two of you back together," Dad said, beaming. "Your mother is thrilled."

"Yeah, a year is a long time," I said. He obviously didn't know about our monthly rendezvous while I was in Africa.

##

After we arrived at our apartment, Alex began unpacking our suitcases while Dad and I found cold drinks and a plate of sandwiches Mom had placed in our refrigerator.

"What are your plans, hon?" Dad asked as he placed paper plates on the table.

"I need to contact Ross. I have no idea where they've hidden him or why."

A knock on the door made us look at one another. "It's your mother." Dad smiled as he opened the door.

A whirlwind of energy flew through my door and into my arms. "Sloan! Oh thank God, Sloan," she said, sobbing. "And Alex!" She reached for my wife and pulled her into the same tight hug.

She planted multiple kisses on our faces and then stood back to look at us as if trying to make certain we were truly there.

I laughed out loud as I gazed into eyes that mirrored my own. My mother is a fifty-six-year-old version of me. Her hair is still thick and blonde. Her lips are full and beautiful, but her most striking feature is her green eyes. Eyes that look like they could dissect one's soul. As a child, I was certain those eyes could melt anything if she stared at it long enough.

"Tell us what's going on with you two," Mom instructed as she pulled chips from the cabinet and condiments from the fridge.

We spent the next two hours describing our escape from Africa. We moved to the living room, where Alex sat close to me. Mom watched her with a sly smile.

"So, you two . . ." Mom looked from me to Alex and back again. "You are . . . ?"

"Married," Alex said, her face beaming. "We renewed our vows in Italy. We're legally married in every country."

"Twice." I grinned as I squeezed her hand.

"We need to let these young people get some rest," Dad said, getting to his feet. "They must be exhausted."

I nodded. I wasn't exhausted, but I did want to be alone with my wife.

While Mom and Alex whispered in the kitchen, Dad led me into the foyer and gave me the keys to the pickup he had procured for me. Mom and Alex joined us, and we walked my parents to mom's car, thanking them profusely for all they had done for us.

##

"What were you two whispering about?" I slipped my arm around Alex's shoulders as we walked toward our bedroom.

"Girl things," she said. "Nothing you need to know."

"I'm a girl." I pouted. "Why can't I know?"

She rose on her tiptoes and kissed me. "Your mother was telling me how glad she is you married me."

"Umm, that makes two of us."

##

I leaned against the headboard of our bed and watched Alex dress—fitted jeans, pullover, and boots.

THREE TIMES AS DEADLY

"What do you have planned for today?" I asked as she leaned down to kiss me.

"Horseback riding," she answered with a twinkle in her eye. "You shower while I fix breakfast, and then let's go horseback riding."

"Okay," I said as she swayed out of the room.

We loved riding. Our Texas home was on Lake Granbury, where we owned a little over a hundred acres of waterfront pastureland and six quarter horses.

I was certain the agency was watching our home and any other place they thought we might visit. I needed to do something quickly to resolve my situation. Alex was not the kind of woman to sit still for very long, and I was getting antsy too.

My memory had returned except for the most recent months before my accident. God, if I could only remember where I shipped the information I had gathered and who my handler was. Although I'd been told that Leigh and Ross were part of my team, I couldn't recall either of them.

I turned off the blow-dryer as Alex slipped her arms around my waist and hugged me tight. She felt good against my naked back.

"Breakfast is ready, baby," she said, kissing me between my shoulder blades. A tremor ran through my body.

I turned in her arms and kissed her, desperately trying to convey how much I loved her. The way she kissed me back told me she already knew.

##

"Sloan, could we go to the ranch?" Alex said as she refilled our coffee cups. "I miss our horses, and we're out of cash."

"I know, honey, but that's risky. Why don't we drive around the area and see if we spot anyone surveilling our place?"

She rubbed her hands together. "I'd like that."

"You know, both of us are adrenaline junkies." I laughed. "You're getting excited at the thought of encountering a bad guy."

"Hmm. I do like it when you use your whip—on other people." She giggled as she tugged at the whip wrapped around my waist.

"I think it's ingenious how you make it look like a fashion accessory. If anyone ever realizes it isn't a belt, women will buy whips by the thousands to emulate you."

She made me laugh. We both knew she was the trendsetter in our family, the one other women imitated.

On the way to the ranch, Alex informed me that I kept a "runner's kit" ready at all times.

"A runner's kit?" I raised an eyebrow for further clarification from her.

"You always keep several hundred thousand in cash, a pistol, ammunition, and a dozen phony IDs," she explained as we parked on a hill overlooking the ranch.

"Do you see anyone?" Alex asked.

"No, but I don't think we should go to the ranch. Let's drive around and observe."

My burner phone buzzed as I pulled back onto the road. "What's up, Dad?" I put him on speakerphone so Alex could hear.

He informed me that his home was under surveillance, and every time he or mom left the house they were followed.

"That means they don't believe we're dead," I said. "Try to get their license plates. Maybe I can find out what agency they're from."

We drove around the area for a couple of hours without encountering any suspicious-looking vehicles.

"Let's come back tomorrow," I said. "If we don't see anyone, we'll go for a horseback ride."

"Okay." Alex grabbed my hand. "Then you get to take me dancing tonight, missy."

"Boot scootin' or ballroom?" I quipped.

"The country club." She pursed her lips and flashed her eyes at me. "I'd like to dress up and torment you for a few hours."

"That works both ways," I said, using my sexiest voice.

She leaned close and whispered into my ear. "Yes, yes, it does."

##

Chapter 22

"God, you're gorgeous," I said as I watched Alex glide into the living room. "How can you walk so gracefully in those heels?"

"It's easy, darling, when that's all one wears. I must admit, I do feel a bit out of practice after following you all over Africa in flat-heeled boots."

She was wearing a silver lamé dress—it stopped just below her thighs—and matching heels. The dress was backless but modest in the front.

"I love that outfit," I let my eyes slide down her long legs, "but it doesn't leave much to the imagination."

"Umm, but it does make you drool, so it has achieved my goal." She took my hand and twirled me around.

"You look beautiful." Her face lit up as she examined my emerald-green gown with a slit up to the thigh. "I'm certain your dress will turn some heads too."

"Perhaps we should be more low-key."

"Perhaps, but I love the way you look when you dress like this. I want to spend the evening with the most beautiful woman in the room."

"As do I." I brushed my lips across hers. I just wanted to taste her without smudging her lipstick.

##

Dancing with Alex was an exercise in self-control. She pressed herself against me and whispered in my ear, a combination that made my heart rate skyrocket and breathing impossible.

"Are you as turned on as I am?" she whispered as she slid her hand down to the small of my back and pressed further into me.

I didn't even try to suppress the moan she elicited.

"We should go," she whispered. "I need to be alone with you."

I nodded and followed her to the valet stand.

"Ladies," the valet said with a lopsided grin as he matched our ticket with the keys, "I'll be right back with your car."

I didn't have the heart to tell him it was a pickup.

"What's keeping him so long?" Alex squirmed as she checked her watch. "I'm dying to get home."

Ten more minutes passed, and the valet was still missing. "I'll walk around to the side and get our vehicle myself," I muttered. "Wait here, baby."

There was no sign of the valet, but the keys were in the truck, so I started it and returned to Alex.

There was a commotion at the valet stand. I got out of the truck to see what was happening. The valet was sitting on a stool while a waitress dabbed his head with a napkin. He had a nasty gash from his hairline across his forehead.

"Oh thank goodness you have your truck!" The valet grimaced as he stood. "I thought someone was stealing it. They knocked me out when I opened the door and—"

THREE TIMES AS DEADLY

Ice water infused my veins. "Alex! Alex!" I yelled as I looked around for my wife. "Where is my wife?"

The blank stares on everyone's faces told me they had no idea where she was.

A single silver lamé stiletto lay on the curb in front of the valet stand. I picked it up.

"I've called the police," the maître d' informed me before scurrying off to calm the patrons.

I jumped back into my pickup and left. I called my father. "Dad!" I fought the panic that was rising inside me. "Dad, they've kidnapped Alex."

"Where are you?" he asked.

"Headed to our apartment."

"I'll meet you there, Sloan."

"Bring my LC," I told him. "I need a fast car, not this pickup.

I gunned the pickup truck through traffic, barely avoiding several accidents. There's a reason I liked fast cars; they got me where I wanted to go in a hurry. Trucks, not so much.

Mom and Dad were already at the apartment when I arrived. They followed me into the foyer.

"Sloan, what happened?" Dad asked.

"You look ravishing," Mom interjected.

"We went out. When I went to get the truck, they kidnapped Alex."

"They who?" Dad said, his voice thick with worry.

"I'm pretty certain it's the people I work for."

"Who the hell do you work for, Sloan?" Dad was getting worked up.

"I have to go." I charged into the bedroom and returned minutes later in what Alex calls my soldier of fortune outfit, complete with the bullwhip. Dad and I traded car keys, and I gave them both a hug. "You haven't seen me," I reminded them.

"When will we see you again?" Mom called after me.

"When I find Alex!"

##

It was after midnight when I parked on the hill overlooking our ranch. The night-lights were on in the arena and the barn. For over an hour, I watched for anyone who might be observing my home.

I finally thought it was safe to enter my house but decided to approach on foot. It took me over an hour to slip into the back door.

I had no idea where I kept my runner's kit or how heavy it might be. I recalled the layout of the house and quickly located our bedroom.

The room was so . . . Alex. Exquisite furniture surrounded a king-size bed. I searched through the closets and found nothing but clothes and shoes. I collapsed onto the loveseat and looked around the room.

Out of the blue, it hit me—there was a false wall at the back of my closet. I located the lever to open the hidden door and found myself in a room that looked more like a military arsenal than a woman's safe room.

I grabbed a Glock 17 with a standard eleven-round magazine, a couple of 33-round clips, and three boxes of bullets. A duffle bag sitting inside the door caught my eye. I opened it and found money, along with passports, driver's licenses, and credit cards in various names. A stun gun, six grenades, and a cylinder of pepper spray were tucked into an interior zippered pocket. I stuffed the guns and bullets into the bag.

A pair of custom-made, leather knee boots were in the bag. I examined them and was surprised to find that the attractive decoration that ran down the sides of them held long, slender knives. I changed boots.

I must lead one hell of a dangerous life.

I looked around the bedroom and memories flooded my mind: Alex laughing; Alex teasing me until I begged; Alex poised above me in the dark.

I hefted the duffle bag over my shoulder. I had everything I needed to get my wife back, and God help anyone who stood in my way.

##

Chapter 23

I was almost back to Dallas when Dad called. "Sloan, a woman just called and said for you to call her at this number. It's urgent."

I pulled to the side of the road and dialed the number Dad gave me.

"Leigh Redding," the voice on the other end of the line said.

"Leigh, this is Sloan." I tried to remain calm.

"Sloan, where are you?" she asked in a hushed voice.

"Where do I need to be?" I replied.

"Here, in Washington. You need to bring in your evidence." Leigh was almost whispering. "Honey, everyone is searching for you. I don't know what you have, but there has been a steady stream of African leaders through here since you disappeared. None of them look very happy."

"Where's Ross?" I asked.

"I don't know that either, Sloan. I can't find out anything. You two stirred up a hornet's nest in Africa."

"Leigh, I have no idea what we uncovered. I do know that someone has kidnapped Alex. I must find her."

A long silence greeted my declaration.

"Leigh, who is my handler?"

"I don't know," Leigh huffed. "All three of us have a different handler to prevent corruption in our agency."

"Is there corruption in our agency?" I asked. "Is there a mole?"

"I don't think so. Sloan, please come in, for your safety."

"I've got to go."

"San Antonio," Leigh whispered quickly. "She's in San Antonio."

I hung up the phone and slipped the battery from it, just in case they traced my call.

##

The first light of day reminded me that I hadn't slept in over twenty-four hours. I pulled into a Holiday Inn Express behind a Cracker Barrel in Burleson.

Using a Texas driver's license and a credit card I hoped would work, I requested a single room. To my surprise, everything went without a hitch.

"I hope you enjoy your stay with us, Miss Denton," the clerk said as she returned my credit card and driver's license along with a receipt. "Per your request, I have put you on the third floor next to the stairwell."

I stared at my driver's license as I waited for the elevator door to open. Dixie Denton! I wondered who in the hell gave me a name like Dixie Denton. I'll probably be mistaken for a stripper.

I showered, lodged a chair under the door handle, and fell into bed. I was surprised at how fast thoughts of Alex merged into dreams of Alex as I fell asleep.

##

THREE TIMES AS DEADLY

I awoke and reached for Alex. Something twisted in my stomach when I realized she wasn't there. It was the first time I'd awakened without her beside me since we escaped the African hospital. It was a cold, lonely, gut-wrenching feeling.

I stared at the ceiling, trying to formulate a plan to get her back. Life wasn't worth living without her.

The only reason anyone would kidnap my wife was to use her as leverage to get the evidence I had—somewhere. I racked my brain trying to recall where I would send something so important.

Most of my memory had returned, except the last year or so and some chunks of my college days. I remember the day I stumbled into my dorm room and saw Alex propped up on her bed reading. She was the most beautiful creature I had ever seen. Even now I became slack jawed when I thought of her.

My stomach growled, and I looked at the clock. It was six in the afternoon. I decided to eat at the Cracker Barrel across from the hotel and then head to San Antonio. I dressed and took one last look around my room to make certain I wasn't leaving anything.

If Leigh knew Alex was in San Antonio, that told me the agency—whoever that is—had my wife. I intended to go to San Antonio, flash around Alex's photo, and ask if anyone had seen her. That should result in a contact from her captors.

Out of habit I pulled back the drapes and checked my car. The coupe looked like a luxury vehicle but was greased lightning on four wheels. The ten-speed automatic transmission could go from zero to sixty miles per hour in four seconds. The silver color helped it blend in with the millions of other silver cars on the road. With a 470-horsepower engine, it could outrun just about anything with wheels. I was even beginning to like the front grill that looked like a giant bug catcher.

Alex and I had purchased the Lexus LC before I left for Africa. I was itching to get it on the road and open it up.

What the . . . ? As I peered from behind the drapes, three Mexicans—two men and a woman—walked to my car and looked around to make sure no one was watching them. One of the men stooped down and placed his hand under the rear end of the car. I was certain he had attached a magnetic tracker to my gas tank. I was sure they weren't with the agency. I wondered how many people were after me.

The trio moseyed across the parking lot and entered the Cracker Barrel. They weren't worried about watching me, knowing their tracker would allow them to catch up with me somewhere down the road. Losing my appetite, I grabbed my duffle bag and hurried to my car.

I tossed my bag into the passenger seat and walked to the back of my car. I bent down and looked under the vehicle. The tracker was easy to spot. *The three must be amateurs.*

I pulled the tracker from my gas tank and slapped it onto the side of a horse trailer as it slowly moved through the parking lot. I watched as the horse hauler turned onto I-35W and headed north, the opposite direction from my planned route.

I stopped at a Walmart on my way out of town and purchased another burner phone. I put the battery back into the phone that Alex would dial, just in case she tried to call me. She hadn't, but I had a call from my Dad.

"Thank God," Dad exclaimed as he answered the phone. "Sloan, you need to contact Leigh. She's worried sick about you. She says it's an emergency. She has news about Alex, but she said she couldn't share it with me."

"I'm on my way to San Antonio," I told him. "I'll let you know when I get there. Call if you need me."

I texted my parents the number to my new burner phone using our standard cryptic method—the first six digits to my mother and the last four to Dad.

The one-word text, "Good," from my father told me he had the new number.

I pulled onto I-35 headed to San Antonio and dialed Leigh's number. The phone rang several times, and I was about to press the button to end the call when Leigh answered.

"Leigh, it's Sloan. Dad said you have information on Alex."

"Sloan, I'm so glad you called. I couldn't talk earlier. People were in my office."

I grunted. I was in no mood for small talk.

"Alex is being held in a deserted quarry somewhere around San Antonio," Leigh informed me. "I'm trying to find out the exact location."

"There must a hundred deserted quarries in Bexar County," I thought out loud. "Leigh, who has kidnapped her and why?"

"I'm not certain," Leigh said, "but it must be someone who believes she's still important to you."

"She is the most important thing in the world to me," I declared. "I'll call you when I get to San Antonio."

"Sloan, listen to me—"

I hung up the phone and removed the battery.

I reached San Antonio a little after one in the morning and checked into a motel for a good night's sleep. Tomorrow I would find my wife.

##

Chapter 24

I showed Alex's picture up and down the River Walk then went to the San Antonio Visitor's Center, where I was lucky enough to get a map of all the quarries in Bexar County. I scowled as I searched through the pages of listings for operating and abandoned quarries.

San Antonio had done an incredible job of converting old quarries into shopping malls, complete with movie theaters and high-end restaurants. Chic apartments and lofts now enhanced old concrete walls and silos. Whoever had the foresight to convert old eyesores into beautiful, updated shopping malls deserved a pat on the back.

I spent the rest of the day showing Alex's photo to employees at every shop in the Rivercenter. After trudging through over a hundred shops and talking to more than three hundred people, I slumped into a chair at Tony Roma's and ordered a rack of ribs

I was hungry, exhausted, and heartsick. The more the memories of my life with Alex returned, the more it hurt to be away from her.

By the time I finished my dinner, lights were dimming in the Rivercenter. The giant shopping mall closed at nine. I hopped a river taxi and went to the Marriott River Center Hotel at the end of the river.

THREE TIMES AS DEADLY

The hotel was one of our favorite places. It had special meaning for Alex and me. We loved the piano bar on the second floor overlooking the hotel lobby. Alex loved Rachmaninoff's *Rhapsody on a Theme of Paganini*. I always slipped the piano player a twenty with a note to play the piece for her. Alex would hug my arm between her breasts as she whispered into my ear how much she loved me.

I sat down at the table we always shared and ordered a Dubonnet on the rocks. I scribbled my request on a napkin, folded it around a twenty, and asked the waitress to give it to the pianist.

I sipped my drink as he played the rhapsody and recalled how this was the exact setting where I'd asked Alex to marry me. *God, I must find her.*

I tossed enough money on the table for my drink and a nice tip and headed for the elevator. As the door slid open, a hand shoved me into the elevator and pushed the Stop button as soon as the doors closed.

As I whipped around, my hand shot behind my back and gripped the handle of the Glock tucked into my waistband. I was face to face with my waitress. "May I see that photo again?" she asked.

I pulled the picture of Alex from my hip pocket and held it out to her.

"I haven't seen her in person," the waitress said, "but I think I overheard two black men talking about her last night. They had foreign accents—British, maybe."

"What makes you think they were talking about her?" I asked.

"They spoke of her beauty, and they had a ring that looked like the one you're wearing."

My heart stopped beating as I gasped for breath. "It must be Alex. Do you know where they are?"

"I believe they're staying in the hotel," she said. "They signed their check to their room last night. Come back to the bar, and I'll see if I can find their bar tab."

I nodded. "I'll get off in the lobby. You go back to the bar, and I'll walk up the stairs and return to my table."

"Another Dubonnet?" She raised her eyebrows.

"Sure," I said.

Soon after I returned to my table, she served me another drink, placing it on top of a cocktail napkin. "Their room number," she whispered.

I finished my drink, tossed a fifty on the table, and slipped the napkin into my pocket. I took the stairs down to the lobby and checked into the hotel. I requested a room on the same floor as the two men.

I was surprised to find myself in the room next to them. I listened for several minutes, trying to hear any conversation the two might be having. I racked the Glock, replaced it in the waistband of my jeans and tried to formulate a plan.

If they had Alex, the easiest thing would be to follow them, but I had no idea what kind of vehicle they were driving or where it might be parked. I knew I couldn't retrieve my car and follow them. I opted for the direct approach.

I heard the shower turn on and thought the gods might be with me. Grabbing the can of pepper spray from my duffle bag, I shook it as I walked into the hallway and knocked on their door. I turned so only my profile would be visible through the peephole.

"Well, aren't you a pretty thing?" the man said, leering at me as he opened the door.

He was muscular and over six feet tall. I knew my only chance was to surprise him. I soaked his face with the pepper spray, and he went to his knees, clawing at his eyes and gasping for breath. I hit him as hard as I could with the butt of the Glock. He sprawled on the floor at my feet.

I unfurled the bullwhip and pressed my back against the wall as his partner charged from the bathroom.

"What the hell?" He growled scanning the room. As he turned, the whip wrapped around his throat, and I yanked it downward, pulling him to his knees.

By the time he realized what was going on, I had the barrel of the Glock pressed into the space between his eyes.

"You have my wife," I hissed. "Alex Cartwright. Where is she?" I pulled hard on the whip, and he clawed at it with his hands, trying to slide his fingers between the leather and his throat.

"Tell me!" I demanded as he gulped for air. His fingers worked frantically at the leather cutting into his skin. "One more pull and I'll crush your windpipe," I warned him.

"Tejas Quarry," he said, sputtering out the words.

I had seen the Tejas Quarry listed in the abandoned quarries pamphlet. I wanted so badly to kill him, but opted for giving him a concussion instead as I swung the butt of the Glock into his temple.

I checked the pockets of both men. Alex's ring was in the pants pocket of my first victim. Their wallets gave me no clue about the country employing them. I took their wallets, guns, and cell phones. I slipped a knife from my boot and slit the sheets into strips. I tied their feet and hands, rolled them over on their stomachs, and tied their hands to their bound feet. I stuffed a wash cloth into their mouths and tied gags in place so they couldn't spit out the cloth or call for help. I trussed up both men like Christmas turkeys.

I grabbed my can of pepper spray, closed the door to their room, and hung the *Do Not Disturb* sign on their door. I needed all the time I could buy to get to Alex.

I retrieved my duffel bag and headed for the car.

I keyed Tejas Quarry into my GPS and pulled out of the Rivercenter parking garage as Siri began talking to me. The GPS showed the quarry to be an hour and a half from my location.

##

The land around the quarry was flat and covered with brown grass and low-growing cedar bushes. I knew the cover of darkness was my only hope of sneaking up on Alex's captors if they were in the quarry.

I pulled my car between two tall cement walls and listened. The only sound was the hot Texas wind blowing through abandoned buildings. There were no lights anywhere. I scanned the land for any sign of footprints or vehicle tracks. I saw none.

Moving from building to building, I found nothing to indicate another human had been in the quarry. I opened the door to the largest crumbling building. A single candle burned, lighting the area around it.

"Alex!" I gasped as my wife turned to face me.

Something hit me in the chest. In a stupor I stared down between my breasts where a dart had lodged. I recognized the handiwork of one of Africa's elite hit squads.

I fell to my knees. The last thing I thought before pitching forward was, *I hope it's a sedative and not a poison.*

##

Chapter 25

"Sloan! Sloan, honey, wake up." Soft hands slapped my face as I struggled to open my eyes. "Come on, baby, wake up," the voice insisted.

I tried to focus my eyes but squeezed them shut as the bright sunlight hit my retinas, causing excruciating pain.

"What time is it?" I mumbled. None of my body parts wanted to cooperate. My lips felt numb and I couldn't feel my limbs. My eyes fought opening, and my throat felt as if it might constrict at any moment.

"Sloan, wake up, honey." The soft voice continued to coax me from my stupor as strong arms lifted my shoulders and pulled me into the warmth of someone's lap. I inhaled slowly, not trusting my throat to allow the action. The scent of the woman filled my senses. It was soft and exciting. Fragrance in which one could lose one's self.

I knew without opening my eyes that the arousing scent didn't belong to Alex, but I did recognize it.

"Leigh?" I moaned.

"I'm here, Sloan," Leigh whispered. "I've got you, baby."

I struggled to sit, but Leigh pressed my head back into her lap.

"Be still, Sloan," she insisted. "We don't know what's in your bloodstream. We don't want to kick up your heartbeat and pump something deadly throughout your system. The ambulance is here."

"Alex," I muttered. "I found her."

Leigh nodded without replying. I swear I saw her wince before my eyes slammed shut again.

##

For the second time in less than a year, I awoke in a hospital room. I listened as a doctor talked to Leigh. "Be sure she drinks a lot of water and relaxes. No strenuous activity," he instructed. "We couldn't identify the toxins in her system, so we don't know how they will affect her. Hopefully, they'll completely pass from her bloodstream in the next twenty-four hours. I gave her a wide spectrum antidote to counteract the toxins."

I closed my eyes and pretended to be asleep. I wondered why Alex wasn't with me. "I'll release her around eight in the morning," the doctor continued. "I want to keep her here tonight for observation. Just in case there's a reaction we haven't anticipated. She'll need someone with her for the next few days."

"I'll be taking care of her," Leigh informed the doctor in a tone that didn't allow for argument. "I'll stay with her tonight and then take her home with me in the morning." ##I kept my eyes closed as I tried to put together the pieces of the strange puzzle I was working. I had remembered that Leigh and Ross were my partners and that we formed an elite group of US Treasury agents who worked multi-billion-dollar fraud cases.

Ross and I worked under cover of being hard-news reporters and documentary producers. Leigh's cover was a job in the New York governor's office. Both of my partners were outstanding.

I could now recall my life with Alex up to the time I had left her to do the documentary in Africa. Then my memory still had large pieces missing.

I groaned and opened my eyes. Leigh was close to me, watching my every move.

"How do you feel?" she asked.

"Not bad." I grimaced. "Whoever hit me with the dart didn't intend to kill me, or I'd be dead."

"I'm glad you aren't," Leigh said, smiling. "We arrived as they were dragging you to a panel van. They wanted you alive. I'm thankful we arrived when we did."

"Yeah, me too." I looked around the room. "Where's Alex?"

"She evaded us," Leigh said.

"Evaded? You make it sound like she's a criminal."

Leigh hesitated. "I just meant she wasn't at the quarry when we arrived."

"Did you even look for her or try to rescue her? My God, Leigh, she was kidnapped!"

Leigh shrugged.

"How did you know where I was?"

"You turned on your GPS to locate the quarry," Leigh said. "That was the break we'd been anticipating."

I glared at her. "Well, now that you have me, what are you going to do with me?"

"What would you like me to do with you?" Leigh trailed her fingernails down my arm.

"Take me to Alex," I said.

"Sloan." Leigh's exasperation was obvious in her tone and on her face. "Why are you so obsessed with Alex? I thought you were over her."

"Over her?" I snorted. "How could anyone ever get over a woman like Alex? Besides, she's my wife."

"No, she isn't," Leigh hissed. "She divorced you while you were in Africa. She sent you a "Dear John" letter."

I couldn't stop my mouth from gaping open. Leigh's statement was like a stab in the heart. "Divorced me?"

"I guess that part of your memory hasn't returned either," Leigh mumbled, "or you're still in denial"

I dragged my hands down my face, trying to figure out what was happening. "I don't believe you. Alex would never leave me."

"She divorced you and took everything," Leigh was without mercy. "She left you penniless, and now all she has to do is crook her little finger, and you go running back to her."

"Oh, man, don't tell me I was fool enough to cheat on her?" I knew Alex loved me. I didn't know what game Leigh was playing, so I decided to go along with her.

"No one knows why she divorced you," Leigh's expression was sympathetic. "You simply received a packet of papers to sign while you were in Africa. You were devastated and wouldn't talk about it. Ross said you were inconsolable.

"Yes, that would have destroyed me," I said.

"So, you are a free woman." Leigh watched my eyes as she traced the back of my hand with her fingers. "I want to help, Sloan. Please let me help you."

"I will," I said, more confused than ever.

##

Chapter 26

"How did you get here so quickly?" I asked Leigh as she unlocked the door to her motel room.

"As soon as I learned Alex was here, I flew down," she said. "I knew she would lead me to you."

I looked at my duffle bag on the bed then glanced at Leigh.

"One of the officers drove your car back to the motel when they took you to the hospital. I brought your things here. Your bullwhip is in there too.

"As soon as the doctor releases you, we'll fly to Washington. Your handler needs to debrief you."

"Leigh, I still can't remember what evidence I have or where I sent it." I sat down in one of the two chairs in her room.

She studied me for a long time but seemed to believe that I couldn't remember.

She sat down in the chair next to mine. "What do you remember?"

"I remember going to Africa," I said as I tried to recall the things that had come back to me. "I know that Ross and I had over five hundred hours of video for our documentary.

"I remember preparing to leave Africa," I thought out loud as new memories filled my mind. "Ross and I were shooting some last-minute footage when men in black Hummers attacked us. Their gunfire enraged a mother rhino, and she shoved our jeep off the cliff. The next thing I knew I was in the hospital."

Leigh nodded. "Ross wasn't as badly injured as you, and he managed to get to the embassy where we picked him up and brought him home.

"I was sent to make certain you were safe and to bring you home as soon as you were well enough to travel," Leigh said, narrowing her eyes at me. "Imagine my surprise when Alex showed up claiming to be your wife."

"She is my wife. I—"

"Do you remember how to use a computer?"

"Of course," I said, rolling my eyes.

Leigh pulled a laptop from her suitcase and placed it on the small desk. She opened it and logged onto the motel's internet.

"Here." She stood, offering me the desk chair. "The internet is full of information about you and Alex. See for yourself. Just type in Alex and Sloan Cartwright."

I pulled the laptop toward me and typed in our names. Photos of Alex and me flooded the monitor. I looked at our wedding photos and pictures of us sailing. Photos of us in Africa, Alex sitting in the back of a jeep while I struck a Great White Hunter pose. Alex laughing as we played with a pair of lion cubs at Camp Elephant.

There were pictures of us accepting awards in our respective fields. Videos of us dressed in gorgeous gowns and holding hands as we walked on red carpets.

Hundreds of photos and in every one of them, we only had eyes for each other. She never would have divorced me.

I typed in *Alex and Sloan Cartwright divorce,* and there it was, all over the internet. Alex on a popular talk show announcing to the world that we had gone our separate ways.

"Why?" The talk show hostess grilled her mercilessly.

"People change," a distraught Alex replied. "Our relationship had simply run its course."

"But just last month the two of you were seen cavorting in Spain," the woman said, continuing to push for the sordid details.

"We met to hammer out our divorce agreement," Alex mumbled. "Look, I can't do this." She stood and left the set as tears filled her eyes.

The talk show hostess tried to cut to a commercial, but her camera operators were too busy consoling Alex to pay the hostess any mind.

I turned off the computer. I couldn't bear to watch any more. I fought the urged to throw up as I stumbled to the bathroom to throw cold water on my face.

"Do you believe me now?" Leigh touched my elbow. "The agency sent me to get you. I pretended to be your wife so the hospital would release you to me, but Alex interfered with that."

I nodded. "Where do we go from here?" I mumbled. Before she could answer, I flung out another question. "And what about Amarosia? Who is she?"

"She's a mystery to me," Leigh said, sighing. "Never heard of her before. I was as shocked as you when the three of us showed up claiming to be married to you."

"I'm not like that," I said, glancing at Leigh. "Am I? I mean, I'm not the type to cheat on my wife?"

"No." Leigh snorted. "You are all about commitment and loyalty. I don't know why Alex divorced you, but I do know you would never cheat on her as long as you were married."

"After our divorce . . . " I stopped for a minute, blinking back the tears I felt pooling in my eyes. "Would I seek solace in another woman's arms?"

Leigh shook her head. "No. Believe me I tried to console you."

"Oh, um, I'm sorry." I bowed my head.

"Don't be. When you finally get over Alex, I'm certain you will be just as devoted to me."

I had to laugh at her confidence. She was a beautiful woman, and honestly, if I weren't insanely in love with Alex, I would probably be with Leigh.

"So, we both agree that Amarosia is an unknown in our equation?" I asked, still trying to figure out the whole convoluted mess.

"She is for me," Leigh said.

My stomach growled, and we both jumped at the sound before bursting out in laughter. "I think I'm hungry," I said.

"Why don't I take you out to dinner?" Leigh said. "On the company credit card, of course."

"Of course." I walked to the bed and dug in my duffle bag for my bullwhip.

"Are you going to carry that thing?" Leigh said.

"No, I'm going to wear it." I watched her eyes widen as I draped it around my waist. "How's this?"

"Unbelievable," she said with a chuckle. "It looks like a fashion accessory."

She looped her arm through mine, and we headed out the door.

"Just for tonight, Sloan," she glanced sideways at me, "can we pretend to be a couple?"

"Okay, but just during dinner. The game ends when we return to this room."

Leigh agreed, but not before I caught the look of disappointment in her eyes.

We walked arm in arm along the Riverwalk until we stopped at Boudro's and waited for the maître d' to seat us. "Want to dine riverside?"

"You order our wine," she said as we were led to our table. "You always order the best wine."

The waiter appeared as soon as we were seated. "I'm going to have the filet," I informed him. I salivated as I recalled the thick, tender steaks for which Boudro's was famous. "So, let's pair it with a nice 1960 Faustino 1 Gran Reserva."

"Now you're just showing off," Leigh said, shaking her head. "They probably don't even carry it."

"Oh, but we do, senorita," the waiter assured her. "We have over seven thousand bottles of wine in The Wine Cellar."

"The Wine Cellar is another restaurant connected to Boudro's," I explained as the waiter returned with two wine glasses and our wine in an ice bucket.

"Oh my goodness!" Leigh's whole face lit up as she sipped the wine. "I was right; you do know how to select wine."

We dined and drank two bottles of the wine. "Hey, I muttered as the wine relaxed me, "if the agency wants to send us all over the world, the least they can do is pay for fine wine."

The evening was pleasant. A breeze ruffled the trees along the Riverwalk, and soft music floated around us. Leigh looked up at me through long lashes. The twinkling lights that lined the Riverwalk danced in her eyes. She truly was a beautiful woman. I found myself wanting to lean in and kiss her full, red lips.

I shook my head. I was certain I belonged to Alex. The wine, in combination with the lingering toxin in my body, made me dizzy and threatened to impair my judgment.

I closed my eyes.

"Are you okay?" Concern filled Leigh's voice.

"I, um, uh, just a little dizzy," I mumbled. "Drinking a bottle of wine right after being shot with a toxic dart wasn't my best decision."

"We should return to the hotel so you can lie down," Leigh said.

"No, let me sit here for a few minutes." I motioned for the waiter and ordered coffee for us and the check.

As the coffee did its best to offset the effects of the wine and my head cleared, I asked Leigh the question that had been bothering me all day.

"Leigh, what is being done to locate Alex?"

She pursed her lips and paused as if organizing her thoughts. "She is none of our concern. The agency's purview doesn't include Alex."

"Whether she's married to me or not, she's an American citizen whose life is in jeopardy because of her association with me. She's been kidnapped to use as leverage against me."

Leigh cocked her head at me. "Sloan, can't you forget Alex for one evening?"

"How can I? How can you? Her life is in danger."

"As soon as her captors realize she means nothing to you, they'll release her—"

"Or kill her," I said. Both of us knew she was spewing bullshit.

"Dammit, Sloan, she divorced you!" Leigh raised her voice, and diners sitting around us tuned into our conversation. "What part of *she wants nothing to do with you* don't you understand?"

I jumped to my feet, causing my head to spin. I gripped the table to steady myself. Leigh leaped to my side.

"Sloan, honey, let me help you!"

"I'm fine," I mumbled as my vision cleared, and I started walking back to the motel.

Leigh linked her arm through mine to steady me. "I'm sorry, Sloan. I didn't mean to be insensitive to Alex's predicament. I'm still angry that she showed up in Africa and the two of you ran away together."

I said nothing, concentrating instead on putting one foot in front of the other.

"Why was she there?" Leigh asked.

"Maybe she still loves me." I snarled at her, making no effort to temper my snarky attitude.

"Or maybe she was trying to locate the evidence you have amassed." Leigh was having no part of Alex loving me. "That evidence is worth millions to the criminals involved. Hell, to the countries involved."

We walked in silence for a while. *God, I wish I could remember where I sent my evidence.*

171

"Alex is incredibly wealthy," I pointed out. "I seriously doubt she would get involved in anything as criminal as stealing my evidence and selling it to the highest bidder.

"Her life is in danger, plain and simple, and it's our fault." My voice was a low rumble as I tried to control my temper.

Before we got much further, I heard a wolf whistle behind us. I looked over my shoulder as a group of young Mexican men approached us.

"Hey, mama," one of them said to me. "You lookin' for some fun?"

"I've had all the fun I can stand for one night," I growled as my hand slid to the stock of the bullwhip.

"Hey! No, problemo." He grinned, his perfect white teeth gleaming against his dark complexion. He held out his hand as if to shake on it. His dark eyes begged me to take his hand. For some unknown reason, I did.

As we shook hands, he transferred a scrap of paper into my palm. "You enjoy the evening, mama." He winked at me and sprinted to catch up with his posse.

I slid my hands into the pockets of my jeans. "I'm exhausted," I said to Leigh. "I need a shower and a good night's sleep."

##

Chapter 27

I dug through my duffle bag and laid out clean clothes for the next day. I placed my car keys on the top of my bag. I locked the bathroom door, turned on the shower, and pulled the small square of paper from my pocket. I unfolded it and read the message written on it: *Alex in zombie town.* The words were printed, childlike.

I showered and donned the white robe provided by the motel. "Did we pass an ice machine on our way to the room?" I asked Leigh. "I need some ice and a Dr. Pepper."

She studied me for a moment and nodded. "I'll get it for you."

"No, no," I said. "I'm not an invalid. I'll get it myself."

"Seriously, Sloan, get ready for bed. I'll get your drink and ice."

I nodded and pulled on an old T-shirt as she grabbed the ice bucket and headed for the door.

When the door clicked behind her, I fired up the laptop and typed in *zombie town, San Antonio, TX*. To my surprise, there were images and a video of a housing addition that had been abandoned halfway into completion. The developer was serving prison time for defrauding the bank. He'd obtained a construction loan and then used the funds to support his lavish lifestyle and pay for his son's wedding.

The housing project had come to a halt when the bank discovered the developer had never filed plats with the city and had no plans for roads, sewer, water or electricity to serve the addition.

I memorized the directions and turned off the computer. I was in bed when Leigh returned.

"Thank you." I flashed my best good-little-girl smile as Leigh poured the Dr. Pepper into the glass of ice and handed it to me.

She sat down on the side of my bed. "Sloan, I don't like arguing with you." Her look was grave. "You must know how I feel about you."

She leaned in and kissed my lips. I forced myself to kiss her back. "I took a cold shower," I said. "Perhaps you should too."

She chuckled and nodded. "Perhaps I'd rather go with the heat and see where that leads us."

I waited until I was certain she was in the shower. Then I dressed, tossed the laptop into my duffle bag, grabbed my car keys, the bullwhip, Leigh's purse and slipped out the door.

It took me a few minutes to find my car, but it finally beeped when I kept pushing the fob. I cranked it, turned off my GPS system, and sped away from the motel.

In the dark I had more difficulty locating the abandoned housing addition than I'd anticipated, but I didn't dare turn on the GPS.

As daybreak filled the sky with faint blues, yellows, and magentas, I spotted the outline of the deserted houses rising on a hill. I pulled my car into the unfinished garage of the closest building.

There were about thirty homes in various stages of construction. None were completed, and the glass was broken out of every window. Obviously, vandals had destroyed a large part of the construction. I located the most-finished house and headed for it. As I approached, I could see the flickering light of a lantern. I crawled to the window, attracting stickers and cactus like a magnet. God, sometimes Texas—like Africa—could be hard and unforgiving.

I settled beneath the paneless window and listened to the voices inside.

"I'm telling you," a gravelly voice croaked, "they aren't married anymore. Sloan Cartwright doesn't care if this woman lives or dies. She won't come looking for her."

"She'll come," a deep baritone voice replied.

I fought the urge to peep over the windowsill. I didn't recognize either of the voices.

"She won't come for me," I heard Alex declare. "She hates me. I left her penniless in the divorce."

"Yeah? Then why did she escape from Africa with you?"

So she *did* divorce me! A whirlwind of emotions twisted through my mind. But it was her idea to renew our vows in Italy legally. That means we're now married.

"She kidnapped me," Alex said.

"If you don't shut up," the gravelly voice threatened, "I'm going to shut you up."

I crawled to the corner of the house. I was trying to decide on my course of action when I poked my head around the corner and found myself staring at a pair of steel-toed army boots.

The last thing I saw was the boot heading toward my face. I turned my head just in time for the blow to land on the side of my head instead of my nose.

##

I kept my eyes closed as I slowly became aware of my surrounds. I was sitting in a chair. My hands were bound behind my back. My captors had tied my ankles to the legs of the chair. I tugged at my restraints, trying to ascertain their strength. *Damn, I hate zip ties!* Handcuffs were easier to escape. The ties cut into my wrists.

"You've killed her," Alex said, sobbing. "A blow to the head is a death sentence for her. She had a severe concussion in Africa. She hadn't recovered from it."

"Shut up," the gravelly voice barked. A loud slap and the cry from Alex told me he'd hit her. "We don't need you anymore now that we have her. The boss said she would come for you."

The baritone agreed with Alex. "She's right, you know. If the blonde dies, the consortium will skin you alive."

"If she dies, her evidence dies with her," the gravelly voice said.

The two men continued to argue. I opened my eyes just enough to get a look at the men. One was short and bald and the other had a dark beard.

"I doubt it," the bearded one said. "She's too smart for that. You need to get her to a hospital. We have to get that video."

176

THREE TIMES AS DEADLY

"Are you nuts? Half the world is looking for her." The other man started pacing the floor. "If I take her to a doctor, we'll be arrested. We need to bring a doctor here."

"You go get the doctor. I'll watch them," the bald man suggested.

One of them yanked hard on my restraints. I could tell by Alex's sharp intake of breath that he had done the same to hers.

"They aren't going anywhere," the bearded man grunted. "We'll both go get a doctor. No way am I leaving you alone with the brunette."

I was glad to learn they didn't trust each other. The door slammed, and I heard a deadbolt jammed into place. I listened for their vehicle to leave. I could hear them arguing outside the window. They finally cranked a car and drove away.

"Oh dear God!" Alex cried. "Sloan. Sloan, baby, can you hear me?"

"I'm okay," I answered as I raised my eyes to look at her. "Are you okay? He hit you."

I gasped as I saw blood trickling from her beautiful lips. An explosive rage ran through me. I knew I would kill her assailant before this was over.

"Can you get your hands free?" I asked.

"No. I've been trying for two days. The zip tie is even tighter." Alex squeezed her eyes shut to hold back the tears.

"It's going to be okay, honey," I assured her. "I have knives in my boots. I'll try to get my feet up to your hands. See if you can get the knife." I nodded toward my boots. "There's a knife in each zipper pouch.

THREE TIMES AS DEADLY

Alex blinked away her tears and nodded at me

I hopped and scooted my chair until I was directly behind Alex. I rocked my chair until I turned it over backward, lifting my feet even with Alex's hands. The back of my head hit the cement floor and pain shot through me.

Alex screamed, unable to see me. "Sloan, are you okay?"

"I'm good," I croaked. "Can you stretch your fingers just a little bit? You're almost touching the zipper."

She tried but was unable to reach the top of my boot. "Can you push closer?" Alex asked.

"Alex, this will hurt, but if you can hook your hands over the toe of my boot, I can use your arms as leverage to pull myself closer."

She took a deep breath and hooked her tied hands over the toe of my right boot.

"This will hurt, honey," I said. The thought of hurting Alex made me sick to my stomach.

"As you know, I can take a little hurt," she said in an effort to lighten the mood. It didn't work. "It's better than dying. Do it, Sloan."

I felt her brace herself, and I arched my foot, pulling the toe of my boot back toward me. Alex cried out, and my chair moved about two inches.

I lay still. I wasn't sure I could do that to her again. I was certain I had dislocated one of her shoulders.

"I've got it, Sloan," Alex's voice was dripping with pain. She inched the zipper down and fumbled around until she found the handle of the knife. I felt it slide from my boot.

"What now?" Alex said.

"Cut the zip ties binding my feet. Keep your hands away from the blade. It's extremely sharp."

It took her a long time to cut the ties, but she finally cut my feet loose. I struggled to my feet and backed up to her so she could free my hands.

"Just hold the knife, honey. I'll slide the ties back and forth over the blade." I knew that every movement she made was killing her shoulder.

The zip tie separated with a pop. I took the knife and cut Alex loose from the chair.

"God, Sloan!" She fell into my arms, sobbing against my chest. "I thought you were dead. I saw them shoot you with a dart before they brought me here."

"It was toxic enough to make me ill without killing me." I hugged her tight. "God, you're an armful of woman," I murmured into her ear as I gloried in the softness of her.

"We need to get out of here," I said, pulling her toward the broken window of the house. "We'll have to go out this window. They locked the door from the outside. My car is about three blocks away."

"Fix my shoulder," she said, her face etched with pain. "It's killing me."

"It'll hurt like hell," I huffed.

"Fix it, baby! I can't stand jostling around like this."

I found a bedroom door to use as leverage. As Alex flattened her torso against one side of it, I put my foot on my side and pulled hard on her arm. She screamed and went to her knees."

"Oh God, that hurt," she cried. Tears filled her eyes as she struggled to remain coherent. I've seen men twice her size faint when I pulled their shoulder into place.

I placed my hands around her rib cage and lifted her to a standing position. "Can you walk?"

She leaned against me and nodded. I scooped up the bullwhip and led Alex to the window.

"Let me go out first so I can help you when you come through," I suggested. "There's a drop from the window. I can catch you and let you down easy."

"You always do," she said. She gave me a lopsided smile that didn't reach her eyes.

##

Chapter 28

I floored the accelerator, and the LC sprang into action. I pitched Leigh's purse out the window. *That should keep them busy for a while.*

"What are we going to do?" Alex asked as she rubbed her shoulder.

I glanced at her. Blood covered her and matted her hair. The dark circles under her eyes told me she was exhausted. The thugs had ripped all the buttons from the blouse she was wearing.

"Your blouse . . ." I said, swallowing hard. "Did someone—"

She snorted. "No. They fought over me. I'm just thankful the two of them weren't smart enough to agree to share."

Her voice dropped to a low murmur. "I thought I was going to die, Sloan."

A shiver ran through my body. The thought of losing Alex was unbearable.

Both of us looked like we'd been set on fire and stomped out. We didn't even have a comb to remove the tangles from our hair. We looked like homeless women.

"We need to lay low for a while, but I doubt any reputable hotel will welcome us. There is a Buc-ee's in New Braunfels," I informed Alex. "Let's stop there and pick up some toiletries and clothes. They sell T-shirts and casual clothes. With the traffic they have through there, no one will notice us."

The New Braunfels Buc-ee's' claim to fame is their induction into America's Best Restroom Hall of Fame. The 68,000-square-feet convenience store-service center offers travelers everything from gas to beaver nuggets—*I'm afraid to guess what that is*—and eighty-three commodes.

Alex headed for the ladies' room, and I grabbed jeans and T-shirts in our size, toothbrushes and hair paraphernalia. By the time we left the restroom, we were halfway presentable.

"We need a place to hide for a few days while we heal and formulate a plan of action," I thought out loud.

"What about Scurlock Farms, that little bed-and-breakfast we loved so much in Georgetown?" Alex hugged my arm between her breasts. I could tell she was thinking of how we had made love in the secluded cottage.

We stopped at Walmart in Georgetown and purchased two burner phones and enough supplies to last a week.

Alex called Scurlock Farms to see if we could reserve the cottage. For once, luck was with us.

After taking care of the reservations, Alex shuffled through the dozen identifications I had in my duffle bag. "Dixie Denton, Ruby Glass, Daisey Darling." She laughed. "Who thought up these names?"

"Draco, the best counterfeiter in the business. He thought it would be fun to embarrass me. He said he always fantasizes about me being a pole dancer. He keeps me out of trouble and works for me, not the agency."

She leaned over to kiss me but gasped as the weight on her elbow shot pain into her shoulder.

"Are you okay?" The look of agony on her beautiful face made my heart ache.

"I forgot you almost tore off my arm." Pain clouded her eyes as she moved her arm.

Alex waited in the car as I took care of checking us into Scurlock Farms. I didn't recognize the person who waited on me, and my Draco-produced ID and credit card worked without a hitch. The guy was good.

"We're on county co-op water now," the desk attendant informed me. "You won't be bothered with the well pump going out."

"Good to know," I said as I turned to leave. "Thanks."

##

Alex headed for the shower as I unloaded the car. By the time I'd put away the groceries and made sandwiches, Alex had showered and dressed. She entered the kitchen still towel-drying her hair, dressed only in a T-shirt and panties. She was more beautiful than I remembered. I ached to hold her but knew she was hurting, so I placed the Advil and a glass of water on the kitchen island along with a sandwich.

"Eat before you take the Advil," I said. "I can't wait to get into the shower."

I let the hot water beat down on my head. I couldn't remember the last time I had washed my hair. I shampooed it twice and then rinsed it thoroughly. The problem with long, thick hair was that it took a lot of time to rinse the shampoo from it.

Alex was sitting on the bed when I entered the bedroom. "The sandwich was wonderful," she said. "Thank you."

"No problem," I said, trying not to look at her too long.

She patted the spot beside her, motioning for me to sit down. "You know those movies where the hero is shot, run over by a bus, and dropped from a ten-story building?"

I laughed out loud as she repeated the words I had spoken to her in the hospital.

"And the beautiful woman drags him from the street to her bed, patches him up, and he makes mad passionate love to her?"

I continued to chuckle at her antics.

She stood, straddled my lap and gazed into my eyes. "I am that guy, Sloan."

"Oh God!" I moaned as she pushed me back onto the bed. "I want you so badly. I just didn't think you'd be up to it. You've been through a lot the past few days."

"But I'm not dead," she murmured against my lips.

I placed my hand behind her head and pulled her lips tighter against mine. I flicked my tongue over the cut in her lip. "Does that hurt?"

"No," she hissed as she pressed her lips harder against mine and took control of my mouth with her tongue. "I need you, Sloan."

I slid my hands under her T-shirt and moaned as my fingers found her soft, taut breasts. Her nipples were erected and begged to be sucked. I responded to their request.

"It's been too long, baby," she whispered into my ear.

I pushed her onto her back and began to explore every inch of her glorious body. Over the years I have touched her a million times, but she always thrills me.

I kissed her lips, careful of the cut, but she pulled my mouth hard against hers. "I am that guy, Sloan!" She growled. Her eyes sparkled like a million stars as she pulled my body down on top of her.

I slid my knee between her legs, and she slowly began to grind into my thigh. "Don't tease me," she begged.

I didn't.

Much later, I lay on my back beside her, waiting for my heart rate to return to normal. She turned onto her side and threw her arm and leg over my body. Then I asked the question that had haunted my thoughts since I read about our separation on the internet.

"Why did you divorce me?"

She chuckled. "Because you told me to." She slid onto my body and trailed kisses from my cheek to the pulse point in my neck.

"Why would I do anything that stupid?" I asked. "I am hopelessly in love with you."

"You feared the criminals you were about to expose would harm me if they thought I was important to you. You thought a public divorce would put them on notice that you no longer cared for me." She began to grind into me, and all thoughts of anything but making love to her flew from my mind.

Loving Alex always drove everything else from my thoughts and left me at peace with the world.

The joyful sound of a bird welcomed the sunrise, and I did too, as I snuggled into the arms of the beauty sleeping beside me. *God, I've missed this.*

Alex stirred and pulled me into her.

"How is your arm this morning?" I asked as she pulled my face between her breasts.

"Much better. A little more exercise like last night, and I'll be healed."

"Please consider me your personal trainer," I said, chuckling as I kissed her pert nipples.

"Oh, I do." She giggled as she fisted my hair and pulled me tighter against her.

"I need to know two things," I said as I watched Alex make pancakes. "I need to know who my handler is and where I sent the videos.

"Do I maintain a storage facility somewhere?" I queried Alex.

"Not that I know of, baby." She leaned over and kissed me as she placed the plate in front of me.

"You've never told me anything about your agency work, because you didn't want criminals to go after me to get to you. You had an awful time with politicians after you broke the sex trade story."

"I remember that," I said. "I remember almost everything except the two things that will keep us alive."

She refilled our coffee cups and joined me at the counter. "Eat your breakfast and let's go for a walk. It's lovely outside."

"Do you know who those two thugs were that tied us to the chairs?" I rinsed our plates and put them in the dishwasher.

"They spoke English when they conversed with one another, but the guy with the beard spoke a foreign language when he was on the phone. It wasn't Spanish or French, but I don't know what it was."

"Probably Afrikaans," I surmised. I rattled off several sentences in the language. "Did it sound like that?"

"Yes," Alex said.

"That means we have thugs from Africa, the US, and Asia after us," I informed her. "The sooner I get my evidence to the agency the better off we'll be."

"Does your dad know we're okay?" Alex asked as we explored a path in the woods outside our cottage.

"No. I'm sure my parents are worried to death about us. When we return to the cabin, I'll call him.

"I'm sure your corporate people are going crazy without you," I added. I thought about how much everyone depended on Alex. She had strong, smart

187

women in high positions in A&S Cosmetics, but they all turned to her for guidance.

"This will be a good test of their strength and decision-making capabilities," Alex said as she squeezed my hand tighter.

"Honestly, I've been scared to death since Ross called and said you were in the hospital," Alex admitted, "but I have never felt more alive. When we get out of this, I want to travel more with you."

"I was thinking about settling down behind a desk with you," I said. "I believe the excitement comes from us being together—wherever we are."

"You may be right." Alex brushed my lips with hers.

##

Chapter 29

It was dusk when Alex whirled me around and pressed my back against an ancient oak tree. "Sloan, kiss me and then look over my shoulder. I saw a movement at the corner of the cabin."

I buried my face in her hair, surveying the cabin and the woods around it. "Yes," I whispered in her ear. "Someone is watching us. I can't get a good look at them. Damn, you smell good."

She giggled like a teenager, pushed me away and slapped me on the shoulder. "Would you do that to me right now?" she said loud enough for anyone close by to hear.

"If you'll let me," I answered just as loudly as she broke free from my arms and ran toward the cabin. I chased her, and we both made it into the cabin without any interference from whoever was skulking around our cottage.

"Perverts," Alex whispered. "They didn't interfere because they want to watch us. Follow me into the bedroom. Don't turn on any lights."

"How many did you see?" I asked as I coiled my whip.

"I counted three."

THREE TIMES AS DEADLY

"That was my count too. Two at the front and one at the back door. Let's see if we can draw them to the side window of our bedroom."

"Time to give the performance of your life," I said, wiggling my eyebrows at her. "Make those sounds that always make me salivate. Feel free to scream my name while you're at it."

I pulled the Glock and silencer from my duffle bag and walked to the front door.

"Oh my God, Sloan!" she yelled with an appropriate mix of passion and moaning. "Do you have any idea what that does to me?" She began a rhythmic chanting of my name. "Sloan, Sloan, Sloan. Oh God, Sloan.

It took all the strength I had to walk away from her. As she continued the audio performance, I slipped out the back door and screwed the silencer onto the barrel of my gun. As I did so, the agency's training motto jumped into my mind: *Never give anyone a second chance to kill you.* I knew the three men surveilling us were now at the bedroom window on the side of the cabin, trying to see what we were doing.

Alex got louder, heading toward a crescendo by the time I reached the corner of the cabin. I stepped into the open and fired three perfectly placed shots. The voyeurs never knew what hit them. They wouldn't get a second opportunity to kill me.

I kicked the bodies to make certain all three were dead. The man with the gravelly voice was still moving. His eyes opened wide as he realized who held a pistol pointed at his head.

"Remember me?" Without mercy I stared into his eyes. "You slapped my wife."

THREE TIMES AS DEADLY

The fear in his eyes was palpable. "Who sent you?" I placed the cold gun barrel against his forehead.

"The Consortium," he mumbled.

"Which one?" I snarled.

"Save the Rhino Consortium.".

"The same group that hired me to do the documentary?" I asked.

"Yeah." A coughing spasm shook his body as blood oozed from his lips. He knew he was dying and took his parting crack at me.

"I raped your woman." His grin was evil.

"No, you didn't." My smile was just as evil as I pulled the trigger one more time to put him out of his misery.

I tapped the windowpane with the barrel of my gun and Alex raised the window.

"Everything's okay now." I leaned in and kissed her. "I'm going to look around. I'll be inside shortly."

"I love you," she whispered.

I stuck the pistol into my waistband and dragged the dead men to the well about twenty feet away. I removed their identification, guns, and cell phones and then dropped the bodies down the well shaft.

Inside the cabin, I removed the cell phone batteries and bagged the items I'd removed from the dead men's bodies. I wanted to be able to identify them when I filed my report.

"Do we need to leave?" Alex asked. "I like it here."

"No," I said. "We're safe here."

THREE TIMES AS DEADLY

Alex walked over and wrapped her arms around me from behind. "Oh my God, Sloan," she said. "Do you have any idea how much I want you?"

I turned around and pulled her close. "Do you have any idea how badly I want to hear you chanting my name again?"

"That all depends on how good you are." She nipped at my neck. "The better you are, the louder I scream your name."

##

Chapter 30

"Did you know who Leigh was when you arrived at the hospital?" I asked as I rubbed Alex's shoulder with something called Olbas Oil.

"Yes, you had introduced me to Leigh and Ross. I figured the agency had sent her to get you. I wasn't certain what was going on, so I seduced you to run away with me."

"Seduced me, huh?" I pulled her into my arms. "It's not like you had to try very hard. I was eating out of your hand the minute you whirled into my room."

"Uh-huh." She hummed as she kissed me and pulled back from me. "A little more oil here, please."

"Who is Amarosia?" I asked, continuing to rub the soothing oil into her sore shoulder.

"I have no idea," Alex said, her brow furrowed. "She was a surprise to me too. I do know she was also after the videos.

"She and Makin were working together. I overheard them talking in the hospital lobby. I think you must have some incriminating evidence against him. He told her she must get the videos or he would go to prison.

"So Amy, Leigh, Ross, and you were the only ones who knew about the evidence you'd collected.

How did the men who tried to kill you find out about it?"

"That is the question that's driving me crazy," I said as I poured more oil into my palm. "My handler also knew. I wouldn't be on an assignment without his approval."

"Your handler is a man?" Alex said. "Do you remember who he is?"

"No." I wrinkled my brow trying to recall my handler's name. "I'm not certain it's a man, but that just seems right.

"You said Ross had my cell phone," I recalled. "Let's try calling him on it."

Alex kissed me. "Why didn't I think of that? That's why you are an undercover agent, and I simply keep the women of the world beautiful." The twinkle in her eyes sent a rush of fire through me.

I reached out for her, but she eluded my grasp.

"Call Ross first," she said, winking at me.

##

"Hello?" a voice answered on the second ring.

"Ross?" I said, punching the speakerphone button so Alex could hear.

"Sloan? Damn, girl, is that you? Jesus, I thought you were dead! Are you okay? Where are you?"

"Hey, slow down," I said. "I'm fine. I'm in Texas. Where are you?"

"I'm hiding out too," he whispered, as if he feared being overheard. "The agency is keeping me in a safe house until this is settled."

"Ross, do you have any idea what we uncovered?"

194

"Not we, Great White Hunter. You! You're the one who met those people in secret and recorded every meeting with that concealed camera. You didn't share with me. You said it was too dangerous."

"Obviously I was right," I grumbled. "Someone is trying to kill me."

"Yeah, the agency sent Leigh after you, Sloan. Why didn't you come in with her?"

"I . . . well, I—"

"Don't tell me you let Alex get her claws into you again?" Ross said, disgust dripping from every word. "After the Dear John letter she sent you and serving divorce papers on you while you were up to your ass in African crocodiles?"

I didn't say a word, so he continued.

"She is something," Ross said.

"Yeah, she is." I grinned as Alex settled herself on my lap.

"Are you in our usual safe house?" I asked.

"Yes. Sloan, you must come in. You need the agency's protection. Leigh came in today, and all hell is breaking loose."

"Ross, I appreciate your loyalty," I said, "but things are not what they seem between Alex and me. She's my wife. I'll explain when I see you."

"So, you're coming in?"

"Yeah, but not until I have my hands on those videos. I'm hanging up now."

##

I lay on my back with Alex's head resting on my shoulder. I looked at my arm where she had dug her nails into it to make me know what she wanted from me.

"You really do have your claws in me," I said with a snicker.

She raised on her elbow. "You'd think that after all this time you would know what I want without so much direction." Her eyes twinkled with mischief. She laid her cheek on my breast, and I stroked her hair.

We lay like that for a long time. I was searching my mind for any clue about the evidence I had accumulated. My mind drifted to the incredible animals that were being hunted to extinction.

"Care to let me into that beautiful mind of yours?" Alex murmured.

"I was just thinking about the atrocities being committed in Africa for the sake of the almighty dollar," I said.

"Share with me," she whispered.

"Honey, some of the situations I encountered in Africa are too ghastly to repeat.".

"Maybe, just maybe,"—she raised her head and brushed her lips against mine—"it might help to share the things that haunt you with someone who loves you."

"I . . . I have video." I squeezed my eyes shut, trying to recall where that video was. Again, I failed.

"Poachers will stop at nothing to obtain rhino horns," I said. "They slaughtered the last female rhino in the Krugersdorp Game Reserve. She had a nine-month-old calf by her side.

"In the KwaZulu-Natal province, poachers cut off the entire nose of a white female rhino to get the horn. Miraculously, she survived, but her one-month-old calf was so frightened by the attack on his mother that he ran into the bush and couldn't be found. By the time he was located, he had died from dehydration."

Alex groaned. "Oh, no! I understand why you're haunted and why you want to help."

"The tragic thing is that in most of the cases, the people who were supposed to be protecting the animals actually aided the poachers for a few dollars." I paused, choking back the lump in my throat.

"The poachers are brazen because in most cases, they are working with someone on the inside who is willing to look the other way.

"They broke into a French zoo and shot the four-year-old rhino who was just a big pet. They cut off his horn with a chainsaw."

"I think I'm going to be sick," Alex mumbled as she jumped from our bed and ran to the bathroom. I heard her brushing her teeth a few minutes later and knew she had thrown up.

She sat on the bed beside me. "I will never again complain about you leaving me to work on your African documentaries." She leaned down and kissed me between the eyes as if trying to drive away any thoughts that might be hurting me.

I tucked a stray strand of dark hair behind her ear and pulled her on top of me. "You are the most beautiful woman I have ever met," I whispered in her ear, "inside and out."

She rolled off me, into her prior spot, and nestled against my side. "What is so special about rhino horns?"

"Honestly? Nothing. The Vietnamese, Asians, and Chinese believe that rhino-horn dust has curative and aphrodisiac powers.

"The horns are made of keratin, the same thing as our fingernails. Consuming rhino dust is the equivalent of consuming fingernails."

"That is just disgusting," Alex said as she crinkled up her nose.

"Even so," I pointed out, "an ounce of rhino dust sells for the same amount of money as an ounce of gold."

She nuzzled further into my arms, and I held her tightly. Alex had a way of making the world go away.

One should never marry someone they can't talk to. It is important to have that one person who will share your deepest thoughts and return them to you with their own perspective.

Sometimes Alex and I talk a problem to death, but together, we always find a solution.

##

Dawn was breaking when soft lips began kissing their way up my shoulder and into the crook of my neck. I lay still, trying to suppress the smile that wanted to cover my face. "Sloan?" Alex's velvet voice purred my name. "Wake up and play with me."

"Are you going to play nice?" I murmured.

"No-o-o-o," she said in that sexy drawl I loved.

"Okay, then I'd love to play." Already breathless, I pulled her on top of me.

##

Chapter 31

We spent a week at the cabin, giving Alex's shoulder time to heal and enjoying each other's company. We finished proofing the manuscript I had written about our African adventure and emailed it to my publisher.

An instant email shot back. "I thought you were dead!" Dee always jumped straight to the point.

"I may be after you read my newest novel," I emailed back. "Let me know what you think. Right now I'm hiding out from everyone, so please don't let anyone know you've heard from me."

She replied a few minutes later. "My lips are sealed, my little moneymaker. LOL. I can't wait to read this. Contact me when you can."

"She'll love it," Alex said with a confidence I didn't quite feel. "I do."

"Umm, but you're prejudiced." I turned off my laptop and wrapped her in my arms, savoring the thrill that was Alex.

##

A feeling of déjà vu swept over me as I did a quick walk through the cabin to make certain we had everything. Memories filled my mind: Ross yelling at me to hurry; driving my jeep alongside a running

199

rhino; bullets hitting the jeep and falling, falling into nothingness.

"Sloan?" Alex shook my arm, "Sloan, are you okay?"

I gave her my best smile—one I hoped would cover my troubled thoughts, though I have never been able to fool Alex.

"What's wrong?" she said, studying me.

"I think I should leave you with Mom and Dad until I get this mess settled," I informed her. "I'm concerned for your safety."

"No way am I leaving your side." She glared at me. "I only feel safe when I'm with you. I know you can handle anything that arises."

"You're right," I said, "and I don't trust anyone else to protect you." I grabbed my bullwhip and duffle bag and headed for the car. "New York, here we come."

We drove for hours, stopping at fast-food places along the way.

"I need to get out and walk," Alex said as the day grew long. "Let's eat dinner at a restaurant. I'm sick of fast-food."

I agreed with her. "Watch for anything that looks decent," I said.

"I keep seeing signs for Mama's Place." Alex pointed out a billboard that guaranteed Mama served good home cooking at exit 98B.

"Mama's Place it is." Alex rested her hand on my thigh, and I could feel her studying my profile. A warm blush spread from my chest up to my face.

She giggled. "I love the way you blush."

"You're staring at me," I ducked my head but kept my eyes on the road.

"You truly have no idea how gorgeous you are," Alex whispered as she stroked my cheek. "Just gorgeous."

"There's Mama's Place," I said, still amazed at how Alex could turn me into a burning inferno with a simple touch.

"After dinner, let's go to that Penney's store across the street and see if we can find something to wear that isn't a walking advertisement for Buc-ee's," Alex suggested. "These T-shirts are fine in Texas, but I'm not sure how they'll play in New York."

I draped the bullwhip around my hips and followed Alex into the restaurant. It was cheerful and inviting. A jovial woman standing behind the counter welcomed us and motioned for a young woman to give us menus and seat us in one of the faux-leather, café-style booths in the corner.

"Chicken-fried steak!" Alex pretended to swoon. "I can't remember the last time I had chicken-fried steak." She scooted against me and stroked the inside of my thigh.

"Behave." I moaned as she took joy in my reaction to her touch.

"Want me to stop?" she whispered in my ear.

"Not really," I mumbled.

"You should try some of Mama's homemade pie," our waitress said as she prepared to take our order.

"Do you two own this place?" Alex asked the young woman.

201

"My mother owns it," the girl replied. "It'll be mine someday, so, yeah, I guess you could say we both own it."

"It's a nice restaurant," Alex said

The girl beamed, basking in Alex's approval. We placed our order and snuggled a little closer together.

##"We should spend the night somewhere in Arkansas," I said as I motioned for the waitress to bring our check.

As the girl stepped behind the counter to total our tab, four burly men burst through the door. Mama rushed from the kitchen. "You boys are no longer welcome here," she declared.

I could tell from their cuts and colors that they were part of the infamous Bandidos motorcycle gang. I could also tell from the look of pure horror on the face of our waitress that she was terrified of them.

"We're paying customers," the largest and ugliest of the filthy-looking men growled as he reached across the counter and caught the young waitress by the wrist. "We want this pretty little thing to service us."

The raucous laughter of the four filled the restaurant. They leered at the girl as Mountain Man dragged her from behind the counter.

Two other couples dining in the restaurant made a quick exit, leaving Mama, the waitress, Alex, and me alone with the four barbarous men.

Alex's hand tightened on my arm, encouraging me not to get involved. I slowly uncoiled my whip beneath the table, keeping the stock fastened to my side. The feel of the pistol in my waistband gave me added courage.

"Oh my God," one of the thugs said as he glared at Alex. "Look at the knockers on her."

My entire body stiffened as Mountain Man turned his head to leer at my wife. "I bet you could do it on a motorcycle too, mama." His yellow teeth gaped out of his scraggly beard.

Wondering what he meant, I turned to look at Alex. For the first time, I realized she was wearing a Buc-ee's T-shirt that declared, "Beavers do it in a truck" above the picture of the convenience store's adorable little beaver mascot.

"Really?" I mumbled under my breath. *There should be a law against double entendres on T-shirts.*

Mountain Man swaggered toward our table as if he had two watermelons between his thighs. I gripped my dining utensils.

He rested his palms on our table and leaned into Alex's face. "I'm gonna have a good time with you," he said. Halitosis was the word of the day.

"I don't think so," I whispered as I nailed his right hand to our table with my steak knife and buried my fork into the soft part of his throat below his chin.

He roared like a wounded buffalo. I swung my whip, lashing across the faces of the other three who were coming to his rescue as Mountain Man choked on his own blood.

"Get out of here," I growled at Alex.

God bless Alex. She never hesitated to follow my instructions when we were in a bad situation. She sprinted for the door. One of the men moved to block her exit, but I wrapped the whip around his neck and pulled as hard as I could.

THREE TIMES AS DEADLY

He was strong enough to pull me toward him, but I braced my feet against the table pedestal—firmly bolted to the floor, thank God—and tightened the noose around his neck. It was just a matter of time until he fainted from lack of oxygen or he got his hands on me. I managed to maintain the stranglehold until he dropped to his knees.

The other two thugs backed against the counter as I turned toward them. I watched them as I backed out the door. I was happy to see that Alex had left in the Lexus.

I ran around the corner of the building as the three bikers stormed out of the restaurant and mounted their bikes.

"I'll kill that bitch," the man I had choked to his knees screamed as he started his bike.

They never knew what hit them. Three well-placed shots—one in each bike's gas tank—set off explosions that shook the ground and skyrocketed the men into outer space. "How's that for a crotch rocket?" I yelled, even though they were past hearing.

Alex skidded to a stop, and I jumped into the passenger's side as the Bandidos went up in flames.

Alex was silent for the first ten miles. Then she exhaled the breath she'd been holding. "You are such a badass," she gasped. "Where did you learn to fight like that?"

"The agency," I replied, afraid my actions had disturbed her.

"Is it wrong that I'm incredibly aroused?" She giggled like a teenager.

"Only if no one takes care of you." I laughed.

"I'm certain you are up to the challenge."

Chapter 32

The next morning, I checked with Ross and learned he was waiting at the safe house, and everything was still in an uproar.

We donned the least suggestive of the Buc-ee's T-shirts we'd purchased—"Beaver's Rule"—and visited the local strip mall. Alex purchased several nice tops in a ladies' apparel shop, and by nightfall we'd made our way across Tennessee.

Alex turned on the television and clicked on a cable TV news program as I headed to the motel bathroom for a quick shower. I returned to the bedroom less than ten minutes later, towel-drying my hair as she opened the carryout we had picked up for dinner. Mama and her daughter popped onto the TV screen.

"A report from Texas confirms the deaths of four members of the Bandidos motorcycle gang. According to Mary Watson, owner of Mama's Place in Texarkana, Texas, a fight broke out among the four men over who would pay for their dinner check.

"The leader of the group died after a fellow gang member stabbed him in the throat with a fork. The remaining bikers apparently collided in their rush to leave the restaurant parking lot, and one of the motorcycle gas tanks ruptured, causing all three bikes to explode, killing the riders.

"The four bikers were wanted for murder and multiple gang rape charges.

"A little justice from God," the female newscaster noted.

"I'm beginning to think Africa is safer than the US," Alex commented.

"Both can be pretty dangerous," I said.

After dinner, I opened my laptop while Alex showered. I sat back as a cacophony of dings announced the arrival of multiple messages into my inbox.

"God, I love this book," Dee gushed in her email. "When can we get together and start writing teasers on it?"

I scrolled through my other emails, deleting the junk, until an email from Leigh caught my eye. The subject line read "Life and Death Matters." I rolled my eyes as I clicked open the message.

"Sloan, I'll meet you anywhere you like," she wrote. "I must talk with you. It's a matter of life and death—yours and mine!"

Alex read the email over my shoulder. "She'll never let you go," she huffed.

"She'd need to have me to let me go," I said, as I closed my laptop. "You're the only one who has me—heart and soul."

"It's your body I'm interested in," Alex whispered as she straddled my lap. "You know, I've seen a whole new side of you the last six months.

"I've always loved the woman I thought you were, but you're so much more than I ever dreamed. I'm having difficulty keeping my hands off you."

"Don't fight it," I said, pulling her close. "I love your hands on me."

##

"Sloan." Alex's anxious whisper yanked me from dreams of her. "Honey, wake up. Someone is doing something to our car."

I rushed to her side and peeked out the slit in the curtain. The three Mexicans who had placed a tracker on my car in Texas were checking it out again. The shorter of the two men squatted down and fooled with the underside of my bumper. He took longer than it would take to attach something magnetic so I knew he had secured a device to my car.

The three sauntered across the parking lot as if they belonged there and slipped into a pickup parked across the road.

"Do you know them?" Alex asked.

"I'm certain the men are part of the Mexican mafia. I don't know the woman. They tried to put a tracker on my car when I was in Burleson."

"The woman looks familiar." Alex wrinkled her forehead in thought. "Wait! She was at the fundraiser for the Save the Rhino Consortium."

"I don't recognize her. Do you know who she is?"

"She was on the arm of the ambassador of Vietnam," Alex said.

"Do you always scope out the women at those functions?" I said, trying to make light of the situation.

"Only the ones who hit on you. You didn't even notice her, did you?"

I shook my head.

"Vietnam is the worst country in the black-market trade," I told her. "For them it's a status symbol, a sign of wealth, to have a rhino horn prominently displayed.

"It infuriates me that an incredibly docile and beautiful animal has to die to stroke some asshole's ego.

"In many ways, rhinos are just like men," I said.

"How so?"

"For their size, rhinos have tiny brains and big horns, like a lot of men I know." I snorted. "Honestly, just thinking about how some men pillage the earth makes me want to castrate all of them at birth."

"Calm down, Calamity," Alex said, tousling my hair. "You're losing perspective."

I didn't want to tell Alex that I was angry with myself. I was almost certain I had been duped into raising funds for the very people who were responsible for the extinction of the rhinos.

"Do you know that the only predator an adult rhino has is man?" I asked Alex. "Rhinos are plant eaters and are so well-protected by their thick armor-like skin that other predators never bother them. Just humans.

"We have to shake the three across the street," I said, my thoughts bouncing back to the here and now.

"We'll cross from Pennsylvania into New York state tonight," I said. "We need to lose them somewhere in West Virginia.

"Let's drive until we're down to a half-tank of gas then pull into a self-service station. They won't risk pulling into the same station, but they'll be low on gas too. When they're finally forced to stop for gas, we'll drive as fast as possible, pull off somewhere, and remove the tracker. We'll keep it with us so they don't suspect anything.

"First shopping mall we find, we'll pitch the tracker into the back of someone's pickup truck."

Alex beamed like a little kid. "This is so exciting."

"If it weren't such a deadly game, it would be fun."

##

We discarded the tracker in the bed of a pickup and knew we had seen the last of the Mexican mafia. Alex curled up in the passenger seat and fell asleep.

We had traveled for three hours when I glanced in my review mirror and realized the three gangsters were still on our tail. They were following much closer than before and didn't seem to be concerned that I would see them.

I touched Alex's shoulder. "Honey, wake up. We have company."

"What? Who?" Alex wiped the sleep from her eyes and looked around before glancing at her side mirror. "I thought you got rid of them," she said.

"So did I. Apparently they put more than one tracker on our car."

To my amazement, the thugs accelerated and tried to pull alongside me. The passenger in the front seat leaned out the window and pointed a gun at us.

I stomped the accelerator, and the LC almost shot out from under me. It left the truck as if it were standing still.

THREE TIMES AS DEADLY

We were on a straight stretch of highway. Fortunately, there were few cars on the road with us. The pickup was running wide open and holding its own on the open highway. One of the things I loved about the LC was its maneuverability. I spotted a graveled shoulder off the road and slung the little car into it. As my front tires crunched the gravel, I slammed on the brakes and skidded into the shoulder. I pulled hard on the steering wheel and accelerated, throwing the rear of the LC into the gravel. The tires squealed and smoked as the little car fought for traction and switched directions.

We charged the pickup truck heading straight at us. I overcame the childish urge to flash a hand gesture at the thugs and, instead, yanked the wheel hard to the left, avoiding a head-on collision. The pickup hit the gravel and spun off the road.

"Oh my God!" Alex gasped. "My heart is in my throat. Where did you learn to drive like that? No, don't tell me; I know. The Agency."

I nodded.

"Damn, here they come again," I muttered, watching the pickup in my rearview mirror. "Some people just don't know when to give up." I hoped they would give up the chase. I didn't want to engage the three of them in hand-to-hand combat.

A blast from the horn of a huge semi let me know that both of us were in the center of the road. I pulled the steering wheel hard to the right and shot through a toll road entrance.

"I think this is under construction," Alex cried.

The mobsters' pickup roared up the ramp and fell in behind us. "Keep your head down," I yelled as bullets pinged against our bumper.

I pushed the accelerator and the LC leaped forward. Driving a hundred sixty miles per hour, I knew I was at the little car's top speed, and the truck was falling farther and farther behind us. As the pickup became a speck in my rearview mirror, I patted myself on the back, proud of my expert evasion skills. Suddenly, a scream from Alex made my blood run cold.

I didn't even have to look. I knew I should cease forward movement immediately, but it was too late. I slammed on the brakes. Smoke surrounded us as the disc brakes locked into place, and the tires burned rubber as they grabbed at the blacktop in an effort to stop the coupe.

I pulled the steering wheel into a tight circle. The car shuddered, skidded backward, made a one-hundred-and-eighty-degree turn, and abruptly stopped.

I gave my thanks to the powers that be.

I looked at Alex. The wide-eyed look of panic on her face told me we were still in danger. That's when I felt the car rock. Yes, rock! Our car was the fulcrum at the pinnacle of the unfinished toll road, suspended hundreds of feet above a deep canyon. We seesawed precariously as the coupe's rear tires alternated between touching the road and lifting above it. The front end of the car hung in midair.

I glanced at the rearview mirror. The pickup blazed toward us and shot through the roadblock designed to keep drivers from launching their vehicles into nothingness. I didn't even turn my head to watch them careen off the canyon walls. I was afraid to move.

"Sloan, do something!" Alex whispered, as if the weight of her words would disturb the perfect balance that prevented us from plunging to our deaths.

"Don't move," I said as I calculated our chances of surviving the situation.

"Alex, we can try to coordinate opening our doors and jumping from the car. Or I can put the car into reverse, gun the engine the next time the rear wheels touch the ground, and hope the thrust will be enough for the wheels to grab the pavement and shoot us backward."

I didn't add that I had little faith in us living through either of the scenarios.

"I don't think I can jump." Alex's voice shook. I knew she was as frightened as I was.

"I trust you to get us out of this situation," she said with a whimper. "But if we don't make it, please know that I went to my death loving you with all my heart."

I fought the urge to reach out and touch her. I didn't want to do anything to destroy the balancing act the little coupe was doing.

My right foot was still frozen to the brake pedal. All I had to do was shift the car into reverse without plunging us into the abyss.

I blessed Lexus for their perfect engineering as the gearshift moved from drive to reverse in a smooth, effortless motion. I waited for the rear tires to leave the ground and then eased my foot from the brake, hoping the release wouldn't shoot us forward.

I closed my eyes and set the rhythm of the car's rocking motion in my mind. Forward, back, touch the ground. Forward, back, touch the ground. Forward, depress the accelerator, back, by the time the wheels touched the ground time, I had the engine revved as high as it would go.

Tires screamed and rubber burned as the coupe's wheels spun, gripped the road, and shot us backward. The front wheels caught on the end of the unfinished bridge, but the car's backward momentum dragged them up and over. In less than thirty seconds we were sitting on solid ground, all four wheels touching the blacktop.

I killed the engine and collapsed into Alex's arms. We held each other for a long time, shaking and crying against one another.

I could honestly say that I had never been so scared in my life.

We drove in silence for a long time, rethinking our own mortality. I wasn't certain my heart would ever beat at a normal rate again. We clasped hands, our fingers laced together.

Somewhere in Pennsylvania we located a car rental facility and rented a silver Ford Taurus. We left the Lexus on the parking lot of an all-night grocery store.

"I'm certain everyone knew what we were driving," I told Alex as we pulled onto the feeder road, "They won't be looking for this plain Jane."

We crossed the New York state line sometime around midnight.

THREE TIMES AS DEADLY

"Are you going to risk contacting Ross tonight?" Alex said, yawning as we pulled into the first decent motel we could find.

"No, let's get a good night's sleep and get the lay of the land tomorrow. I want to check out the safe house before we go charging in there. It could be a trap."

Alex yawned again. "Sounds good. I don't think I can keep my eyes open much longer."

We showered then tumbled into bed. Clutching each other, we fell into an exhausted sleep.

A slight noise awoke me. I held my breath and listened. Alex was in the bathroom brushing her teeth.

I pretended to be asleep when she slipped back into bed and snuggled into my side. "Sloan?" she whispered into my ear as she ran her soft feet up and down my legs.

I fought to keep an even rhythm to my breathing. I loved it when Alex awakened me.

"Sloan, baby." Her warm breath sent a tremor through my body. She giggled as she entangled her legs with mine, undulating against my body.

"Wake up and play with me," she whispered.

"What do you want to play?" I mumbled.

"Suspect and interrogator," she said, raking my arm with her nails. "You know . . . when you're interrogating me and have to get rough to extract the answers you need from me."

"How rough?"

"As rough as you want." Her voice was deep and sexy.

"I might need my whip," I said, only half-teasing.

THREE TIMES AS DEADLY

"Your imagination is so much better than that." She kissed my nipple.

"You have no idea." I moaned as I rolled her over onto her back and rose above her. "No idea at all."

##

Chapter 33

I roused from a satiated sleep and snuggled closer to Alex. I moaned as I moved to work out the soreness. Somewhere during our lovemaking, our roles had switched, and she'd become the interrogator. My mind kept replaying the intensity of our early-morning passion.

The hotel room was frigid, and I knew a cold front had made its way into New York. As I snuggled into the warmth of my wife and dozed, memories of the two of us filled my dreams.

I was stumbling down a long hallway, my arm draped over a shapely blonde. We were laughing as she was telling me what she had planned for us. I fumbled for my key and finally managed to unlock the door to my dorm room. She shoved me inside, pushing my back against the door as it swung open and banged against the wall.

"We have to make love in your room tonight," she said. "My roommate is entertaining her boyfriend in my room."

"Mm hmm," I hummed as she kissed me. I opened my eyes and realized someone had turned on the lamp on the nightstand beside the extra bed in my room. My eyes went from the lamp to the face of the most gorgeous creature I had ever seen.

THREE TIMES AS DEADLY

Her lips twitched as she tried not to laugh at me and my date. Her eyes danced, and she tilted her beautiful head to the side. I forgot about the woman kissing me.

"Hey, don't die on me," my date growled as she slid her hand inside my jeans. "I've waited all day for this."

"Uh . . . um, we have company."

"What the hell?" My date turned to stare at my new roommate. "Don't think for a minute you're going to share a room with her." She glared at me, daring me to defy her.

"I'll call you," I mumbled as I shoved her into the hallway and locked the door behind her.

"Hey," I showed off my vocabulary as my roommate's face lit up, showcasing the cutest dimples I had ever seen in my life."

"You must be Sloan Cartwright," she said in a voice that dripped pure sex appeal.

I stood there, staring like a fool. I was certain the heat generated by the woman on the bed had melted my vocal cords.

She shrugged as if she were accustomed to dealing with idiots. "I'm Alexandra Roland," she said, "your new roommate."

My mouth snapped shut of its own accord. I swallowed hard and ran my tongue between my lips, trying to find a bit of moisture in my mouth that suddenly felt as if someone had stuffed it with cotton.

"Since that bed was unmade, I assumed this one was mine." A smile teased her lips. It was clear she knew how she was affecting me. I prayed she was a lesbian, but nothing about her indicated she was.

217

THREE TIMES AS DEADLY

Her long black hair curled around her shoulders, and perfectly arched brows raised in anticipation that I would confirm her assumptions. She raised her hand and touched her lips with a professionally manicured forefinger as if deciding whether I was mentally deficient or a mute.

"Bed? Sure. That one is fine, or you can sleep with me. Er . . . uh, I mean you can have the other bed. You can have anything you want."

She laughed out loud, and it was like the gates of heaven had opened and filled the night with music. I stood at the foot of her bed, gaping at her. More than anything else in the world, I wanted to touch her face, to make sure she was real.

She tilted her head and smiled. "Can you recommend a place I might go for dinner tonight?"

"Dinner?" I mumbled.

"Food," she said. "Something to eat. I've been traveling all day, and I'm starving."

"I . . . I just need to go to the . . . ." I kept my eyes on her as I sidestepped my way into the bathroom and closed the door.

I mentally slapped myself for acting like a cretin. I looked at my face in the mirror and was surprised to find myself grinning from ear to ear. God, she must think I'm an imbecile.

I brushed my teeth as my heart rate slowed. I ran a brush through my long blonde hair, touched up my makeup, and sprayed on some perfume.

As I reached for the doorknob, I realized my hand was shaking. I chastised myself for behaving like a Cro-Magnon man. I'd lost count of the women I'd dated. Never had one of them made me lose my cool like Alexandra Roland.

I emerged from the bathroom to find her standing at the door of our room. "Are you taking me to dinner?" she asked.

I nodded and followed her down the hallway.

I've followed her ever since. The thought was bouncing around in my head as I awoke. I pulled her tighter against me and buried my face in her luxurious raven hair. The scent of her made my heart beat faster. "I love you, Alexandra Roland Cartwright," I whispered in her ear.

"Mm," she cooed. "I love you too, baby."

She snuggled into me and sighed. "What's going on in that beautiful head of yours?"

"I'm beginning to remember more about us. I remember the first day we met."

She giggled. "Yes, that was when I found out how articulate you were."

"It took me a week to carry on a coherent conversation with you," I said, chuckling at the memory. "You were just so damn gorgeous. I felt as if I should lay an offering at your feet every time I spoke to you."

"Yeah, and then you discovered I wanted you as much as you wanted me." Alex moved her lips against my skin as she spoke. A thrill shot through me.

"That did even the playing field a little," I admitted.

"Do you remember our first time?" she asked.

I searched my mind for the memory and drew a blank. "Not yet."

"I'm not going to tell you about it," she said as she kissed my breast. "I want you to discover it."

"How long did you make me wait?" I had to ask.

"Oh, at least seven minutes." she snuggled closer.

"Now you're just toying with me." I hugged her tighter. "I know it took me that long to stop gawking at you."

We lay for a long time just holding each other.

"I bet it snowed last night," I informed her. "Are you ready to face the day?"

"As much as I'd rather lie in your warm arms all day," she said, "I know you have work to do. Can I have breakfast before we jump into the world of secret agents and killers?"

I repeated the first full sentence I had spoken to her so long ago: "You can have anything you want."

##

Chapter 34

The safe house was in a brownstone in Queens. Surveilling a multistory brownstone in New York was quite different from spying on a ranch in Texas.

I knew our safe house or apartment was on the third floor, facing the street. I drove past the brownstone twice, looking for a place where we could conceal our car but still have a clear view of the apartments.

I parked down the block and pulled the binoculars from my duffle bag. Everything looked peaceful. I called Ross.

"Are you alone?" I blurted out before he could speak into the phone.

"No, honey. It isn't safe for you to call me," Ross said. "Don't call me again."

I cursed as I ended the call.

"What's wrong?" Alarm covered Alex's lovely face.

"He told me not to call him again. That means they're trying to set a trap to catch me."

A black town car stopped in front of the brownstone housing the safe house. I pulled the binoculars to my eyes and watched as Amarosia and her father, Governor Makin, got out of the vehicle.

I gasped. "What are they doing here?" They looked around before walking up the steps leading into the apartment building. The town car drove away.

"Something's wrong," I said. "Honey, I'm going inside. Drive to the end of the block and then turn around and drive back. Stop in front of the brownstone and wait for me. If things go sideways, drive away. Don't wait for me. I'll catch up with you at our motel."

As always, Alex nodded and followed my instructions. I watched until she reached the end of the block, touched my gun for assurance, and sprinted across the street and up the steps.

It was deathly quiet inside the brownstone foyer. I ignored the elevator and took the stairs two at a time. I opened the stairwell door a crack and watched as Makin knocked on Ross's door.

"Ross, please let me in," Amarosia said, a sense of urgency in her voice. "I'm in danger."

Ross opened his door. A loud blast sent my friend flying backward. The unmistakable smell of gunpowder filled the hallway as Amarosia's father dragged her to the elevator. He held a gun in one hand and her wrist in the other.

I waited until the elevator door opened and Amarosia and her father were inside then I stepped into the hallway.

I didn't hesitate. I placed a clean shot in Makin's forehead. He had murdered my partner. The man lurched forward, preventing the elevator door from closing. The elevator dinged incessantly as the doors kept trying to close, but bounced back when they encountered the body lying across the threshold.

THREE TIMES AS DEADLY

I trained my gun on Amarosia. Her horrified eyes locked with mine and tears ran down her cheeks. "Sloan, please, don't," she begged. "It's me, Amy. Please remember me?"

A movement to my right pulled my attention away from Amy. Ross staggered to the door. "Sloan, are you okay?"

"You're the one that just took a bullet," I blurted as I caught him by the shoulders.

"I am fine," he grimaced, "bullet-proof vest." He turned his eyes toward the elevator. "Amy."

The noise rising from the stairwell sounded like a herd of elephants was headed toward us.

"Come on," I gasped as I pulled Amarosia's father from the elevator. Ross followed me into the car, and I pushed the down button as the stairwell door opened.

"Was he dead?" Ross asked.

"Very," I nodded.

We ran from the brownstone as Alex skidded to a stop in front of the apartments. I had a firm grip on Amy's arm and dragged her into the back seat with me while Ross jumped into the front passenger's seat. Alex floor boarded the accelerator, and we sped away from the scene of the shooting.

"What the hell is going on?" I asked as I surveyed Amy's face. She threw her arms around my neck and tried to kiss me. A growl from our driver stopped her overtures to me.

"What is she doing here?" Amy demanded as she glared at the back of Alex's head.

"I am more interested in what you're doing here," I gripped her wrist tightly. "Why did you try to kill Ross?"

"It wasn't her," Ross gasped. "It was Makin. God, Sloan everything is in an uproar."

"How did Makin know where the safe house was?" I scowled at Amy.

"I didn't tell him, Sloan," Amy's eyes filled with tears. "You know I would never do anything to hurt you or Ross."

"She is our fourth," Ross frowned. "You, Leigh, Amy and I make up our team."

"But, Makin," I frowned. "I thought he was your father. "

"I have been deep undercover for years," Amy explained. "Makin was my lover—the sacrifice I made for our country."

"What country is that?" I glared at her.

"The United States, of course," Amy frowned. "Don't be so high and mighty, Sloan Cartwright. All you need do is pretend to be a reporter. I must pretend to be a heterosexual. Do you have any idea how awful it is to have some man crawl all over you while you pretend to like it when you want to puke?"

Her question made my stomach twist. Her sacrifices were much greater than mine.

I pinched the bridge of my nose between my thumb and forefinger, trying to make some sense of what was happening. I recalled that Leigh had denied any knowledge of Amy.

"Obviously our cover has been blown," I thought out loud. "Who outed us? If half of Africa knows we are treasury agents, we are sitting ducks for the ivory and horn poachers."

"I don't think they know we are treasury agents," Amy said. "They believe you stumbled onto their smuggling and poaching operations during your work on the documentary."

"I am sure our cover as reporters is still intact," Ross added.

"What about you, Amy?" A concerned look crossed his face as he addressed the dark beauty sitting beside me.

"The agency will have to pull me in," she looked down at her hands that were now folded primly in her lap.

"I can't go back to the governor's palace without Makin. They will sell me to the highest bidder or his successor. His protection kept me safe from the other jackals."

Ross and I nodded. Amy was right.

"Where's Leigh?" I asked.

"She's at headquarters," Ross replied. "We need to let her know that we are all in New York."

"Not yet," I said. "Alex, take us back to the motel. We need a plan."

I walked onto the small motel balcony to get some fresh air. We had dissected our situation ad nauseam. Everything hinged on the videos I had taken. Most of my memory had returned except for what I had done with the videos and my own recollection of why Alex had divorced me.

Strong arms slid around me as Alex pressed her soft breasts against my back. She rested her cheek between my shoulder blades. "I love you," she whispered.

THREE TIMES AS DEADLY

I placed my hands over hers and reveled in the feel of her against me. "What are we going to do?" Alex asked.

"With all three agents in one room, our situation is three times as deadly," I repeated the words the nurse Sadie had used to describe having three wives. It all seemed so long ago.

"Whoever is after us could take out all of us in one fell swoop. I think you, Ross and Amy should go into the agency and let them protect you."

"Like they protected Ross," Alex bit into my back. "If you hadn't been there, Ross would be dead."

"Ouch, that hurt," I whined.

"But you liked it, didn't you?" Alex purred.

"Too much," I laughed as she nibbled at my shoulder blade.

"Please, stop torturing me," I begged. "The four of us are going to be together, sleeping in one room for a while.

Alex moaned and bit me harder then giggled at my gasp of pain.

"We should join the others," she said in a pouty voice.

##

Chapter 35

It took us a week of scouring the newspaper, but we finally found a listing for a two-bedroom apartment for lease.

Alex and I met with the landlord and made the arrangements to rent the ground-floor apartment. He practically salivated as he gave us the tour of the place. Honestly, we would have rented a tent to get out of the one-room motel suite. Three beautiful women and a man in one room is not the ideal situation. I felt sorry for Ross. One of the many nice things about being a woman is that it isn't so obvious when we become aroused.

The new living situation was better for Alex and me, as we had a private bedroom. Amy took the second bedroom, and Ross, always the gentleman, insisted on sleeping on the sofa.

##

We took turns showering, and then Ross and I began reconstructing our year in Africa, hoping it would jog my memory.

Nothing worked.

"I do have a question." I looked from Amy to Ross. "Why did both Leigh and Amy show up at the hospital claiming to be my wife?"

THREE TIMES AS DEADLY

"The agency sent Leigh to get you," Ross said. "They were afraid the African mafia would abduct you."

"Makin insisted I bring you to the governor's palace," Amy added. "He had no idea both of us were with the US Treasury Department. He only knew that you had videoed him exchanging funds and rhino horns with one of your US senators.

"If that information got out, it would cause them a great deal of trouble, possibly even prison time for the senator."

"I decided the easiest way to have you released into my care was to claim I was your wife," Amy explained. "Then Alex showed up."

"Ross, why did you call Alex?" I watched his eyes as I asked the question.

Ross shook his head. "I didn't call Alex," he said, scowling at me.

"Yes, you did," Alex insisted.

"I . . . I promise you, I didn't," Ross said.

"You had Sloan's cell phone. You called me from it." Alex's forehead furrowed as she tried to recall the sound of the voice on the phone.

"Are you certain it was me?" Ross asked. "I was hurt too. I managed to crawl into a clump of bushes before the human jackals descended on Sloan.

"They stripped her of everything, her cell phone included. They took her watch, boots, camera, wedding ring—although I don't know why she still wore it." His eyes narrowed as he glared at Alex. "After the sorry way you dumped her."

Alex opened her mouth to defend herself but snapped it shut when I shot her a silencing glance.

THREE TIMES AS DEADLY

"Do you trust your handlers?" I asked Ross and Amy.

"Yes," they answered in unison.

"Do you have any idea who my handler is?" I said, my eyes begging for a yes.

They both shook their heads.

We all sat lost in our thoughts. I knew Ross was lying, but I didn't know why. He'd answered my cell phone when I called him at the safehouse.

"Let's see if there is anything on the news about Makin's death." Amy pushed the button on the remote.

We continued to talk as the news played in the background.

I turned my attention to the TV when Alex gasped.

"In a surprise move today," the newscaster read, "the parents of Alexandra Roland Cartwright have filed papers in court to take over their daughter's vast cosmetic empire.

"The Roland's have filed to have their daughter declared legally dead and have asked the courts to give them power of attorney over her assets. We are fortunate to have Alex's mother, LaRue Roland, with us today."

Alex's mother put on a fake smile as the newscaster turned to her. "Didn't your daughter and her wife, Sloan Cartwright, co-own the cosmetics company?" the woman asked.

"Last year, Alex had the good sense to divorce Sloan Cartwright," LaRue Roland said, flashing a smug look at the camera. "Alex took everything and left Cartwright with nothing but her *stellar* reputation. I still can't believe she cheated on my daughter."

THREE TIMES AS DEADLY

LaRue patted away her crocodile tears with a tissue and turned her best side to the camera.

"Son of a bitch!" Alex said. "Leave it to my parents to go after the money. Sloan, how can we stop this?"

She continued before I could comment.

"And telling the world you cheated on me?" Alex seethed. "The lying bitch!"

"Let them spin their wheels, honey." I slipped my arm around her shoulders. "She thinks we're dead, and that's just fine. It will take seven years for the courts to declare us officially dead. Hopefully this nightmare will be over long before then."

"Could this get any more screwed up?" Ross groaned as he raked his fingers through his hair. "They're coming at us from every direction."

We continued to watch the news as Alex fumed beside me. "They legally disowned me when I married you," she said. "They haven't even spoken to me since then. They are selfish, self-centered vipers.

"My father has cheated on my mother for as long as I can remember. She knows how I hate that. She thinks I'm dead and still has to sling hurtful arrows at me and my relationship with you."

"She's a bitter woman," I said.

I had hated LaRue Roland from the first moment I met her. An incredibly beautiful woman, she was supercilious and cruel. She was a grotesque caricature of Alex. Her beauty hid a heart as black as sin. The pain she had caused my wife was something I would never forgive. I had often daydreamed of ways to humiliate her, but then I realized the woman had no shame. I concentrated, instead, on ways to show Alex how much I loved her and to make her feel secure in my love.

Alex's father, Raymond, was a career politician. For the past twenty years, he had been a state representative, and LaRue acted as if he were president. She was certain she would make the perfect first lady.

I had flashes of Raymond's smug face. He was as egotistical and condescending as his wife. I suspected he was also a petty crook. I often wondered how such self-centered, callous people had produced a woman as wonderful as Alex.

Alex never discussed her parents, so my knowledge of them was the little bit I had gleaned from my first and only meeting with them and what I saw on television. The more I learned about them, the less I liked them. Their latest shameless actions had reinforced my contempt for the couple.

"I must let our corporate officers know I'm alive," Alex said. "It's bad enough that they're forced to run the company without me. They shouldn't have to deal with my parents too."

"Honey, it's good that most of the world thinks we're dead," I said. "It lessens the number of people trying to kill us. If you show your face, I'm afraid they'll come after you again to get to me.

"You could call your parents and let them know you're alive," I suggested.

"Seriously?" Alex snorted. "They would tell the world I was alive just to put me in danger. No, you're right; it's best we remain dead."

Amy had been sitting in silence, watching our reaction to the TV interview. When we stopped to catch our breath, she jumped into the fray. I guess she just couldn't stand it anymore.

"So, why *did* you divorce Sloan, Alex?" she asked.

"It's complicated." Alex shrugged and looked away. "I'd rather not discuss it."

##

Chapter 36

It was after midnight when Alex and I returned to our loft in New York. Wearing hoodies and dark caps, we hoped we would be unidentifiable on the security cameras around our building.

Alex unlocked the door, and we both breathed a sigh of relief as it snapped closed behind us.

Huge stacks of mail and packages covered our foyer table. "Looks like our mailbox ran over," Alex commented.

We quickly checked to see if any of the mail was from me. There was nothing. We kept a post office box for our personal mail and decided we should check there too.

"I just want to crawl into bed with you and forget about the rest of the world," Alex leaned against me.

"Don't tempt me." I chuckled as I pulled her into my arms for a much-needed kiss.

"Then don't kiss me like that," she whispered.

I nodded and backed away from her. We walked through the loft, peeking in closets and flipping on lights just to make sure everything was okay. It was.

##

We located a twenty-four-hour store that carried prepaid phones and purchased six of them. A check of our post office box revealed nothing. Our last stop was at our favorite Chinese restaurant where we picked up an order we had called in earlier.

Amy and Ross acted like we had procured an eight-course gourmet meal for them, as we all shared the various Chinese dishes.

"What now?" Ross asked as he examined his new cell phone. "Can I call my wife? As far as she knows, I'm still in the safe house."

"They'll have her phone tapped," I pointed out.

A look of sadness flashed across Ross's face. "You're probably right," he said.

Alex and I cleaned up after our meal while Amy and Ross sat down in front of the TV. All the news stations were reporting on how quickly the Roland's were moving to force A&S Cosmetics into receivership. They were arguing that with Alex dead or missing, there was no one to manage the affairs of the company. They were petitioning the court for the authority to manage the company until Alex either returned or was pronounced dead.

The newscaster who was interviewing Raymond and LaRue glanced at a note someone handed her. "Our research department has come up with an estimated worth for A&S Cosmetics," she said. "According to the latest issue of *Fortune 500*, your daughter's net worth is somewhere near thirty-five billion dollars."

Silence blanketed our hotel room as we watched the Roland's salivate over the wealth of the daughter they had disowned.

"I'm going to take a shower." Alex nudged me. "Want to join me?"

THREE TIMES AS DEADLY

I gulped, avoided making eye contact with my cohorts, and followed her out of the room.

"Sometimes you are just evil," I whispered in her ear as we made love in the shower.

"Um, just for you." Alex moaned.

##

Alex was restless. Her constant wiggling and sighing told me something was bothering her.

"Do you want to talk about it?" I whispered.

"What?"

"Whatever is keeping you awake." I turned on my side and slipped my arm around her waist, pulling her tight against me. "Something is troubling you."

"My parents," she mumbled. "They are the most greedy, despicable people in the world. Why couldn't I have loving parents like yours?"

"You do deserve better parents than LaRue and Raymond," I said.

"Some people simply aren't meant to be parents," I continued. "But look at the bright side. If my parents had been your parents, we would be sisters. And despite how hot you are, no way would I be making love to my sister."

"You always have such a unique perspective on everything." She laughed, raised up on her elbow, and kissed me. Tears fell from her eyes onto my face. I raised my head from the pillow pushing our lips into a deeper kiss. "Make me forget them, Sloan," she whispered.

##

Afterward, I held Alex stroking her back as she slept with her head pillowed on my shoulder. I had seen Alex cry only twice during our years together. The fact that her parents hurt her that deeply made me hate them even more.

##

My first move of the morning was always to reach for Alex. I hated it when she left our bed before I awoke. This morning she was gone, and my hand rested on a cold sheet where a warm, soft body should have been.

I lay there for a long time, listening to the murmur of voices from the common area of the apartment. Ross and Amy were discussing something in low voices. I didn't hear Alex's voice so I knew she was just listening.

After half an hour of trying to jolt my memory, I decided to get dressed. No matter what I did, I couldn't jump-start certain segments of my life. There were still big holes concerning Alex and me. I did have a brief flash of me punching her father in the face, but then it was gone. I wasn't sure if that was something that had happened or just wishful thinking.

A disturbing vision of me and Leigh played through my mind. In it, I was kissing her intentionally and with a seriousness that almost alarmed me. I wondered if Leigh was okay.

I tucked in my pastel-blue blouse, fastened my jeans, and opened the door. Ross and Amy looked at me, their eyebrows raised as if waiting for me to answer a question.

I looked around the room. "Where's Alex?" I asked.

Amy and Ross exchanged glances. "She left about an hour ago," Amy said. "She said she had to take care of some business."

"Did she take the car?"

"Duh," Ross answered, as if I were a dullard.

I called Alex on her burner phone, and the call went straight to voicemail.

"Did she say where she was going?" I asked.

"Just that she had to protect her company." Amy grimaced. "Do you think she would endanger all of us?"

I shook my head but wondered what Alex was doing. I returned to our bedroom and walked out onto the balcony. The New York morning was crisp and cold. I googled the law firm of Masters and Wilde then pushed the phone number on the screen.

The woman who answered was cheery and professional. "May I speak to Marty Masters, please?" I asked.

"I'm sorry. Miss Masters is in a meeting with a client. May I ask her to call you?"

"Tell her Sloan is on the phone," I insisted.

"She's with an important client," the receptionist insisted. "She gave me strict orders not to interrupt her. Please give me your number, and I will have her call you."

"Is her client the most beautiful woman you've ever seen?" I asked.

"Maybe," the receptionist whispered.

I hung up. I was certain that client was my wife. Marty Masters had nursed a crush on Alex since college, but she was an excellent attorney. I dialed Uber and requested a pick up at the intersection a block from our apartment. I rummaged through sacks of clothes Alex had purchased and found a nice blazer. It made my jeans and blouse look like I had put a little effort into dressing.

"I'll be back shortly," I informed Amy and Ross as I walked to the door. "I think I know where Alex is, and I need to get to her before someone else does.

"Her parents and the news media trumpeting her wealth will give our enemies another reason to abduct Alex. Poachers and smugglers are not above kidnapping women for ransom."

##

I looked up at the skyscraper that housed the law firm of Masters and Wilde. Smartly dressed women and men in expensive business suits kept the revolving door whirling as they entered and departed the building.

I glanced down at my jeans and knee boots. I wasn't exactly dressed for a meeting with our high-powered attorneys, but I knew Marty wouldn't care.

The receptionist looked me up and down as I exited the elevator in front of her desk. Her shy smile told me she liked what she saw, even if I wasn't wearing a Dolce & Gabbana blazer. "Nice belt accessory," she said with a nod toward my bullwhip.

"I need to see Marty Masters," I said. "Don't bother getting up. I know where her office is."

I practically sprinted to the lavish corner office and only slowed down when Marty's secretary stepped in front of her door. The door opened, and a news team and cameraman walked out of the office.

I turned my back and busied myself with looking at the exquisite artwork Marty had on her walls. The news team thanked the secretary and entered the elevator. The secretary waited until the elevator had started downward and then spoke to me.

"Sloan Cartwright?" The woman asked.

"Yes. I need to see Marty," I said in a tone that would have cowed a lesser woman.

"She just left," the secretary said. "I'm surprised you didn't run into her on your way up."

"Was Alex with her?"

"Miss Cartwright, you know all of our client interaction is privileged."

I took a step toward her and she squealed. "Miss Masters left alone."

"That's all I wanted to know," I barked as I headed back toward the elevator.

I slipped into one of the many tiny coffee shops in New York and ordered a cup of coffee while I waited for Uber to come for me. I hated not having a car, but cars were almost useless in Manhattan anyway.

I called Ross to see if he had heard from Alex. He had not. A call to my wife resulted in another instant redirect to voicemail. She had her phone turned off.

By the time I reached our apartment, I was almost frantic. No one seemed to know where Alex was.

I walked onto the balcony of our bedroom and called Leigh.

"Leigh Redding," she snapped into the phone.

"Leigh, it's me. Sloan," I said.

"Sloan, thank God! Are you okay?"

239

"Yes. Are you okay?"

"I'll be much better when you come in," she answered. "Sloan, I care about you. I worry about you. Please come in and let us straighten out this mess."

"I can't. Not yet."

"Are you still with Alex?" Leigh didn't try to hide the disgust she felt.

"Yes."

"Sloan, please listen to me." Leigh's brusque tone commanded my attention. "Don't trust Alex. Don't trust anyone."

"I don't," I said. And that included Leigh.

"Gunmen compromised our safe house," Leigh continued. "They murdered Governor Makin, and we can't find a trace of Ross. We think they have him."

I considered telling Leigh that Amy and Ross were with me, but decided against it. "How is Amy?" I asked.

"How would I know?" Leigh huffed. "We don't keep track of every woman who claims to be your wife."

"Come on, Leigh," I chided her. "I know Amy is one of us."

A long silence passed before Leigh spoke again. "Amarosia is not one of our agents." She was emphatic. "Don't get involved with her. She is as dangerous as Alex."

A firm knock beckoned me from the balcony as Ross stuck his head into my room. "Alex just pulled into the parking lot," he whispered.

"I have to go," I told Leigh. I disconnected the call and walked into the living room.

"We're going for a walk to make certain no one followed her." Ross said as he and Amy left.

I sat down on the sofa and waited for Alex. I couldn't remember ever being angry with her, but I was furious. She had left without discussing it with me and had endangered all of us. Most of all, she had put herself in harm's way.

She opened the door with her usual flourish and stepped into the apartment. She was gorgeous. She had dressed for her meeting with the attorneys and was picture-perfect in her tight skirt, silk blouse, and dark blazer. High heels that always made her shapely legs look even longer were the starting point for my eyes as they inched up her body before coming to rest on her flawless face.

Her blue eyes sparkled as a sexy smile played across her glorious lips.

I realized I was holding my breath. *What . . . ? Oh, yeah, I was furious with her. Maybe.*

I shot her my most daunting look and watched as she sauntered toward me.

"Are you angry with me?" Her silky, soft voice sent a tremor through me.

"I think so." I blushed as what I was thinking pushed everything else from my mind.

Alex settled on my lap and slipped her arm around my neck. Her other hand drifted across my breasts. Her kiss was slow and searching. Her tongue glided along my bottom lip, seeking a response from me. Damn me; my response was instantaneous and passionate. *God, I love this woman.*

"We should take this into the bedroom," Alex whispered in my ear. "I would hate for Ross and Amy to walk in on us."

I nodded and stood with her in my arms. "I love your strength," she whispered, caressing my ear with her tongue. "So strong."

##

I lay on my back, gasping for air. Alex snuggled tighter against me.

"I am sorry," she whispered.

"For what?" I said, still mesmerized by the feel of her.

"For leaving this morning without discussing it with you."

"Oh, that." I tried to recreate the anger I had felt at finding her gone. I failed, realizing it hadn't been anger but concern. "Please don't do that again. I was worried sick about you."

"I know, darling." She traced her fingers between my breasts. "I simply couldn't let LaRue and Raymond steal our company. Marty is putting several things in place to stop them."

"I knew where you were," I admitted. "I just couldn't catch up with you. I tried."

"I knew you would try to stop me," she murmured.

"Yes, I would have."

Voices in the living room told me Ross and Amy had returned. I ignored the pang of guilt that stabbed me. I knew they had left Alex and me alone because they had expected us to argue, not make love.

THREE TIMES AS DEADLY

"We should get up. I'm certain they didn't expect us to end up in bed," Alex said. "I think they expected you to give me a good tongue lashing."

"I thought I did!" I blushed at my audacity.

"Oh God, Sloan," Alex said, one eyebrow cocked at me. "You certainly did."

##

Chapter 37

"I don't think anyone followed her," Ross informed us as we walked from our bedroom. "What were you thinking?" He glared at Alex. "You could have gotten us all killed."

"I was very careful," she said. "No one saw me. I had to talk with our attorney. I had to stop my parents."

Ross shook his head in disbelief. "I know Amy and I don't move in the same world of high finance that you and Sloan travel in, but I believe living trumps a hefty bank account any day of the week."

"I . . . I know." Alex hung her head. "It won't happen again."

"Until you feel like it," Amy muttered.

"Hey, that's enough," I said. "We're turning on each other like a pack of jackals. We have to pull together if we're going to survive this."

Everyone nodded.

"I'm going to take a shower," Amy announced. "Maybe the two of you can do something constructive today and get us dinner."

"Amy certainly has a stick up her—"

I cut off my wife's tirade by placing my fingertips against her lips. "Let's get dinner," I said. "Ross, would you like to go with us and help select the evening's cuisine?"

"No, surprise me," he said. "I think I'll watch the news and see if there is anything flying across the airwaves about us."

Dinner was a quiet affair, with Amy seething and Ross casting apprehensive glances at Alex. The TV was on but muted so we could exchange occasional thoughts.

After dinner, Amy and Alex cleaned the kitchen, I retrieved a notebook and pen from my duffle bag and gathered everyone around the table.

"We need to go over the chronology of events," I said. "There is something we're missing."

"Obviously, someone wanted us dead before we left Africa," Ross frowned. "They tried to kill us as we videoed the rhino."

"They tried to kill Sloan in the hospital," Alex added. "That was when I knew we had to get her out of there."

So far, so good. "So, the source of our would-be assassins is Africa," I said, scribbling in my notebook. "Judging by the characters we encountered in Texas, they've sent their henchmen to America.

"Will Makin's death slow them down?" I asked Amy.

"Doubtful. Makin was involved with politicians from the States. I don't have names, but I think you did manage to get them.

"I know that the night after you attended the embassy party, all hell broke loose. I heard talk of a burglary. Apparently, someone broke into Makin's safe and copied documents that were in it. They believed it was you."

I tried to conjure up visions of me breaking into a safe. "I've got nothing," I said.

Ross was watching the silent TV over my shoulder. I saw his eyes widen in surprise. "Alex!" he hissed.

I moved my chair so I could see the television as a camera zoomed in on my wife and our attorney, Marty Masters, talking with the host of the highest-rated talk show on TV. *So that was why the camera crew was at Marty's office*, I said to myself.

I glared at Alex, but she refused to meet my gaze. I turned back to the TV, picked up the remote, and unmuted the sound.

"I am delighted to have Alexandra Roland Cartwright, cofounder of A&S Cosmetics, and her attorney, Marty Masters, with us today. As many of you know, Mrs. Cartwright's parents have petitioned the courts to give them control of Alex's company because they believe she is dead. As you can see, they are wrong."

The camera zoomed in on Alex's face. Her nervous smile showcased the little dimples at each corner of her lips. She looked like a gorgeous angel.

"Sloan and I have taken some time off to enjoy an adventure with one another." Alex tilted her head a little to the left. "This year we renewed our marriage vows in Italy. Many of you thought we had divorced, but we did not. I have loved her from the moment I first saw her and have never stopped.

"My parents and I are estranged. They disowned me when I married Sloan Cartwright. For some reason, they decided to try to take over the company co-owned by Sloan and me. Our attorney, Marty Masters, will be handling everything moving forward, including a countersuit against LaRue and Raymond Roland.

"I wanted to do this interview to let my friends and those of you who count on A&S products know that I am still at the helm of our company, and that Sloan and I are still very much married."

I stared at Alex as the talk show host questioned Marty.

"I saw the divorce papers," Ross said. "Sloan, I watched you crumble when you realized what they were."

Alex reached for my hand. "Yes, she was served, and the papers were signed and returned to me. I shredded them. It was Sloan's idea. She knew she was in danger and was afraid that danger would extend to me. She wanted a public divorce so criminals would believe I wasn't important to her. I couldn't bring myself to file the papers."

"That didn't work, did it?" I mumbled.

"It did until she showed up in Africa." Amy snarled at Alex. "You should have stayed home. We would've taken care of Sloan."

"I saw the great job you two did taking care of her." The look of contempt Alex gave Amy and Ross let the pair know she had no confidence in them.

"I've got to get some air," Amy said. "Ross, do you want to join me on my balcony?"

The two left the room. Ross shook his head in disbelief as he closed the door to Amy's bedroom.

THREE TIMES AS DEADLY

Alex turned to me. "Do you think they are—"

The rest of her words were lost in an explosion of shattering glass. I wasn't sure what was happening, but I knew it wasn't good. I shoved Alex to the floor and covered her body with mine.

An explosion deafened me, and I felt as if my head was being ripped from my shoulders. I protected Alex's head with my chest, burying her face between my breasts. Darkness was the last thing I saw.

##

Chapter 38

The ringing in my ears felt like a buzz saw cutting through my brain. I kept my eyes closed, knowing that even a pinpoint of light would increase my pain.

Along with the pain came a flood of memories—memories that I had lost. Memories of my life with Alex. Memories of our divorce. She had divorced me, and it was my idea!

What Alex had said was true; I had insisted on it to remove her from danger. I was glad she couldn't bring herself to file the divorce papers. Somehow, the thought of Alex not being my wife for even a moment distressed me.

I tried to move my arms and discovered they were tied behind me. Something warm and solid was resting against my back. It took me a moment to realize Alex was tied to me.

God, is this nightmare ever going to end?

Summoning all my strength, I slowly opened my eyes. Thankful that we were in a dark room, I whispered, "Alex, are you okay?"

"I'm fine, baby," she whispered back.

Relief shot through me and ricocheted off the back of my skull. I tried to regain some semblance of composure. I didn't want Alex to know how frightened I was.

"Do you have any serious injuries?" I asked.

"I don't think so. You shielded me from most of the blast."

"Good. Do you have any idea where we are?" I moved my legs and was surprised to find my ankles weren't bound.

"A boxcar or shipping container, I think. I didn't lose consciousness but pretended I was out cold so I could see where they were taking us."

"Where are Amy and Ross?

"I don't know," she answered. "Four men grabbed them and dragged them out first then came back to get you and me. I don't think Ross and Amy were affected by the explosion.

"They tied us up and threw us into the back of a black suburban."

"Do you have any idea who they are?" I asked.

"None."

"Are your feet tied?"

"No."

"Let's try to stand. We'll have to trust each other to support the other's back," I said. "Are you okay with that?

"If you don't know how much I trust you by now," she said, "you'll never know."

"Okay, on the count of three."

We pulled our legs beneath us. Using our backs for leverage, we pushed hard against each other and got to our feet. I thanked God that we were both in excellent condition. Alex groaned.

"What's wrong?" I asked.

"Nothing. You're taller than me. You pulled my arms up behind my back for a moment. I'm okay now. Are you wearing those wonderful boots?"

"Yes. Let's get against a wall so we can balance ourselves while I retrieve the knife."

It took us a good half hour to get the knife and cut the ropes. We gave each other a quick hug, and then felt along the walls to determine if we were in a shipping container or a boxcar.

We located a crack that felt like a door, but I couldn't budge it. We weren't moving, so that was something in our favor. I kept thinking my eyes would adjust to the darkness, but that never happened. Whatever we were in was sealed tight. Not even a sliver of light slipped inside. I didn't know if it was day or night.

We huddled into the far corner of our prison. I scooted my back into the corner and pulled Alex between my legs, her back resting against my chest. The ringing in my ears was maddening, but I didn't want to worry her, so I kept that bit of information to myself.

We dozed and finally fell into a deep sleep.

I awoke to find my eyes had adjusted to the darkness or it was daylight outside. Alex jerked awake when a jarring blow to our container shook it from one end to the other.

I listened as the screech of scraping metal and the huff and puff of air brakes echoed around us. I thought my head was going to explode.

"Damn it! We're in a boxcar," I said. "We're being hooked to a train."

251

I looked around us and was surprised that I could make out objects. Light squeezed in around a sliding door and through a vent on the roof of the boxcar. It was daylight.

Various boxes and heavy-looking objects rested against one wall.

I tightened my arms around Alex as she dug her heels into the boxcar floor and pushed back against me for reassurance.

"It's okay, honey," I cooed in her ear. "We've been in worse situations than this." The scary thing was that our lives had become one continuous dangerous situation after another. The last few months of our lives read like a frickin' James Bond novel. We could call it *Die Daily*. Right now, I was just worried about living another day.

I could tell by the swaying of the train that we were moving fast. "I need to stand up, honey." I pushed Alex up and accepted her hand to help me to my feet.

The train went into a curve, tossing me against the wall. Alex slammed into me, and I wrapped my arms around her, bracing for the next sway, but it never came.

Walking in a fast-moving boxcar is even more difficult than walking on the deck of a sailboat. Both require excellent balance.

"Maybe we can crawl through there and jump off the train," I said, gesturing toward the air vent in the top of the boxcar.

We stacked the boxes high enough for me to climb to the vent and then pull Alex up with me. Just as I reached the vent, the train swayed, sending the boxes and me flying into the boxcar wall.

Suddenly, my mind flooded with images and memories. Everything came back to me. "Oh my God, Alex!" I exclaimed. "I know where the video is."

Alex's eyes narrowed, and she studied me for several seconds. "Don't tell me," she said. "I don't need to know. Just get us off this damn train!"

That settled the question nagging at the back of my mind. I could trust Alex. She wasn't after the evidence I had. She was only there because she loved me.

I had the overpowering urge to sleep. I couldn't keep my eyes open.

"Sloan!" Alex patted my cheeks. "Sloan, baby, don't go to sleep. Oh God! You have another concussion."

It seemed like I drifted in and out of sleep for days, as Alex shook me awake and kept me from falling into a deep sleep. She tried to support me and walk me, but the unexpected swaying of the train threatened to slam us both against the walls.

She gave up and backed into a corner, pulling me sideways between her legs. I don't know how she stayed awake, but she kept me from sleeping as blackness filled the boxcar and then faded into daylight again.

Exhausted, we both fell into a troubled sleep.

"Honey?" I kissed Alex and looked around, trying to decide what to do.

Alex jerked awake. "Are you okay?"

"Much better," I said. "I do believe you saved my life."

"I have never been so scared," Alex said, her tears leaving visible tracks on her grimy cheeks. "I was so afraid you would go to sleep and never wake up."

"Thanks to you, I'm okay." I held her close as she sobbed against my shoulder.

By the time Alex pulled it together, I had a plan. A crummy plan, but a plan nonetheless.

"You'll need to hold the boxes while I climb onto the top of the train." I calculated our chance of success as we began stacking the boxes again. "I'll see if I can open the door from the outside."

Alex breathed a sigh of relief. "Good. That way we won't have so far to jump."

I had to laugh. Leave it to Alex to see the bright side of our situation.

Alex held the boxes to keep them from sliding out from under me, and I struggled up them, grabbing hold of the vent and pulling myself through it to sit on top of the boxcar. The fresh air made me dizzy.

I looked around, hoping to spy a landmark, anything that might give me some idea as to our whereabouts. I saw nothing useful.

I wrapped the end of my whip around the walk-bar that ran the length of the train roof and backed to the roof's edge. I looked down for a foothold. The ground was speeding by at an alarming pace.

As soon as my stomach settled, I moved to the metal ladder that ran down the side of the boxcar. I yanked my whip loose from the roof's bar and descended the ladder. Once I was just above the door lever, I popped my whip and lashed it around the metal bar. Pulling with all my strength didn't budge the heavy metal bar. I slid the stock of the whip through the ladder rails and used them for leverage. The movement of the bar was painfully slow. I kept tightening the whip's leather around the ladder until the bar pulled away from the door. Alex gave the door a hard tug from the inside, and it slid open enough for her to ease out. I shook the whip loose from the bar and pulled it back to me.

We were traveling through a pine-tree forest. I prayed the pine needles weren't covering rocks or other hard, sharp objects.

Alex looked down at the ground speeding past. She gave me an "are you crazy?" look, saluted me, and nodded for me to jump. She jumped moments after I did.

We both rolled away from the tracks, thankful we were still alive.

"Do you have any idea where we are?" Alex asked as she brushed debris from her pants and blouse.

"Well, Dorothy, we aren't in Africa anymore." I grinned as I pulled pine needles from her hair.

"Not funny." Alex frowned.

"It is a little warmer, so I think we're south of New York," I noted. "We've been traveling for over thirty-six hours. I think we're in Tennessee. It's a godforsaken area, for sure. Maybe the Appalachian Mountains."

We surveyed our location. Stark mountains seemed to rise for miles before touching the sky. Looking the other direction, we spotted smoke curling above the trees. It seemed to come from the other side of the ridge. We headed in that direction. After walking for hours we found the house producing the smoke.

THREE TIMES AS DEADLY

We were cold and hungry. Hopefully, the homeowners would be hospitable.

"They'll ask how we got here," Alex pointed out as she clung to my arm. "What should we say?"

We both looked like the losers of a horrible gang fight. Our clothes were ripped and filthy. Our hair was filled with dirt and pine needles. In New York, we would be dubbed "bag ladies." Here we might pass for moonshiners.

"We should hide these," I said as I pulled my wedding ring from my finger and nodded for Alex to do the same.

"I've never voluntarily taken it off," she said. "Those two thugs took it from me so they could pawn it.

"I'm going to hide them in my boots," I reassured her. "Otherwise they might be stolen. I have no idea what we'll run into here. I know an entire team of treasury agents works Tennessee like a gold mine. Drugs and illegal liquor are a way of life here."

Alex shot me a begrudging glance and handed me her ring. After securing them in the bottom of the zippered knife pocket in my boot, I kissed her. "It's also best that we don't look like lesbians in this part of the country. Matching wedding bands would be a dead giveaway."

##

Chapter 39

We approached the wood-frame house and stopped when a huge hound dog bayed like a foghorn.

"Will he bite?" Alex slipped behind me as I fingered my bullwhip.

"I'm not sure," I whispered as the dog moved closer and blasted the hills with another bark.

The door of the house opened, and an elderly woman stepped onto the porch, a shotgun leveled at us. "Lonso, come here!" she yelled to the dog. "Leave those girls alone."

"She's going to shoot us," Alex whimpered.

"Good evening, ma'am," I called to the woman. "We were hiking the Appalachian Trail and got lost two days ago. Can you point us in the right direction to town?"

"Come closer," the woman yelled as Lonso decided to sniff us in the usual places dogs stick their noses. He was particularly enamored with Alex, as she tried unsuccessfully to shove his nose from her crotch.

I fought the grin that threatened to take over my face.

"If you laugh," Alex growled under her breath, "I will kill you."

257

We walked closer to the porch, our hands in the air.

"Oh, for heaven's sake," the woman said., "Put down your hands. This thing ain't even loaded. You two are a fright, but you look harmless."

Still trying to avoid Lonso, we walked up the steps to the porch. The woman kicked at the hound dog, still right on our heels. "Leave those girls alone," she hissed. "Just like a male . . . always sniffin' around beautiful women."

She flashed a toothless grin and held the door open for us. "Come in! Come in."

The woman headed straight for the sink, took a set of dentures from a glass on the counter, and slid them into her mouth. "Sorry. I wasn't expecting company," she said.

Alex was still behind me with a death grip on my arm. I shook her loose and held out my hand to the woman. "I'm Judy Lane and this is my . . . uh, friend, Alice Lewis." Alex held out her hand too.

The woman shook our hands and scrutinized us for several seconds. "Why don't you girls go clean up, and I'll fix you something to eat. If you've been wandering around for two days, you must be starving."

She pointed to a door off the kitchen. "I've only got one extra bedroom, but you're welcome to use it for the night. There's a washroom connected to it.

"You'll have to sleep together. I hope you don't mind."

"That should be interesting." Alex giggled. "It's been a long time since I went to a slumber party."

"There's a bunch of my daughter's clothes in the closet and the dresser," she added as we moved toward the bedroom. "Feel free to use any of 'em. She won't be needing 'em. God rest her soul."

We stopped and turned to commiserate with our hostess. "I'm sorry for your loss," I put on my saddest face.

"Oh, she ain't dead. She ran off with that good-for-nothing traveling preacher that passed through here last summer. Left me with all the chores around this place."

We thanked her again and went into the bedroom. As soon as I closed the door, Alex was in my arms. She blew out a deep breath and hugged me.

"Why don't you wash up first?" I pointed to the makeshift shower that seemed to hang off the side of the room.

"It won't hold both of us," I added when Alex grabbed my hand and tried to tug me along with her. She pretended to pout and stripped off her clothes.

"God, you are one beautiful woman," I enthused.

The sparkle in her eyes told me the feeling was mutual.

When we returned to the kitchen, something delicious-smelling was bubbling on the stove.

"I hope you girls like stew," our hostess said as she ladled a thin soup into bowls for us and cut a pan of cornbread into squares.

"We love stew," I said.

"This looks wonderful," Alex said as she dipped her spoon into the watery stew. "Oh my gosh! It tastes as good as it looks.

"Your daughter's clothes fit us perfectly," Alex commented between bites. "Thank you for letting us borrow them."

"You can have 'em," the woman muttered. "They ain't doing nobody any good sittin' in that closet. You two sure make 'em look better than Bridget ever did."

"May we know your name?" I asked as I finished the last bite of my stew.

"Oh, where are my manners?" She wrung her hands and pushed her hair back from her face. "My name is Marguerite Johnson. You can call me Mazie. Everyone does."

"I like the name Mazie. It sounds happy." Alex offered he woman her million-watt smile and Mazie blushed.

As we visited with Mazie, we learned that she was a widow.

"Do you live out here alone?" Alex inquired.

"Oh, no," Mazie said. "My two sons live with me. They work in the fields. They'll be home any minute now." She placed two more bowls on the table, along with spoons and glasses of water.

As if on cue, heavy boots stomped up the stairs and to the door. Two burly men clamored into the room, arguing about whether it would rain. They stopped in their tracks and stared at Alex. Men and women always reacted to Alex that way.

I rose from the table and waited for Mazie to introduce us. Both men licked their lips as they stared at Alex. Having experienced that same reaction, I knew what they were thinking. My hand rested on the grip of my whip.

THREE TIMES AS DEADLY

Mazie broke the silence. "Boys, we have guests, Alice and Judy. They wandered off the Trail and have been lost for two days."

Both men snatched the caps from their heads and nodded at us. "These are my boys," Mazie continued. "They're twins, Colt and Sig. Ain't they pistols?" Mazie burst out laughing at her own little joke.

The men blushed and hung their heads for a second before joining their mother in raucous laughter.

I moved around the table to stand between them and Alex as I extended my hand to shake theirs.

"Your mother was kind enough to take us in for the night and feed us," I said. "I apologize for not waiting on you to eat, but we hadn't eaten in two days."

The men shook our hands then looked at their mother as if asking for guidance. I noticed they both reeked of marijuana, but they didn't have the glassy-eyed gaze of one who had been smoking it. I wondered if they were mj farmers.

"Don't just stand there like dolts," Mazie chided them. "Wash your hands and join the ladies and me for dinner."

The two practically knocked each other down getting to the sink to wash their hands. They sat in the chairs across from Alex and me, while Mazie sat at the head of the table.

"You give thanks, Colt," Mazie instructed.

Colt mumbled a few incoherent words, followed by a loud "Amen."

I am certain the men had been identical twins at some point in their lives, but fist fights or other altercations had changed that. Colt had a broken nose, and Sig was missing his two front incisors. Both had various scars and cuts on their faces. They were six feet tall and weighed over two hundred pounds.

"I thought you boys could drive these ladies into town in the morning," Mazie said as she passed the cornbread to her sons and cut slices of apple pie for Alex and me. "Maybe take them to the train station or the bus station."

"You got any money?" Colt asked.

"Enough for a bus ticket," I answered.

"Where you headed?" Sig said.

"Nashville," Alex interjected. "We're supposed to meet our friends in Nashville."

"Huntsville is the closest town with a bus station," Sig informed us. "It's on the other side of Punkin Hollow Cemetery."

The two brother exchanged glances. "We're going to a barn dance in Punkin Hollow tonight." Colt's broad smile revealed yellow teeth that had never had a relationship with a toothbrush. "You girls should come with us. We'll show you a really good time."

"We're exhausted," Alex said. "We must have wandered ten miles today before your mother was kind enough to take us in and feed us."

"Aww, come on," Sig wheedled. "We'd be so proud to show up at the dance with lookers like you two on our arms."

"That is very kind, but honestly, we'd much rather sleep than dance. We truly are worn out."

I stood and began clearing the table, signaling the end of the meal and the conversation. Alex joined me at the sink carrying the rest of the dishes.

"You girls leave those dishes," Mazie said. "I ain't got nothing else to do. You get some sleep. Boys, you need to clean up if you're going to the dance. No gal is gonna look at you twice the way you look now."

The men shuffled from the room, mumbling about how unsocial we were. I was glad they left without causing us trouble. Mazie had been nice to us. I didn't want to hurt her sons.

We finished cleaning the kitchen, and Colt and Sig returned dressed for the dance.

"You boys are just too handsome," Mazie said, her facing glowing as she looked her sons over. "Don't you think so, girls?"

We nodded and then stood around until the men left, again refusing one last invitation to join them.

Mazie listened as the pickup pulled away from the house. "Don't you like my boys?" The painful look on her face made it clear we had hurt her feelings.

"They are handsome fellows," Alex said.

"I thought they were very nice and polite," I added.

"Then why didn't you go to the dance with them? It would have made them so proud."

"We are so tired we can barely make decent conversation," I sighed as if it took more energy than I had to talk.

Mazie narrowed her eyes and scrutinized Alex and me. "Nah," she snorted. "You're both too pretty to be lezzies. You ain't lezzies, are you?"

"Lezzies?" I raised my eyebrows as if I didn't understand her question.

"You know," Mazie grunted. "Girls who have sex with other girls."

"Is that even possible?" I looked at Mazie as if she had sprouted another head.

Mazie studied us for a minute then burst out laughing. "You wouldn't even know how, would you?"

We shook our heads as if we had no idea what she was saying. "Would it be okay if we go to bed now?" Alex asked.

Mazie settled into a chair with a book. "We don't own a TV," she informed us, "but you're welcome to my books if you see anything you'd like to read."

"That is kind of you but I would fall asleep before I read a page," I admitted. "We'll just go to bed now, if that is okay with you."

"Of course, sweetie." Mazie nodded as she turned a page of her book.##

I locked the door and pushed a rickety chair under the door handle. When I turned around, Alex threw herself into my arms.

"Oh Lord, I wanted to touch you," she said. "I hate being near you without touching you."

"Wait," I whispered. "You're not one of those lezzies, are you?"

"Yes," Alex hissed. "I'm in disguise as a real woman."

I buried my face in her thick, luxurious hair to keep from laughing out loud. Alex was an armful of woman, and I loved every voluptuous inch of her. The way she felt against my breasts and in my arms was pure heaven.

Erin Wade
THREE TIMES AS DEADLY

"We should sleep in our clothes," I told her. "I don't trust the pistol brothers. We need to be able to fight our way out of here if necessary."

Alex rolled her eyes "I've been dying to get you naked," she said, moaning.

I put a finger to my lips to shush her. "These walls are as thin as tissue."

Alex turned back the bedspread and slipped off her shoes, still scowling about sleeping in clothes.

We took turns in the small washroom and then slipped into bed. The sheets were rough and the mattress was lumpy, but it was much more comfortable than the boxcar where we'd spent the previous night.

Alex snuggled into me, and we quickly fell asleep.

##

Soft kisses on the back of my neck woke me as the sun was rising. Naturally, I turned over and pulled her into my arms.

"Shh," she whispered. "Mazie and the two shotguns are in the kitchen."

"Pistols," I said, chortling. "They're named after pistols."

"We should get out of bed." Alex continued to whisper. "Unless you have something better in mind."

"No, you make too much noise." I grinned.

"I promise to be quiet," she whispered.

"A promise you can't keep. We need to get moving." I slid from the bed and held out my hand to her.

I slipped on my boots and silently thanked Bridget for wearing the same size jeans as Alex and me. I

265

draped the whip around my hips and listened at the door as Mazie assured her sons that Alex and I were not lezzies. "They're girly girls," I heard her say.

I opened the door and entered the room that served as a combination kitchen and living area. "Good morning," I said with a smile. "Mazie, thank you so much for letting us sleep here. I feel much better."

"We were wondering if you would sleep all day," Colt said, his yellow teeth on full display as he poured two more cups of coffee for Alex and me.

"What time is it?" I asked.

"Seven," Sig barked, "but we got up at five thirty." He puffed out his chest like a proud peacock.

"The early bird gets the worm," Mazie said. "My boys don't let no moss grow under their feet. They're really hard workers. They'll be real good providers for some lucky gals."

I agreed.

The men's eyes swung to Alex as she entered the room. I hated it when men—or women—looked at her that way. I took a deep breath and sipped my hot coffee, ignoring the urge to throw it on Sig and Colt.

"After breakfast, we'll take you girls to the bus station," Sig informed us.

"May I have your mailing address?" Alex asked Mazie. "Y'all have been so nice to us. I want to send you something when I get home."

"You don't need to do that, dear," Mazie said as her cheeks reddened. "We were glad to help two ladies in distress. Weren't we boys?"

The men nodded and looked us up and down. I had an uneasy feeling.

THREE TIMES AS DEADLY

We started to help clean the kitchen, but Mazie shooed us away. "You best be going," she said. "The next bus from Huntsville leaves at noon."

We thanked her again, said our goodbyes, and followed the pistol brothers to their pickup. Sig opened the rear door and I climbed in. I scooted over to make room for Alex, but Sig jumped in beside me.

"You ride up here with me, pretty lady," Colt said to Alex, grinning as he patted the bench seat beside him.

Alex looked at me as if expecting me to do something then shrugged and jumped into the truck.

"That's more like it." Colt laughed as he shifted gears and gunned the truck.

"Do you fellows know Mary Jane?" I asked as Colt pulled onto the highway.

"I might know her," Sig said. Colt's stern glance in the rearview mirror silenced him.

"I wasn't born yesterday, guys," I said with a chuckle. "I smell it. We could get high just sniffing your upholstery."

Colt squirmed in the driver's seat. "We may have transported it, but we never keep it in the truck. Ma would kill us."

"But you do grow it, don't you?" My treasury agency training kicked in, as I tried to find out how much of the cannabis the boys produced in a year.

"We grow it," Sig volunteered. "But we don't use it. Ma would skin us alive and feed our bones to Lonso."

"So if that highway patrolman behind us pulls you over, we're good?" As I finished my sentence, red and blue lights started flashing.

"Shit!" Colt said, his eyes on the rearview mirror. "Pardon my French, ma'am." A sheepish look crossed his face as he apologized to Alex.

"You have no weed in this vehicle, right?" I reiterated.

"None," Colt and Sig chorused.

"It's that son of a bitch, Leon." Sig grunted. "He's gonna shake us down."

Colt slowed down and pulled the truck off the road. "Stay in the car with the girls," he said to Sig. "And y'all keep your mouths shut."

A highway patrolman walked to the truck as Colt rolled down his window. "Please step out of the truck, sir," he said.

Colt complied.

"Put your hands on the hood and spread 'em," the officer directed. Colt obeyed.

The patrolman frisked Colt, and then pulled his nightstick from his belt and placed it between Colt's legs. "I believe I have probable cause to search your vehicle," he barked as he lifted the club against Colt's crotch.

Colt stiffened and stood taller, trying to avoid the club between his legs.

"May I search your car?" the officer growled.

Ignoring Colt's warning to stay out of it, Alex rolled down her window. "What is your probable cause, Officer Leon?" she asked as she read his name tag.

I dragged my hands down my face, trying hard to think of a way out of the situation headed our way.

"Maybe you should step from the vehicle too." Leon leered at Alex. "Let's see if the rest of you is as pretty as your face."

"Leave her be," Colt growled. "You can search my truck. I ain't got nothing to hide."

Leon glared at Colt. "I need all of you to get out of the truck," he snapped. "All of you, out!"

Sig got out and offered Alex his hand to help her down. As I slid out of the back seat, another patrol car pulled in front of our truck. A short, scrawny officer—Titus, as per his name tag—got out and swaggered toward Leon. A younger man dressed in Levi's and a sweatshirt followed him.

As the officer approached, Leon pitched a Ziploc baggie full of marijuana onto the floorboard of Colt's pickup.

"What's up, bro?" Titus asked as he scrutinized Alex.

When Leon turned to answer the man's question, I grabbed the baggie and tossed it from the vehicle.

"I believe these folks have marijuana in their vehicle," Leon blustered. "Help me search it. You take the front, and I'll take the back."

Leon pulled the floor mats and back seat out of the truck. He searched through the seat pouches and, of course, found nothing. He straightened and looked at the other officer.

"Nothing here," Titus said as he completed his search.

"Did you do a thorough search?" Leon frowned as he moved to the front of the pickup.

"See for yourself," Titus said.

I moved closer to Alex and watched as Leon threw the floor mats on the ground and ripped up the carpet in search of the baggie he had pitched into the vehicle.

"I'm taking them in." Leon's face was almost purple with anger.

"On what grounds?" Alex demanded.

"Resisting arrest." Leon's smug look dared us to argue.

"Leon, I don't think these folks have—" Titus snapped his mouth shut as Leon dragged him away from us.

We waited while the two argued about what to do with us. The officers continued to undress Alex and me with their eyes as they talked.

"You two, into my car." Titus jerked his thumb toward his patrol car and squinted his eyes at Alex and me.

"Don't hurt 'em," Colt yelled. "They ain't done nothing. They're just hitchhikers we picked up."

"What were you planning on doing to 'em?" Leon gave us a lecherous look.

"Nothing," Sig answered. "We were just giving 'em a ride to the bus station in Huntsville."

"That's right," Alex added. "These men have been perfect gentlemen."

Leon snorted. "Colt and Sig, perfect gentlemen?"

He zip-tied the brothers' hands behind their backs and shoved them into the back seat of his patrol car.

Alex and I sat in the back of Titus' car as the young Levi's wearer climbed into Colt's truck to drive it to the station.

##

Chapter 40

Titus and Leon herded us into the jail's three cells. They put the brothers in a cell together but separated Alex and me. Alex was between the brothers and me.

She clung to the bars separating us and whispered to me. "I don't like this, Sloan. What are we going to do?"

"Let me see if I can reason with them." I wrapped my fingers around hers and squeezed her hand.

Titus strolled into the area and stopped to look at Alex for a long time.

"What are you charging us with?" I asked.

Titus ignored my question. "I need to see some identification for you two," he said, stroking his stubbly chin with his thumb and index finger as he gawked at Alex.

I glanced at Colt and Sig. I needed reaffirmation that Titus was as dangerous as I suspected. The look of terror on both men's faces told me I was right.

"We were hiking the Trail," I said. "A rockslide knocked us over a cliff. We managed to land on a ledge, but our backpacks went over the edge and out of sight. Our wallets and identification were in the backpacks.

"We made our way to Mrs. Johnson's house, and she was kind enough to give us a place to stay for the night. Colt and Sig were driving us to the bus station when your friend pulled us over."

"So, you're vagrants?" Titus declared.

I bristled. "No, we're American citizens who were hiking the Appalachian Trail. This isn't some backwater, Third World country. This is the United States. We are citizens. We have rights. I want my phone call. Now."

"Yeah, right." Titus snorted. "You got a quarter? All we have to make outgoing calls is a pay phone."

He moved to stand in front of Alex's cell. "You might be the prettiest woman I have ever seen," he said, leaning against the bars of her cell.

"Did you boys get a piece of this action last night?" His grin was malicious as he taunted Colt and Sig.

Colt moved as close as he could to Alex's cell. "Leave her alone, Titus," he snarled. "She ain't no two-bit whore like you're used to rutting. She's a lady."

"Maybe I've moved up in the world." Titus licked his lips as he unlocked Alex's cell door. "Yeah, maybe I'd like a lady."

"Leave her alone, you bastard," Colt howled.

"She's your girl, ain't she?" Titus smirked at Colt. "Then you should enjoy watching this."

He unfastened his nightstick from his belt and scowled at Alex. "Be nice to me, and I won't need to use this on you." A hateful grin curled his lips.

Alex pressed her back to the bars between us. "Do what I say," I whispered in her ear.

"I don't want any trouble," Alex said. "If I do what you want, will you drop us at the bus station?"

"Did you hear that, Colt?" Titus yelled. "Your girl just propositioned me. She'll do whatever I want for a ride to the bus station."

The bars bit into Alex's back as Titus pushed himself against her and tried to kiss her. Alex turned her head away from him.

"Drop!" I growled.

Alex fell to the floor like a sack of potatoes, and when Titus jerked his head up to glare at me, I hit him in the throat as hard as I could.

He grabbed his throat and whirled around, trying to scream. No sound came. I knew I had crushed his larynx. He fell back against the bars, and blood dripped from his mouth onto Alex, who was still lying on the floor. I reached through the bars, wrapped my forearm around his neck and choked him. Blood spurted everywhere.

Alex scrambled to her feet, eyeing her bloodstained clothing. Her face seemed to crumble as she looked at me.

"You ready to have some fun, Titus?" Leon said as he strode into the room. "What the hell? What do you think you're doing?" he shrieked at me. "Let him go, you crazy bitch!" Then Leon made the biggest mistake of his life: he unlocked my cell and charged me.

Using my grip on Titus for leverage, I kicked Leon in the crotch with all the force I could summon. He doubled over and fell to his knees. I dropped Titus, clasped both my hands together, and brought them up under Leon's chin, snapping his head backward and knocking him out.

I could hear his teeth clash together and the crunching of bones.

Blood spurted from his mouth, and he hit the floor with a thud.

I grabbed the keys from Leon and pitched them to Alex. "Unlock the boys," I said to her. Alex appeared dumbstruck, still looking from Titus to me and back to Titus. "The keys, baby," I said. "Unlock the cell door."

I pulled Leon's gun from his service holster, shoved it into the back waistband of my jeans, and pulled my sweatshirt down to hide it.

As if in shock, Alex moved to the other cell and released Colt and Sig. Colt ran to the key board where his truck keys were hanging beside my bullwhip.

"Go," he growled. "Take my truck. Hurry before they come to."

"They ain't coming to anytime soon," Sig said as he kicked Leon. "He ain't never gonna be the same."

I insisted that they come with us. "If you stay here, you'll be blamed for this . . . this—"

"Carnage," Alex mumbled.

"Yeah, carnage." I didn't look Alex in the eye. I knew my actions had disturbed her. She had seen me defend us with a gun or a whip, but she had never witnessed me in hand-to-hand combat. I have to admit my take-no-prisoners attitude in a fight was extremely brutal. When I hit someone, I didn't intend for them to hit back.

We locked the jail cells and took the keys. I grabbed my whip and draped it around my waist.

"We'll take the front seat," Colt said. "You two can sit in the back together."

I slid in beside Alex and slammed the door as Colt's truck laid rubber leaving the parking lot.

"Where'd you learn to fight like that?" Sig asked, a new look of respect on his face as he turned to look at me.

"I went to a rough high school," I replied without taking my eyes off Alex. I slid my arm around her, and she slumped against me.

"Are you okay, honey?" I whispered.

She nodded but didn't make eye contact with me.

I sensed that Alex had indulged in all the secret agent life she could tolerate. I decided to call Leigh and have the agency pick us up at the bus station. I knew where the video was hidden and had recalled some of the atrocities recorded on it. If I sat down with my team and viewed the evidence, I knew everything would come back to me.

The ride to the bus station was a short one. Sig insisted that Alex take his shirt to cover her blood-soaked blouse. We bid Colt and Sig goodbye and thanked them. When it counted, the men had come to our aid. We owed them.

Inside the bus station, I talked a man into letting me use his cell phone and I called Leigh.

"Thank God you're all right!" she said the moment she heard my voice. "Where are you?"

I heard Leigh suck in a breath when I told her our location. "How in the hell did you get to Tennessee?"

"It's a long story. I'll tell you when you get here."

I gave her the bus station's address and looked around as she repeated it back to me. "There's a coffee shop across from the waiting area," I told her. "We'll be there."

THREE TIMES AS DEADLY

I could hear Leigh typing on her keyboard. "I've requested a helicopter. We'll be there as soon as possible. Sloan, don't leave! I'll look like a fool if I arrive in an agency chopper and find you're not there."

"We'll be here," I was too weary to run.

Alex got a table while I ordered coffee and sandwiches. I glanced at my wife as I waited for our order. She was watching me with a strange intentness.

I touched her shoulder as I placed the food on the table. She glanced up at me then looked away. I wondered if she thought I was a monster. I had lost track of the lives I'd taken in our efforts to stay alive. She probably thought killing came easy for me. It didn't, but I'd never hesitate to do whatever it took to protect those I love.

I leaned over Alex and brushed my breasts across her shoulder as I placed a straw into her drink. A slight tremor ran through her body, and she blushed. At least her body still had a positive reaction to me.

We ate in silence as we waited for the agency to show up en masse. I chanced quick glances at my wife. She looked tired and a little pale. The thing that bothered me most was that she wasn't flirting with me. Alex always flirted with me.

We finished eating and moved to more comfortable chairs in the waiting area. Without a word Alex curled up in her seat and let her head rest on my shoulder. Soon her soft, steady breathing told me she was asleep.

Alex knew I was an undercover agent for the US Treasury Department. She knew about the dangers and challenges of my job, but she'd never witnessed it up close and in action like she had for the past year.

THREE TIMES AS DEADLY

She knew how passionate I was about protecting the animals that are being destroyed by humans. She knew I would do anything to protect my loved ones and my country. She had always been proud of my dedication to the things I believed in.

She accompanied me on book and documentary tours. She had always been a part of the glamorous side of my job and loved it. She loved that side of me. Now she knew the dark side of my job, the dark side of me.

I tried to imagine myself in Alex's place. It must have been disturbing to have found out that your wife of ten years was a ruthless killer.

It was one thing to know your wife was trained in all phases of combat, and another thing to see her in action. In all our time together, Alex had only seen me dressed like her and interacting politely with society.

We attended movie premieres, charity fundraisers, and boardroom meetings dressed in the current fashion styles and high heels. During the past year, she'd only seen me in jeans and boots and she'd seen me kill more than once.

I believe that, for the first time, Alex realized all the facets of my personality—who I really am. I wondered if she could love both sides of me as passionately as she has always loved the woman she thought I was.

I rested my cheek against the top of Alex's head and drifted off to sleep.

##

Chapter 41

"Sloan?" Gentle hands shook me awake. I tightened my grip on Alex's hand and opened my eyes.

Leigh stood over me. "Wake up, honey," she said as Alex stirred beside me and hugged my arm between her breasts. She jerked away when she realized Leigh was there.

"Would you like a cup of coffee?" I asked Alex. She nodded, and Leigh followed me to the coffee shop counter.

"Thank you for getting here so quickly," I said. "I'm tired of running."

"I've been so worried about you," Leigh said. "We knew you were in this area. We picked up the police report about a blonde woman beating the hell out of two highway patrolmen."

"They were going to molest us and probably kill two men who were nice enough to give us a ride here," I said. Leigh knew who I was and how dangerous I could be.

"I figured as much," she said with a crooked smile. "Let's get that coffee and board the chopper. We need to stop by that highway patrol station. You probably want to file charges against the officers involved."

That sounded like a good plan to me.

"Everyone is waiting at the agency," Leigh said. "You know they'll want to debrief you and Alex."

I raised my eyes to Alex. She was watching Leigh and me. "Can't they wait until Alex has a good night's sleep? She's pretty beat. This has been a real ordeal for her."

Leigh snorted. "Alex is tough. She'll be fine."

##

I watched out the chopper window as the helicopter lowered to the parking lot beside the State Highway Patrol office. Once the pilot killed the engine, I jumped out and reached up to help Alex. She hesitated for a moment, her eyes locked on mine, before moving so I could wrap my hands around her waist and lift her from the chopper. I swear I saw a trace of a smile on her face. She stood for a moment with her arms around my neck, looking at my face, and then pulled away from me and followed Leigh.

I thought this nightmare was coming to an end, but a worse one was beginning. What if Alex couldn't handle all there was to know about me?

What if she couldn't reconcile the woman she'd followed all over the world the past twelve months with the woman she had lived with for the past ten years?

Chapter 42

I was surprised to see Leon and Titus still huddled in the corner of their cells. As I walked toward them, a back door opened and my partners marched into the cell area.

"Ross, Amarosia," I said. "It's so good to see you, but what are you doing here?"

Before I knew what hit me, Leigh had stripped the bullwhip from my waist, and Ross had his gun pointed at my head. With one hand I grasped the back of the desk chair in front of me.

"What the hell is going on here?" I said as I shoved Alex behind me.

"You really don't know, do you?" Leigh snorted from behind me. "You truly don't remember what's in those videos?"

I shook my head and narrowed my eyes. "Why don't you tell me?"

"Why not?" Ross grunted. "You're going to die anyway.

"You discovered that the mole in our operation was Leigh," he said. "When you informed me, I told her. We work together. Leigh sent the men in the Hummers. I jumped from the jeep just as you went off the cliff."

THREE TIMES AS DEADLY

"But why?" I said, the knot in my throat all but choking me. "How could you be a part of killing such magnificent beasts?"

"For the money, stupid." Ross bared his teeth as he rubbed his thumb and fingertips together.

"I could never kill a rhino—especially a cow with a calf. That's dispicable." I had a sinking feeling they'd kill us as easily as they killed the rhinos.

"That's easy for you to say. You're the great Sloan Cartwright. You have it all: a gorgeous wife, fame, fortune. It was easy for you to be magnanimous.

"You raked in the book sales and the appearance fees, while we took home our paltry paychecks from Uncle Sam."

"You could have written books. You could have gone on tours," I pointed out. "You made damn good money from our documentaries. I always shared with you."

"Not everyone is as gifted with the written word as you," Ross grumbled.

"Enough!" Leigh snapped from behind me. "The point is, you have enough evidence on those videos to blackmail half of the world leaders, and you're going to turn it over to our government."

"How do you fit into this?" I glared at Amarosia.

"Ross always hid the rhino horns in the boxes you shipped the agency. I provided letters on Governor Makin's official letterhead with his forged signature, exempting your boxes from inspection. Leigh removed the horns before turning your reports over to the agency."

"We had a nice racket going until you discovered what was going on," Ross added.

I felt Alex pull the pistol from my waistband. I dropped my hands to my sides. "So, you're going to kill Alex and me?"

"And those two." Ross flicked his gun barrel toward Leon and Titus. "It will look like you got into a shootout with them and killed each other."

In an instant, I shoved the chair into Ross, and Alex slid the pistol into my hand. I kicked Ross's gun from his hand and placed my gun against his temple.

"Drop the gun, or I'll shoot you in the back!" The familiar voice echoed throughout the room. I let the Glock slip from my fingers. It clattered to the floor. "Not you too," I sobbed.

"Not you, you little jackass." Sadie laughed as she strode into the room. "Leigh, drop the gun, or I'll shoot you where you stand."

Armed men filled the room and handcuffed my former partners. I watched in silence as the three were led away.

"You? You're my handler?" The relief I felt was unfathomable. "Sadie, thank God you're here." I pulled Alex into a hug and looked at Sadie over my wife's shoulder.

"Why didn't you tell me in the hospital?" I demanded.

"We knew we had a mole," Sadie said. "We just weren't certain which of you three it was. It turns out it was your two partners."

"And Amarosia? She isn't even with the agency?" I was unable to hide my joy at seeing Sadie.

"Now your brain is working," Sadie said. "Amarosia was in cahoots with Leigh and Ross. They had a sweet money train going. You were about to derail it."

"I never expected your woman to show up to take you home." She looked at Alex. "You threw a wrench into the works when you stormed that hospital room."

I exhaled as I recalled Alex's magnificent entrance into my room. It seemed so long ago.

Sadie issued orders as her agents arranged for Titus and Leon's transportation to the hospital. I held Alex's hand as we headed for the helicopter.

We were almost out the door when I remembered my whip. I ran back to collect the most dangerous weapon in my arsenal.

##

Sadie and I spent the next two weeks going over the videos I had compressed onto the flash drive and hidden in the stock of my bullwhip. I hated debriefings. When being debriefed, one was cut off from the rest of the world. I wasn't allowed to see anyone until the agency was satisfied that I had given them all the information I had. I was missing Alex like crazy.

"This will gut the US Fish and Wildlife Service," Sadic said. "It looks like they were helping facilitate the poaching."

"Not to mention these senators and representatives." I ran my finger down the list of names on my notepad, all elected officials who had fallen prey to their greed.

"You know Alex's father is on that list, right?"

"Yes," I said. "I'll tell her. May I see her now?"

"You can see her anytime you wish," Sadie said, "but she isn't here. She left with her lawyer last week."

I was stunned. "Did Alex ask to see me before she left?"

"Yes, but you were in the director's office, and her attorney assured her she would keep in touch with you."

I returned to my agency-provided room, showered, and dressed. I packed the few things I had, including my bullwhip.

I had slept the last two weeks without Alex, and I was going crazy. I wasn't certain where we stood. Her cool reactions after my fight with Leon and Titus had me worried. I had to find out what was going on in that beautiful head of hers.

##

I slipped into the Uber vehicle and gave the driver the address of our apartment. I didn't have a key, so I hoped Alex would be home. She wasn't. I sat down by our door, leaned my back against the wall, and waited for her to return.

I propped my arms on my knees and rested my forehead on them. I must have drifted off, because the dinging of the elevator startled me. I couldn't see the women who got off, but both voices were familiar. My heart thudded in my chest as I listened to their laughter.

"Do you want me to break the news to Sloan?" Marty Masters said.

I heard Alex sigh. "No, it's my problem. I'll talk to her. Thanks for dinner."

They must have been standing by the elevator. I didn't hear footsteps, and their voices remained distant.

"I could come in for a nightcap," Marty suggested.

I held my breath until Alex declined Marty's offer.

The elevator dinged again, goodbyes were said, and then there was silence in the hallway.

My stomach turned inside out. I lowered my head to my knees.

"Ahem."

I opened my eyes and let them travel up the woman who owned my heart and soul.

"What are you doing out here?" A tiny smile played on Alex's lips. "Why didn't you go inside?" She offered me her hand and pulled me to my feet.

"I, um, don't have a key."

She smiled and unlocked the door to our apartment.

Alex hung up her coat and walked into our kitchen. "I'm going to make a fresh pot of coffee. Want some?"

I nodded and sat on the stool at the counter. I loved watching Alex putter around our kitchen.

"Alex, I—"

She held up her hand to stop my declaration and then placed two coffee cups on the counter. We waited in silence as the coffee dripped into the carafe.

"Sloan, we need to talk," she said as she poured our coffee. She pushed mine toward me then carried hers to the sofa, motioning for me to follow her.

I couldn't swallow because of the lump in my throat. *We need to talk* had always preceded disaster for me. I bowed my head to gain control of my emotions and followed her to the sofa

"I don't know where to start," she said without looking at me. She placed her cup next to mine on the coffee table.

"Alex, please don't—"

"Just let me talk, Sloan." She took a deep breath as if plunging into deep water.

"This past year has been . . . I don't even have words to describe this past year with you." She turned toward me, sadness in her eyes. "I just know I can't do this anymore."

I fought hard to keep from throwing up in her lap. My stomach jumped into my throat, and I clasped my knees with my hands to keep them from shaking. Her words shook me to the core.

"The past ten years with you have been wonderful. I took care of the corporation while you traveled around the world jousting with windmills. I was lonely but fine with that, because you always came home to me. Only you weren't jousting with harmless windmills. You were fighting deadly criminals, people who wanted to kill you.

"This year I learned things about you I never dreamed possible. I have no idea who you are, Sloan.

"You're a lethal weapon in the service of your country. You live a life of death and intrigue. Every day you put your life on the line for the causes you believe in. You are foolishly brave and fearless and always one step this side of death's door. I'm afraid that one day you won't come home to me."

I bowed my head and said nothing. I knew what she said was true. I couldn't argue with her, and I loved her too much to lie to her by telling her I could change.

"I have asked Marty to draw up the papers to set up a board of directors to run our cosmetics company."

"I'm sure she was more than willing to do that." Sarcasm dripped from my lips.

"She thinks I am crazy, but she understands," Alex said.

"She understands that I'm tired of being away from you when you're on assignment. She understands that I want to be at your side twenty-four hours a day; that I want to fall asleep in your arms every night and awaken in them every morning. She—"

"Wait! What? What are you telling me?" I didn't trust my ears and was afraid I wasn't understanding what she was saying.

"I'm telling you, Sloan Cartwright, that I am your wife, and I want to go where you go. I don't want to spend another minute away from you. I—"

"Oh God, yes!" I choked out the words. "Yes. A thousand times yes. That's what I want too."

Her eyes widened and her mouth moved without producing words. Finally, she found her voice. "You do? I thought you liked going your own way and doing your own thing."

"Alex Cartwright, after ten years you still don't know how much I love and need you? How important you are to me? How I adore you?" The hollow feeling moved from my stomach to my heart when I realized I had done a lousy job of letting this gorgeous, marvelous woman know how much I loved her.

"I have always wanted you with me," I said. "I didn't think you would want to leave your world and live full time in mine."

Alex crawled into my lap and soft lips found mine. She kissed me as if it were the first and last kiss of a lifetime.

"You are the most exciting person I have ever met," Alex murmured against my lips. The vibrations shook the foundation of my world. I pulled her closer, pressing her lips against mine as she moved them, lighting a fire in me that only she could extinguish.

##

I leaned my head back on the arm of our sofa trying to calm my breathing. Making love with Alex always left me breathless. Alex lay on my stomach as I caressed her back. "I . . . I thought you were going to leave me because of who I am."

"Sloan, every moment we've spent together has been wonderful, but this past year has been exciting and earth shaking. Maybe it's the danger or the thrill of watching you in action. Maybe it was making love in a BushCat. I don't know." She shifted her weight and raised her head to gaze into my eyes. "One thing I am certain of is that you can protect me and handle any problems that arise. Even in deadly situations, I feel safe with you."

"You know I would die for you," I whispered.

"I know." She sighed, dropping her head back onto my chest. She lay still for a long time, listening to my heartbeat.

"After sharing so much with you," Alex murmured, "I can't go back to the staid existence I've been living. During the past year, I've traveled from one end of Africa to the other. I've ridden a camel, been licked in the face by a feral lioness, and made love with you in places I didn't even know existed."

"You were also almost molested on several occasions, nearly killed by an Egyptian cobra, and threatened by ruthless henchmen who would have killed you in a heartbeat," I pointed out. "Not to mention our brief suspension between life and death as we dangled from the unfinished bridge to nowhere."

"You didn't let that happen," she whispered.

She lay still for a long time.

"Do you have total recall?" she finally asked.

"I do."

"Then you know who Leigh is?" Alex sighed.

"Yes," I said. "The first time I saw you, Leigh was the date I shoved into the hallway and slammed the door on.

"She never forgave you for that," Alex snickered.

"Apparently not," I mumbled. "I could have been more gracious, but the minute I saw you, all I wanted was to be alone with you."

"I suppose that is all we have ever wanted," her lips were warm against my skin, "to be alone with each other."

I was silent as I thought about the list of arrest warrants Sadie and the agency were serving as we lay in each other's arms. I searched for the words to tell her about her father.

"Alex, your father's name was on the list of people Sadie issued arrest warrants for."

"I'm not surprised," she said. "I'm okay with whatever happens to him. I never want to see him or LaRue again."

"So, we're okay?" I asked, still finding it hard to believe that I hadn't lost the love of my life.

"We're more than okay, baby," she said. "We're wonderful."

In one easy move, I stood with her in my arms and walked toward our bedroom. "Good, because I have some desires you can fulfill."

"Um, and I have an entirely new group of fantasies for you to make come true."

I raised my eyebrows. "Like . . .?"

"The bullwhip." Her voice was deep and sultry.

"Oh!" My voice rose an octave.

"And I'll be the one using it," she informed me in the sexiest way imaginable.

"Uh . . . you do know I've been teasing about the bullwhip, right?"

"I might also need a pair of spurs." Her voice dropped lower.

"Um . . . uh, what exactly do you have in mind?" My mind was roaring through fantasies at ninety miles a minute.

"Oh, Sloan Cartwright, I am going to ride you like I bought you at an auction." Her voice was dark and filled with promises.

"I believe this is the beginning of a new era of exploits for us." I grinned as I lowered her onto the bed.

"I can't wait for our next adventure," she whispered, her eyes twinkling as she pulled me on top of her.

Neither can I.

THE END

Learn more about Erin Wade
and her books at www.erinwade.us

Other Books by Erin Wade
Too Strong to Die
Death Was Too Easy
Erin Wade writing as D.J. Jouett
The Destiny Factor
www.djjouett.com

On the following pages you will find the
first three chapters of

Don't Dare the Devil
by Erin Wade

Release Date: March 2018

Chapter 1

Eden Daye fidgeted in the hard, uncomfortable chair across from Detective Wayne Rose's desk. She watched as two officers discussed the information she had just given them. She could tell they thought she was demented or—at best—high on some new designer drug.

Eden thought about the information. Maybe they were right. Maybe she was hallucinating or crazy.

Across the room Rose and his partner spoke in hushed tones. "We need to get the chief involved in this," Rose insisted. "This is too coincidental."

"He'll send us all to the shrink," Rose's partner Dozer Davis barked. "Remember how he reacted when we filed that report on Marian Lewis?"

Rose hesitated. "This is . . . look, Eden Daye isn't some nut case off the street. She is *the* Eden Daye, Fortune 500 Daye, heiress to the Clayton Daye oil and gas fortune.

"It has only been six months since her father was brutally beaten to death. Something is not right in that family."

"The others were ladies of wealth too" Dozer pointed out. "Marian Lewis was also an heiress. We spent six months trying to track her down. You know what we found." Dozer shuttered as if the memory was too horrific to revisit. "We got nothing—no clues, no suspects."

"I say we call in Knight," Rose's tone was the sound one would use to commemorate the dead.

THREE TIMES AS DEADLY

"You know the Commissioner has to approve that." The look of fear in Dozer's eyes was unmistakable.

"Gentlemen," Eden said, raising her voice over the hum of their heated discussion. "Will someone please tell me what's going on?"

"I'm calling the chief," Rose said as he headed out the door.

"Can I get you a bottle of water or soda?" Dozer asked Eden.

"No, I'm fine. I just need to know what you're going to do about the abduction of my sister." Eden appraised Dozer Davis as one would scrutinize a new employee.

Dozer was easy on the eyes. At six feet six and two hundred fifty pounds, he certainly fit his name. Thick blond hair curled over his head, making him look much more angelic than he was.

"Could you go over the abduction one more time?" Dozer encouraged her, trying to kill time.

"Why don't you simply replay the recordings from the first six times I told the story?" Eden said, glaring at him.

Dozer breathed a sigh of relief when Wayne Rose entered the bull pen. "Chief wants us to escort Miss Daye to his office." Wayne motioned for Eden to follow them.

In silence, they rode the elevator to the top floor of the Fort Worth Criminal Building that housed the Special Investigations Unit of Central, Texas. The elevator opened directly into a huge room that housed the chief and his assistant.

Chief Frank Carter rose to greet Eden and the detectives. "I'm sorry we must meet again under such dire circumstances," he said as he shook hands with the woman.

"I suppose you want me to retell my story." Eden scowled.

"No, that won't be necessary," Carter said. "Detective Rose has provided me the details."

"I would appreciate it if you could describe your sister's abductor to me. Please try to recall everything you can. Even the minutest details will help us."

"It was dark." Eden closed her eyes, visualizing the event. "There was a full moon. I was watching my sister from the second-floor window as she walked in the garden. I thought I saw a movement in the shadows. Then there was nothing. I decided I had imagined it. The security around our home is state-of-the-art, impenetrable.

"Suddenly something darted from the shadows, threw Sharon over its shoulder, and jumped the garden wall. Just like that, Sharon was gone. No alarms went off, nothing."

"How tall is the garden wall?" Chief Carter frowned as he made notes.

"Eight feet," Eden answered. "Whatever took my sister was only a little shorter than the wall."

Silence fell over the room as everyone digested Eden's story. Even she was beginning to wonder if her eyes had deceived her.

"You said, 'whatever took my sister,'" Carter reiterated. "You couldn't tell if it was a man or a woman?"

"I'm not even certain it was human," Eden whispered.

Carter looked at his officers. "Detectives, you may return to your office. I've already assigned this case to Special Agent Knight."

As Rose and Dozer turned to leave, the elevator doors whooshed open.

Eden was certain a cold wind blew into the office as the woman stepped from the elevator. She was tall and incredibly beautiful. Her mane of thick dark hair billowed around her face as if battling for a place to rest on her shoulders. Piercing blue eyes and perfectly shaped red lips completed the look of beauty and power.

"Here's Agent Knight now." Carter nodded in deference to the woman who dominated the room. Without taking their eyes off the brunette, Rose and Dozer slipped into the elevator and punched the button to close the doors.

Agent Knight arched perfect brows as she scanned Eden Daye from head to foot. "He took your sister?" Knight's sultry voice hummed. "It seems he left the best one behind."

Eden couldn't break the gaze of the mesmerizing blue eyes that seemed to pierce her soul. Agent Knight was spellbinding. Everything about her screamed power. Her black jumpsuit hugged a perfect body. The knee boots she wore looked as if they could be lethal weapons under the right conditions. A nine-millimeter Glock rested in the holster strapped to her right hip. Agent Knight was both breathtaking and terrifying.

Only when she stepped forward did Eden realize a huge black dog accompanied the agent. "Is he a wolf?" she asked.

A slow smile played across Knight's face, "*She* is. Thank you for recognizing that and not trying to pet her."

Somber, she had been beautiful, but Knight was gorgeous when she smiled. Red lips framed perfect white teeth, and dimples kissed the corners of her mouth. Her blue eyes sparkled. As Eden gasped for breath, she wondered how long ago she had stopped breathing.

Chief Carter broke the silence. "Agent Knight will be your constant companion until we sort this all out."

"My constant companion?" Eden fought back the terror that overtook her at the idea of being in constant contact with Agent Knight.

"Constant," Knight cooed and raised a salacious eyebrow.

"I . . . I don't think that's necessary," Eden said.

"Suit yourself," Knight said in a huff as she whirled back toward the elevator.

"Agent Knight, I need you on this case," the chief said. He narrowed his eyes at Eden and got to his feet.

THREE TIMES AS DEADLY

Knight turned around to face the two. "I'm happy to help, sir, but I won't babysit some spoiled brat with a death wish."

Eden blushed from head to toe. No one had ever called her a spoiled brat. "Who the hell do you think you are?" she snapped at the agent.

"I am all that stands between you and certain death," Knight said. "You want my help or not?"

The truth almost made Eden throw up. She knew she was in danger from something. "Yes, please," she said.

##

Chapter 2

As they rode down the elevator, Knight stood beside Eden. Eden was five eight and the agent towered over her. *She must be six feet tall*, Eden thought. Knight shifted from one foot to the other, and a soft, pleasing fragrance filled the elevator. *She smells good too.* Eden studied the woman beside her from the corner of her eye.

As the elevator door opened, Eden realized that once again she was holding her breath in Knight's presence.

"Where is your car?" Knight asked.

"I . . . I don't have it with me. The police picked me up at my home and brought me here."

"I have mine," the brunette said with a shrug. "Is that okay with you?"

Eden nodded. She was surprised Knight had asked her approval. They walked to the parking garage, where an unbelievable car backed from its parking space and pulled to a stop in front of them.

Knight approached the car, and the front doors opened automatically. The back falcon-wing doors lifted, and the wolf glided into the back seat. The car looked like a giant hawk preparing to take flight.

Eden took her seat and the seatbelt locked around her as the door closed on its own. Knight slipped into the driver's seat and all the doors closed. "Address?" she said, one brow cocked at Eden.

Eden recited her address and watched as the information appeared on the car's computer screen. Without making a sound the vehicle moved forward.

"What kind of car is this?" Eden inquired.

"Electric," Knight answered. "Tesla prototype, test vehicle."

Eden watched as the agent steered the car out of downtown Ft. Worth and onto I-30 West.

With all her wealth, Eden had never ridden in a car as smooth and luxurious. The eerie silence of the vehicle was almost unnerving.

"I'm surprised you drive an electric car," Eden said. "I expected you to be more the hopped-up speedster type. You know, like a Bugatti Veyron SS."

Knight glanced at Eden and smiled. "Tess will go from zero to sixty in 2.5 seconds and tops out at speeds over a hundred and fifty miles per hour. I figure that's all the car I need."

"You call your car Tess?"

"I name everything that is important to me, Miss Daye." Knight narrowed her eyes and looked at the blonde.

Eden glanced over her shoulder. The sleeping wolf lay on her stomach and covered the entire seat. Eden guessed her weight at over a hundred pounds.

"What's her name

"El Cazador. I call her Caz," Knight replied.

"The Hunter," Eden said.

Knight cast an approving glance at the blonde next to her and nodded.

"What about you? Do you have a name?" Eden said.

"You may call me Agent Knight." The brunette smirked. "K-n-i-g-h-t."

"I bet you're no one's white knight," Eden's caustic tone made Agent Knight look at her, again.

Agent Knight didn't respond.

##

The GPS system led them around a beautifully manicured golf course. Knight recognized it as River Crest Country Club. Her family had belonged to the elite club for more years than she could remember. Tess eased to a stop in front of an imposing set of gates. Knight watched as Eden dug thru her purse for a remote device.

"I . . . I'm sorry," Eden muttered. "The gates automatically open when they recognize my car. I've never used the remote before." She finally pulled the small box from her purse and pushed the button. The gates swung open to allow the car admittance then closed behind it.

Agent Knight surveyed the grounds as far as she could see. A winding road ducked behind tall shrubs and trees, hiding the gate and entrance road from sight. They were in their own little world.

"Follow this road to the back," Eden instructed. "You can park *Tess* in the garage."

Knight chuckled. "Thank you, Miss Daye."

##

Agent Knight pulled the Tesla into the garage and the doors opened by some unseen command. Caz leaped from the back seat and stretched. Knight watched the wolf as the animal slinked into the woods around the Daye mansion. *Let me know if you find anything unusual.*

The wolf stopped and looked back over her shoulder as if acknowledging her master's thoughts before disappearing into the woods.

"I need to go home and get a few things," Knight said as she walked into the library of the mansion. "If I'm to stay here, I'll need clean clothes and a toothbrush." Her glorious smile captivated Eden. "I assume you'll take me out in public."

THREE TIMES AS DEADLY

"Probably not," Eden huffed. "I don't even know your name. How can I introduce you to people? Do you want others to know you're with the police?"

"Darke," Agent Knight said.

"You'll be back before dark?" Eden snorted. "That's reassuring. What if that . . . that thing comes back for me?"

"D-a-r-k-e," Knight said. "My name is Darke Knight. I'll leave Caz to protect you. You'll be safe, and I'm not exactly with the police." Knight turned on her heel then hesitated at the door. "Don't leave the house until I return."

Eden walked to the door. Her mouth hung open as she watched the dark beauty getting into her car.

"Darke Knight?" Eden said. "Who the hell names their daughter Darke Knight?"

Eden jumped when Margaret, her estate manager, entered the room. "Miss Eden, there's a huge black dog lying on the back terrace. Should I call security?"

"No, Margaret. That's a guard . . . dog. Her name is Caz. Please inform the rest of the staff of her presence." Eden started up the stairs to dress for dinner. "Oh, and Margaret, a tall brunette will be here in an hour. Please put her in the gold room. She'll be staying with us for a while."

Eden wasn't certain how long she could stand Darke Knight. The woman made her uneasy. Knight was too smug, too self-assured. Eden had been on edge from the moment Knight stepped from the elevator.

Of course, she's confident and at ease, Eden thought. *She's been in her element. She has the police wrapped around her little finger and a wolf and car—Tess—that do her bidding.* Eden chastised herself for using the car's name. *Only children named inanimate objects.*

A soft knock on her door drew Eden from her thoughts. "Come in."

THREE TIMES AS DEADLY

"Miss Eden, are you attending the dinner at the country club tonight, or do you wish to dine at home?" Margaret inquired. "It's the beginning of the holiday celebrations."

"I'll dine at home. No, on second thought, I'll attend the dinner."

Eden walked to her window overlooking the mansion's courtyard. *Yes, dinner at the club will be interesting. Let's see how at ease Agent Darke Knight is in my world.*

Eden surveyed her image in the full-length mirror. She had selected a burgundy dress with long sleeves and a scooped neck. Pearl earrings and necklace complemented the dress. Her long blonde hair fell freely around her shoulders. She examined her reflection and wondered if Agent Knight would approve of her appearance. It troubled her when she realized what Knight thought mattered to her.

Eden located Margaret in the kitchen. "When Miss Knight arrives, please ask her to join me in the clubhouse for dinner," Eden said.

The evening was pleasant with a slight breeze whispering through the trees. Eden decided to walk to the clubhouse. It felt good to get outside and walk. She had been cooped up in the mansion since her sister's disappearance.

Eden was nursing her second drink at her table in the back of the dining room when a hush fell over the merrymakers. She looked up to see what had caused the stillness. She watched as Darke Knight glided toward her table. Eden realized that every eye in the room was on the ravishing brunette.

Darke wore an amber-colored floor-length dress, plunged low in the front to reveal perfect cleavage. A floor-to-thigh slit provided a fleeting glimpse of the woman's long, toned legs.

Darke stopped at Eden's table and waited to be invited to sit with her. Her gaze locked with Eden's as she stood across from her.

Eden cleared her throat. For some reason, she couldn't make her lips move. She nodded at the chair.

Darke's lips twisted into a half smile. Eden knew the woman wasn't going to make this easy. She gulped the rest of her drink and cleared her throat again. "Please join me."

Darke nodded her head and reached for her chair. A man appeared from nowhere. "Please, allow me."

Darke smiled and thanked him as she took her seat. A waiter appeared with a bottle of wine and another glass.

The sommelier joined them and bowed as he uncorked the wine. "It is a privilege to have you with us tonight, Miss Knight." It was obvious Darke was no stranger to those who worked at the country club. He waited as Darke sipped the wine and gave her approval of the selection.

Eden was surprised to see that Darke was as at home with the country club set as she had been with the law enforcement officers.

Darke waited until the waiter took their order and left the table before she spoke to Eden. "I told you to stay in your home."

"You can't order me around," Eden muttered through clenched teeth.

"I wasn't ordering you around." Darke's voice was calm. "I was trying to save your life."

Eden watched, spellbound, as Darke moved her head from side to side and seemed to sniff the air. Her blue eyes turned darker and narrowed. Her nostrils flared. She surveyed the room and settled on the man approaching their table.

The man bent down and kissed the blonde's lips. "Hello, Eden. Have you heard any news about your sister?"

Eden shook her head and watched in silence as Carter Winthrop scrutinized her dining companion.

After what seemed like several minutes, Eden broke the silence. "Carter, this is my friend Darke Knight. Darke, this is my fiancé, Carter Winthrop."

Darke nodded but said nothing.

"She's visiting me for a while," Eden added.

"Miss Knight," Carter said with a slight dip of his head. He opened his mouth as if to say more but snapped it shut without uttering a sound. He seemed stunned by the woman's beauty. She had certainly rendered him speechless.

Eden cleared her throat. "Would you like to join us for dinner, Carter?"

"No, I'm with clients," he said, his eyes glued to Darke's. "I had hoped you would join us, but it would be rude to leave your guest."

"Yes," Darke murmured, her husky voice sending shivers through Eden. "We'll be leaving soon."

Carter turned away from Darke and addressed Eden. "Don't forget we're going horseback riding tomorrow."

"I'm not sure I can," Eden said, casting a look at Darke.

"I would love to go horseback riding," Darke looked up at Carter. "I will be staying close to Eden until the situation with her sister is resolved. Like a body guard."

Carter nodded as an unhappy look flited across his face.

##

"Where's your car?" Darke asked as they left the country club.

"I walked," Eden replied.

"In those shoes?"

Eden reached into her oversized purse and pulled out a pair of tennis shoes. "I wore these."

"You should put them on," Darke instructed.

"I won't need them in Tess," Eden said with a smirk.

"I walked," Darke's tone was flat.

"In those shoes?" Eden gasped as she stared at the six-inch stilettos worn by the agent.

"They're more comfortable than they look." Darke's blue eyes sparkled in the moonlight as if she were enjoying toying with the blonde.

Eden changed her shoes and almost ran to keep up with the other woman. "There's no fire," she grumbled. "Can't we slow down?"

Darke said nothing but shortened her stride and slowed their pace.

Eden suppressed a scream as Caz materialized in the dark and joined them. "She scared me," she explained.

Darke nodded but said nothing.

"Are you angry with me?" Eden moved closer to the taller woman. For some reason, she felt safe next to Darke.

"I don't want you to meet the same fate as your sister," Darke said. "If you want me to protect you, you must do as I say. This isn't a game. It's serious."

Eden was silent. After several minutes, she asked, "Do you know what happened to my sister?"

"Since the chief called me in for your case," Darke said, "I'm certain it can't be good."

"They don't call you in for the normal, everyday cases, do they?" Eden almost whispered.

"No, they don't."

The tone of Darke's voice left a coldness in the pit of Eden's stomach. She wondered what had taken her sister and who had killed her father six months earlier. Even though Darke scared her, she was thankful for the agent's presence.

##

THREE TIMES AS DEADLY

Eden was restless. Nightmares of Sharon's abduction kept screaming through her mind. She walked from her bed to the window. A full moon cast a brilliant light, filling the trees and statues with grotesque shadows.

She caught her breath as she realized two of the shadows were slinking across the lawn. *It looks like Caz has found a friend.* She watched as the two wolves loped across the grass and disappeared into the trees.

##

Darke smiled as Eden joined her in the garden the next morning. "I thought you were going to sleep all day."

"It's eight in the morning," Eden grumbled, rumpling her hair with both hands. "How long have you been awake?"

"Long enough to take Caz for her morning run and convince your housekeeper I would die without coffee."

Eden couldn't suppress her smile.

"She even gave me an extra cup in case you joined me." Darke poured coffee for Eden from a sterling silver carafe. Eden watched as smoke curled upward from the hot coffee.

"When you feel like it," Darke said, "would you show me where your sister was when she was kidnapped?"

Eden suppressed a shudder as she thought about walking in the dark corner of the garden. "After breakfast I'll take you there."

"How long have you been engaged to Carter Winthrop?" Darke asked as she refilled her coffee cup.

"A month," Eden said.

Darke tilted her head to the side and watched Eden. "When is the wedding?"

"We haven't set a date."

"I'm sure you're anxious to marry him," Darke said. "He's quite handsome."

305

"I plan to finish college first," Eden said as she avoided commenting on Carter Winthrop.

They ate their breakfast in silence. Eden was amazed at the amount of food Darke consumed. *I wonder how she maintains her perfect figure.*

"I've finished with breakfast," Eden said, jumping to her feet. "Would you like to see the garden where Sharon was abducted?"

Darke followed the younger woman into the garden on the west side of the house. Eden keyed a passcode into the gate leading into the garden.

"Is this the only entrance to the garden?" Darke asked.

"It's the only outside entrance. We can enter from the house too." Eden swept her hand toward a beautiful patio with two spotless glass doors that opened to the house.

"Where do the doors lead?" Darke said.

"The left door is Sharon's suite." Eden bit her lip, fighting back the tears. "The right door leads into the breakfast room." She turned away and burst into tears.

"I'm sorry," Darke consoled her. "I know this is difficult for you."

Eden nodded, wiped the tears from her eyes with the heel of her thumb, and walked toward the far corner of the garden where yellow crime scene tape still billowed in the morning breeze.

Darke stepped over the tape and studied the tracks on the ground. "Your sister was wearing tennis shoes," Darke stated.

"Yes," Eden said. "She had just returned from the country club and was still wearing her tennis shorts and shoes. The police took her tennis racquet. It was twisted beyond recognition."

"Do you own a large dog?" Darke squatted down to study the huge prints beside those left by the tennis shoes. She picked up a handful of dirt and sniffed it.

Eden trembled. "No. Why do you ask?"

"There are three sets of prints," Darke said as she continued to stare at the ground. "The third set of prints are bare feet. Looks like a man's size eleven."

"I . . . I only saw two things," Eden said. "Sharon and that monster."

Both women watched as Caz slinked along the garden wall and began to dig in the far corner. She looked at Darke and whined.

"What have you found, girl?" Darke bent over and shoved dirt away from the object Caz had uncovered. "A pair of shoes?"

Darke looked up at the garden wall. It was easily eight feet tall or more. "The . . . abductor threw your sister on its shoulder and leaped over the wall?"

"Not over it," Dawn said, her brow furrowed as she recalled the horrifying event. "To the top of it. A wall this tall is also wide. It's about four feet thick. It stood on top of the wall and . . . and—"

"And what?" Darke's voice was low and persuasive.

"Howled!" Eden slapped her hand over her mouth as if trying to keep the words from tumbling out. "It howled like a wolf."

"That wasn't in the police report," Darke said, her eyes locked on Eden's.

"I didn't tell anyone. I was afraid they would rush me to the tenth floor of John Peter Smith Hospital."

Darke nodded. "The psyche ward."

"Yes."

"So, the . . . thing jumped from where I'm standing to the top of that wall with your sister over its shoulder?" Darke said.

The woman is either hard of hearing or she's trying to torture me. "Yes," Eden whispered.

##

Chapter 3

"Dozer, I understand." Darke's voice was hushed and exasperated. "When will he be back?"

"About an hour," Detective Dozer Davis answered.

"Why can't you pick them up by yourself? It's just a pair of shoes. I don't want to break the chain of evidence, so either you or someone in CSI needs to pick them up." Darke couldn't keep the annoyance from sounding in her voice.

"The shoes won't go anywhere in an hour," Dozer grumbled. "We'll get there as soon as Rose returns."

Darke inhaled and counted to ten. "Did you look at the photos I sent you? The paw prints?"

"Yeah. Where did you find a dog that size?"

"Jesus," Darke growled. "Give me the name and number of the CSI agent who worked this crime scene."

"That would be Zeller." Dozer rattled off the phone number. "She knows more about the evidence than I do. She just finished her shift."

"Loraine Zeller?"

"Yeah, Lori Zeller," Dozer said. "Do you know her?"

"I'll just talk to her," Darke grumbled. "Forget I called you."

Darke paced the floor. She hadn't spoken to Lori Zeller in over six months. Although they'd solved their last case together, Lori had refused to report the events as they'd happened. For that, Darke was thankful. She wondered if Lori would work with her again.

THREE TIMES AS DEADLY

Darke frowned when Lori's answering machine picked up her call. She debated leaving a message and was about to hang up when a breathless Lori picked up the phone.

"Zeller," she said.

"I'm afraid to ask what you're doing," Darke said, unable to refrain from teasing the CSI.

"Chasing that damned wolf pup you left with me," Lori said, as she caught her breath. "God, Darke, he's incredibly smart and fast."

"I appreciate that you're taking care of him for me." Darke chuckled.

"A call from you can't be good," Lori's voice was cautious.

"It isn't," Dawn said. "Did you work the crime scene at the Daye mansion?"

"Yeah. Did you read my report?"

"No, it wasn't included in the file they gave me."

"They probably threw it away," Lori grunted. "The boss didn't like my conclusions. He threatened to make me go on vacation. Said I was obviously exhausted."

"Off the record," Darke said, "what did you find?"

"Same as the murders you and I worked six months ago," Lori's voice dropped an octave lower as she gave her secretive answer, "wolves."

##

Made in the USA
Columbia, SC
14 November 2018